Kate shivered with anticipation as she opened the diary and began to decipher Ellen Livingston's faded handwriting:

Wednesday, August 24, 1904

I have finally arrived at the Wolf Hill Hotel.

While I was waiting for my trunks, a man came into the lobby and looked at me with such intensity, almost insolence, that I still feel troubled at the memory. He was tall, dressed in buckskin pants, knee-high leather moccasins and a coarse linen shirt laced with a rawhide thong. His face was hawklike, very handsome in a rugged way, and his eyes were black and piercing.

"You must be the new schoolteacher," he said, holding out his hand as if I were a man.

I shook his hand, trying to maintain a look of dignity while wondering what to do next, as Mama would faint if she knew I'd addressed a man in a hotel before we were properly introduced.

"I'm Joshua Cameron," the man said. "I live west of town."

Kate closed the book, her mind reeling with dates and numbers.

Almost a hundred years ago, she thought. Could the man have been Nathan's great-grandfather? She could ask Nathan, she supposed, then dismissed the idea. The schoolteacher and the frontiersman would remain her secret for now. At least until she learned how the story ended.

Or if there was a story at all.

Dear Reader,

The story of *The Secret Years* is very close to my heart,
partly because two of the characters are based on my own
grandparents. My grandmother was a young Ontario
schoolteacher, with a personality much like Ellen Livingston's,
who came to the prairie at the turn of the century. And my
grandfather, who wooed her and won her heart, was a
handsome and arrogant man just like Joshua Cameron. I've
always loved the stories my mother told me about their
courtship.

But there's another character in this story, as well, less
obvious but equally dear to me, and that's the prairie itself. I
grew up in considerable isolation on a prairie ranch, and fell
in love early with the sights and scents of that magnificent
sweep of land. I hope I've managed in my books to convey
even a small sense of what it's like to stand alone in the
windy center of the world, with the blue horizon circling all
around you.

In your letters, many of you assure me that you understand
and appreciate my efforts, and I want you to know how very
grateful I am. Without all of you to read and enjoy these
books, my life wouldn't be nearly as happy and fulfilling!

Thanks so much to all of you.

Margot Dalton

Margot Dalton

The Secret Years

Harlequin Books

TORONTO • NEW YORK • LONDON
AMSTERDAM • PARIS • SYDNEY • HAMBURG
STOCKHOLM • ATHENS • TOKYO • MILAN
MADRID • WARSAW • BUDAPEST • AUCKLAND

ISBN 0-373-70638-3

THE SECRET YEARS

Copyright © 1995 by Margot Dalton.

The Secret Years

PROLOGUE

KATHERINE DANIELS, aged thirty-one, the lawyer read from the file folder in front of him. No children. Married for ten years and three months to Adam Daniels, world-renowned rock-and-roll musician, whose personal assets were estimated to be approximately...

Lionel Kribbs shuddered and looked at the woman across the desk. She had blond hair cut short, curling around her head with a look of childlike casualness, and blue eyes that often seemed anxious and timid. Her body had an air of fragility, though she was taller than average, supple and athletic.

Dancing lessons, the lawyer thought. And high-school volleyball and lots of hiking in college. She looked like the type.

But the woman wasn't confident in her movements. In fact, she seemed shy and clumsy, and frequently knocked into his expensive end tables and lamps, or dropped things onto the floor. But in spite of her awkwardness, there were times when she lifted her chin to gaze out the window or turned to smile at Lionel's secretary, and in those fleeting moments she displayed an unconscious grace that took his breath away.

She was like a Renaissance painting, he thought suddenly, surprised by his own romanticism. She should be wearing a damask gown and headdress, with a lace handkerchief tucked into a narrow gold belt at her waist. But, of course, she wasn't. Instead, she wore faded jeans, loafers and a bulky sweater the color of her eyes. The sweater had a rather strange gray-and-white pattern at the yoke, partly Norwegian in appearance, partly abstract.

"I knit it myself," she said shyly when she noticed him studying the sweater. "The pattern got all mixed up somewhere along the line, but I thought the effect was sort of interesting so I finished it, anyhow."

He nodded, disconcerted by that shining smile.

When the woman smiled, she lit up the whole room. For a little while he forgot her clumsiness, her moments of tongue-tied silence and especially her annoying refusal to make appropriate demands throughout her divorce proceedings.... He looked down at the check in his hands. "You know, this is practically criminal, Mrs. Daniels," he said, not for the first time. "Very, very misguided on your part."

"Kate."

"Yes, well...Kate, you're aware of my feelings about this settlement. We could probably have gone close to seven figures on this. Your husband certainly has the assets."

Kate Daniels looked calmly across the desk. "I don't see what difference it makes, really."

"The difference," her lawyer said, controlling his impatience with an effort, "is hundreds of thousands of dollars. You're entitled to it, and I could easily have gotten it for you, plus a generous monthly alimony payment. If only you'd given me more freedom in court, and let me bring up some of the more provocative details of your marriage.''

Kate shrugged. "It's Adam's money," she said. "He earned it. I don't want to take any more of his money than I have to."

"It's not just the money. There's the beach house in Nassau, and this sailing vessel..."

"I couldn't take his beach house. It's the only place he's able to relax," she said. "And he loves sailing, and I don't know the first thing about it."

"That may be so, but the cash equivalence would have been—"

"Adam and I talked about it," the woman said, turning her calm blue gaze to Lionel. He fell silent, momentarily thrown off balance by the childlike clarity of her face. "I told him how much I needed, and what I wanted it for, and he agreed. I don't see why I should ask for more."

Lionel nodded, thinking about the famous man who'd briefly appeared in court. Adam Daniels had been quite a lot smaller than he looked on television and his album covers. And the man had seemed further diminished by the fact that he'd been so obviously broken up over the death of his marriage.

In fact, that was one of the things that Lionel had found most confusing about this whole case. Adam Daniels was a world-famous personage, adored by millions of female fans. His wife, on the other hand, was a quiet nonentity, usually dressed in blue jeans, who seldom traveled with him and never appeared with him in public. Yet it was Kate Daniels who'd insisted on a divorce. She'd quietly refused all of her husband's pleas for mediation and reconciliation. The rock star still seemed to be in love with the slim blonde who'd sat quietly at the side of the courtroom while Lionel presented her case. Adam Daniels had looked anguished throughout the proceedings, and had almost broken down when Kate's grounds for divorce were reviewed.

"Won't you miss the fame and glamour, Kate?" the lawyer asked curiously. "The fans and world travel and all that money and excitement?"

"I never wanted any of that," she said. "When I married Adam, I was twenty-one, still in college, and he'd just graduated. We were both working shifts at McDonald's to pay off our student loans. His band played occasionally in a little club in Calgary, but I never thought he'd be famous."

"But what really caused the rift between you? We've never actually discussed your personal feelings in all this. Was it life-style, or his..." Lionel paused delicately. "His infidelities, or what?"

"In looking back on it, I suppose I can't really blame him for being unfaithful," she said quietly. "Adam's quite a lusty man, and I never wanted to travel with him. I shouldn't be surprised that he looked elsewhere for... company while he was on the road."

"But why didn't you want to go on tour with him? Most people would jump at the chance to travel in style, stay in the best hotels and meet famous people."

She smiled absently and turned to gaze out of the window. She was dismissing the lawyer in much the same way she'd dismissed the glamour, the power, all the things that most people would give their right arm to have.

"Well, then," he said in defeat, taking a final regretful look at the check before he handed it across the desk, "what do you intend to do with your settlement, Kate? I would advise a judicious balance of bonds and mutual funds, enough to generate a secure monthly income since you've waived alimony. Perhaps I can give you the names of some..."

Kate took the check, folded it without examining the total and tucked it into her faded leather handbag, knocking a file folder onto the carpet as she did so. She bent and gathered the papers, then looked up with rueful apology and gave her lawyer a shy smile.

"I'm buying a hotel," she said.

CHAPTER ONE

"A *HOTEL!*" Mamie said, her voice rising to a shriek. "Kate, this is the final, absolute last straw. You've always been weird, but now you've obviously gone out of your *mind.*"

"I love you, too, Mom," Kate said. She sat back in her chair among messy piles of wadded newspaper and packing boxes, sighing at the torrent of words coming from the receiver.

Mamie was probably reclining on a velvet couch, in a dressing gown of French silk, polishing her nails while she carried on her vigorous telephone conversation and ate her breakfast of grapefruit and wheat bran. Kate's mother was trim and artfully blond, with the figure of a sixteen-year-old, the face of an angel and a mind like a striking cobra.

"You could have got millions," Mamie said, still outraged. *"Millions."*

"I didn't want millions. I only wanted enough to buy the hotel and do the renovations."

"Take it from me, a woman's a complete fool if she signs on the dotted line without getting every penny that's coming to her. It's hard to get it later, you know."

Kate could hear a gentle whooshing sound coming over the line. She assumed that her mother was blowing on her nails.

"I guess you should know, Mom," she said cheerfully.

"Damn right," Mamie agreed with satisfaction.

Kate smiled and sipped her coffee.

Her mother was a wily veteran of four marriages. She'd left with a hefty chunk of money from each of them and, generally speaking, no hard feelings on either side. By now, Mamie was able to live in luxury in a spacious Vancouver condo on the waterfront, and indulge her expensive tastes in clothes, holidays and leisurely long-distance phone calls like this one.

Kate was an only child, the accidental offspring of Mamie's second marriage. Throughout her childhood, Kate's father, a well-known breeder of racehorses in Washington, had been mostly conspicuous by his absence.

It was a rather strange upbringing, Kate sometimes thought, but not unpleasant. Life with Mamie, though frequently exhausting, was never dull.

"Have you seen Adam?" her mother asked.

"He's on tour in Australia," Kate said, toying with a notepad on which she'd been busy listing the numbers of furniture movers and auction houses when her mother called. "He flew back for the hearing last month, but he could only stay a couple of days."

"Was he pretty broken up about all this?"

"Yes, I suppose he was. Adam's just never been able to grasp the basic fact that things catch up with you eventually."

Mamie chuckled. "Poor dear, he really believes that if he keeps moving fast enough, he can outrun the consequences of his behavior."

Kate was silent, thinking about the high-living, reckless man whom she'd once loved with such passion. Suddenly, she realized with mild surprise that she could hardly remember his face.

"What happened, dear?" Mamie asked, her voice gentle for once. "Between the two of you, I mean. Oh, I know what all the papers said, but what really happened?"

"I guess it's fairly straightforward," Kate said. "I grew up, and Adam didn't."

Mamie chuckled. "Is that so? And buying a rundown hotel in some godforsaken place is a sign of maturity?"

"Yes," she said after a moment. "It is."

"All right," Mamie said with a sigh. "So you're being mature. But have you thought it all the way through, darling? How much of your money is going into this place?"

"All of it," Kate said in surprise. "I thought I'd explained that."

"No, you hadn't. I suppose I was operating on the mistaken assumption that you were at least partially sane."

Kate ignored this. "The divorce settlement is going to be just about enough to buy the hotel and renovate it properly. There won't be much left over, but I won't need any money because I'll have the hotel, you see."

"I see. And the hotel is supposed to generate enough income to support you?"

"Maybe not right away. But after word gets around and people start coming to stay, it should be fairly profitable. I researched the industry, Mom. I even took a college course this winter on running a hotel. And the Realtor says—"

"Realtors!" Mamie interrupted, her voice chilly with scorn. She drew a deep, audible breath. "Until your hotel is…profitable," she began, "what will you do? How do you intend to pay for the little, trivial things, like your rent, for instance?"

"I won't have any rent to pay. I'll be living in the hotel."

"In the hotel!" Mamie echoed in disbelief. "In this…this wolf den place?"

"It's called Wolf Hill," Kate said patiently. "It's a little town about thirty miles southeast of Calgary, on the prairie. The Realtor says—"

Mamie gave another unladylike snort, which Kate again disregarded.

"The Realtor says it's a very good buy. Because it's quite rundown, I was able to get it for a fraction of its real value. And hotels in those small prairie towns can be extremely profitable because they're not only a part of the travel industry, they also provide a social center for the town. After I get my liquor license—"

"Your liquor licence," Mamie repeated, sounding faint.

"The hotel bar will be a good money maker, but there are lots of complications involved in getting the liquor license transferred, Mom. You wouldn't believe the paperwork."

"No, I don't suppose I would." There was a moment's silence. "Kate, you've always lived in cities.

First, Vancouver, then Seattle, and Edmonton after you and Adam were married. How did you come to settle on this...this foxhole?''

"Wolf Hill," Kate said again. "It's quite a nice town," she added. "Although I didn't actually see much of it. I was only there at night. I flew down to Calgary in February and drove out there with the Realtor to see the hotel, but it was dark when we got there. I couldn't tell much about the town, but it seemed like quite a...a cozy sort of place."

"Cozy," Mamie echoed, her voice bleak. "She's bought a crumbling old hotel in a place she's never seen, but she's pretty sure it's cozy."

"Mom, I'm not going to let you discourage me," Kate said firmly. "I'm really, really excited about all this. You know I've sat up here in this penthouse apartment for years, mostly alone, night after night," she added, her voice suddenly quivering with emotion. "I've spent my time looking down at the lights of the city and wondering what it would feel like to be alive. Now I'm going to find out."

Mamie was silent for a moment. When she spoke, her tone was much gentler. "Is there really going to be a lot of work, sweetheart? Painting and wallpapering and all that sort of thing?"

"Quite a lot, I suppose. The building is structurally sound, but it's been badly neglected over the years. It needs a lot of...cosmetic attention, I think was the Realtor's term."

"I suppose I should come out there and help you," Mamie said, sounding glum.

Kate smiled, picturing her mother in designer overalls and a Gucci head scarf, gingerly dabbing paint on the wainscoting.

"I don't think that's necessary, Mom," she said gently. "I've already hired a local contractor who was recommended by the real estate company. He'll be doing all the heavy work, and I'll mostly just be supervising."

"I see," Mamie said with relief. "That's good, because I'd really hate to leave just now. I've met the most delicious man, Kate. He's a retired military type with wonderful posture and a darling little mustache, sort of like Major Dad. He's so cute."

"I'm glad for you, Mom." Kate smiled and twisted the telephone cord around her fingers, thinking that she probably owed a considerable debt of gratitude to this unknown soldier. At least the man would keep Mamie out of Kate's hair for a while.

"But will you be able to manage on your own, Kate? You're hardly famous for organizational skills and business management, you know. Will you be able to oversee all these renovations properly? Maybe I *should* come out there. For a while, at least, until you're established and things are running smoothly."

"You know, I don't understand why everybody keeps assuming I won't be able to manage this," Kate said with some impatience. "I'm an adult, after all, with a reasonable degree of intelligence. Why on earth shouldn't I be capable of looking after my own business affairs?"

"Because you've never done it before, dear. Adam's accountants and business managers have always looked after everything. You haven't had to lift a finger for years. I'll bet you wouldn't recognize an income tax form if it jumped up and bit you. And as for an operating budget..."

Kate was silent, acknowledging the truth of this accusation. "Okay, you might be right," she said at last. "I agree that I haven't been required to take much responsibility for my life until now. But I'm tired of being so dependent, Mom. I really am."

"All right, dear. You may not be the most experienced person, but I of all people should know how stubborn you are."

"Yes," Kate agreed. "When I start something, I don't like to give up. But for most of my adult life, I haven't tackled anything more complicated than a new knitting pattern. I've just been drifting along, letting Adam do all the living for both of us."

"Maybe you should have traveled with him more."

"I hate traveling," Kate said with passion. "I just *hate* it."

"I know you do, sweetie. Maybe if you'd had children..."

Kate felt a familiar twist of pain. "Adam isn't able to have children, Mom," she said quietly. "You know that. And he wouldn't consider adoption, not even when I begged him."

"I know you've been discontented," Mamie said after an awkward silence. "And I suppose your life hasn't been challenging enough. But honestly, I still don't understand this plan, sweetheart. Why a *hotel?*"

Kate frowned, thinking. "I guess I always wanted a home," she said at last. "You and I moved around so much when I was growing up. And the places I lived in with Adam...none of them ever felt like *home*. They were beautiful, but always so temporary."

"And this hotel...it satisfies your craving for permanence?"

"Yes," Kate said simply. "I've never had a real home, Mom. I've never even owned property. It was all in Adam's name. Now, it's like I own this huge house with dozens of rooms. I'll not only have a home of my own after all these years, I'll be making a home for lots of other people, too. I love that feeling."

"The girl is crazy," Mamie said mournfully, returning to the tenor at the beginning of their conversation. "Absolutely, certifiably insane." But most of the disapproval in her voice had faded, replaced by a tone that was fond and indulgent.

For several minutes after they said their goodbyes and hung up, Kate sat by the table, smiling at the telephone. Then she returned to her notepad and her list of furniture movers and auction houses. Despite her cheery confidence when she'd talked to her mother and her lawyer about this plan, Kate certainly did have a few misgivings. As Mamie had pointed out, Kate's personal responsibilities in the past hadn't extended much beyond the purchase of clothes. Adam's business staff had looked after everything else. Money had appeared in the bank accounts as if by magic, bills had been paid, travel reservations made, apartments leased and disposed of.

Even the place she was living in now, a luxurious apartment she'd been occupying in Edmonton as part of the divorce agreement, was no concern of hers at all.

"Just mark the stuff you want to keep," Adam's manager had told her earlier that evening. "We'll look after getting the apartment cleaned and canceling the lease and all that. Hey, Kate," he'd added, peering into a box full of books.

"Yes, Harry?" Kate had looked down from her perch on a stepladder where she was untying a rubber tree from its anchor bolt in the ceiling.

"We'll miss you, Kate, all of us. You're a terrific girl, and you've really helped to steady The Man all these years. As much as that guy can ever be steadied, I guess."

She'd smiled awkwardly from the ladder. For the first time since she'd begun the divorce proceedings, she'd felt dangerously close to tears. "Thanks, Harry," she'd murmured. "You've always been kind to me."

"Are you leaving pretty soon, Kate?"

"First thing in the morning."

Maybe it was the unexpected emotion of saying goodbye to Adam's staff, who'd been like family to Kate that caused her heart to pound erratically. Or maybe it was the vagabond feeling of setting out into the sunrise with all her possessions in her car. Possessions that included wobbly plants, winter boots and a solemn row of stuffed toys in the back seat, sitting wide-eyed like watchful children. It wasn't a dream anymore. She was actually making it happen.

THE GRAIN ELEVATORS were the first thing she saw of Wolf Hill. Tilted crazily in the distance, their crookedness worried her, until she realized that they were still miles away and the leaning was an illusion created by the curvature of the earth.

"Oh, my goodness," Kate murmured in awe. "You can see so *far*. The vastness distorts everything."

She shivered. The prairie stretched off into the limitless distance, implacable and bleak, dull gold under the cool April sunshine. Only a misty smudge of dark purple clouds marked the horizon far to the south and east, and obscured the peaks of the Rocky Mountains to the west.

Kate thought about the people who'd ventured into this forbidding land in covered wagons a century earlier. They'd brought their families and all their possessions in the wagon box behind them, prepared to wrest a living from the unyielding earth.

Like me, she thought, smiling automatically as a fern shifted in the back and tickled her ear.

But she felt small and frightened and very much alone.

The town of Wolf Hill did little to reassure her. Her image of small-town life involved quilting bees, cornhusking parties and church picnics, but the few buildings that hunkered sullenly in the cool afternoon light as she drove up the main street toward the hotel looked dirty and untended. There was a farm supply store, a service station and a boarded-up restaurant, a barbershop and beauty salon and a shabby department store. Beyond the main street, a few residential avenues bordered by leafless trees seemed to contain a mixture of trailer houses, modest bungalows and once-stately old homes.

The Wolf Hill Hotel dominated the entire town. It was three stories high, fronted with old brick that had mellowed through the years to a lovely shade of rosy pink, and much decorated on the upper stories with fluted plaster cornices, cherubs and baroque swirls. A sagging veranda sported a few three-legged wooden chairs. Most of the windows were broken, and the main entrance had been repaired by the expedient of nailing a plywood panel slantwise across the original door.

Kate climbed from her car and stood in the wind-swept street. She felt her heart sink. For a moment, she wanted nothing more than to get back into her car and drive back to the city, far away from the Wolf Hill Hotel with all its problems and challenges.

But then, she reminded herself that challenges were precisely what had been missing in her life. She'd come here looking for a difficult job to tackle, and this run-down old hotel in its windy prairie setting was exactly that.

Besides, it was far too late to back out now. All the papers were signed.

She squared her shoulders, lifted the biggest fern and one of the suitcases from the back seat and marched in through the front door of the hotel. The door opened into a spacious lobby, currently dusty and unused, since no guests had stayed at the hotel in more than a year. She paused and looked around.

She *owned* this place. The realization hit her with a jolt. It was all hers, from the scuffed hardwood floors to the lofty ceilings covered with rusted metal tiles in fancy designs.

Paint was peeling everywhere. Faded, stained wall-paper fluttered in long torn strips, but the molded oak paneling below the chair rails, though badly scuffed and marked, looked essentially sound.

The former owner's liquor license had been suspended six months earlier because of some improprieties that Kate didn't quite understand. As a result, the only part of the hotel presently in operation was a coffee shop opening off the lobby, from which came wafting the smell of frying onions and other greasy foods, reminding Kate that she hadn't eaten since six o'clock that morning.

She cast a wistful glance at the smoky interior of the coffee shop, from which she could hear the sound of voices. Then, balancing the fern carefully in one arm, she humped her suitcase down the hall toward a room at the rear of the building marked Office.

Kate remembered this room from her earlier visit with the Realtor. Its tall leaded-glass windows—mercifully still intact—opened onto the garden at the back of the hotel. Kate planned to commandeer at least two of the guest rooms on this floor and a bathroom, knock out a couple of dividing walls and make a pleasant suite for herself, handy to the office and the lobby.

She'd spent many enjoyable hours poring over decorating books and office supply catalogs, trying to decide between an oak rolltop desk for her office or an old-fashioned rosewood secretary with charming little pigeonholes.

But now, confronted by the reality of the Wolf Hill Hotel, those considerations seemed embarrassingly trivial. There was a whole lot to do before she'd have the luxury of deciding between rosewood and oak. For one thing, the lobby floor was not only full of splinters, there were gaping holes in places. And all those holes and broken windows were letting in snow, dirt and probably other unpleasant things like bats and mice and stray cats. The place certainly smelled as if it might have a substantial population of furry residents in its dark recesses.

"Oh, my," Kate whispered, becoming more anxious by the minute as she struggled toward the office door, which was standing open, flapping dangerously on one hinge.

Suddenly, to her surprise, Kate heard a conversation coming from the office. Some group was apparently conducting a meeting. She paused, listening nervously. She heard a number of female voices, all extremely loud and indignant, and a male voice murmuring soothing monosyllables that were difficult to decipher.

Kate edged closer, wondering what to do. She had every right to be here. After all, the place belonged to her and that included the office these people were using for their meeting. But the Wolf Hill Hotel had been in this town for almost a century, and Kate had just arrived. It would, presumably, take time for the townspeople to recognize her rights as its owner.

She gripped her suitcase in one hand, trying to summon a proper air of authority. What did one say in such a circumstance?

Excuse me, but I believe you people are in my office. *No, too timid,* she decided. *Maybe I should be bright and breezy.*

Hi, there, I'm Kate Daniels, the new owner here! Nice to meet you.

Definitely not my style, Kate thought, her worried frown deepening. Suddenly, she stiffened, hearing her own name spoken from within the room.

"This Daniels woman, does anybody know a single thing about her?" one of the women was asking.

"She's from the city," another female voice said. "She's real rich. She was married to Adam Daniels, that singer with the long hair that Jason likes."

"I heard they got divorced because he was tired of her. It says in the newspaper that he wants to marry that movie star who was in *Tulip Blossoms.*"

"You shouldn't buy those cheap newspapers, Myrna," the male voice said mildly. "All they print are lies, you know."

"I *don't* buy them. I just look at them in the supermarket."

"They did get divorced," another voice contributed. "But the truth is, she fleeced him out of all his money and now he's practically broke. Apparently, she's a terrible person. Mark's cousin knows Adam Daniels's agent's secretary real well."

"Is that right?" the other woman breathed. "And this woman, she's coming right here to our town? She's using her dirty money to cause trouble for us?"

"Now, Jennie," the male voice chided, "there's no need to get so dramatic, is there? We don't know a thing about this woman, and there's no need to jump to conclusions."

"We know what she aims to do in this town. And we want you to stop her, Nathan Cameron."

"Why me?" the man asked so plaintively that Kate was tempted to smile in spite of herself.

"Because it's your responsibility, that's why. Your family's been here the longest, and all the men listen to you. If you say we don't hold with having a nasty drinking place here in Wolf Hill, the other men will back you up."

"But Aggie," the male voice said gently, "I enjoy a beer or two on a weekend night. I don't see any harm in it at all. I believe you've got the wrong man, ladies."

Kate heard an exclamation of outrage followed by a rising gabble of voices as the group of women went on the attack. She edged past the crooked door and dragged her suitcase into the room.

Three steely-eyed women, all wearing quilted ski jackets, sat gripping handbags tightly in their laps. They faced a man who leaned back in an old office chair, with his booted feet on the desk and a Stetson tipped low over his eyes.

"Hello," Kate said shyly, moving toward the group. "I'm . . . I'm Kate Daniels. I think you—"

An ominous ripping sound told her that her jacket was caught on one of the broken hinges. Flushing scarlet while the women exchanged glances and the man rose from his place behind the desk, Kate tried frantically to free the trapped cloth. In the process, she dropped the fern and the planter cracked, spilling dark potting soil across the hardwood. Kate sighed and watched in silence as the suitcase slowly tipped over, crushing the fern under its weight.

"I'm afraid that plant's a goner," the man said at her elbow, where he was working dexterously to untangle her jacket sleeve.

Kate looked up at him and her eyes widened.

The man was like nobody she'd ever seen before, tall and lean, with a hard-muscled body, a tanned hawk-like face and piercing dark eyes that reminded her of some noble bird of prey. In fact, everything about him brought animal metaphors to mind. Kate thought of tigers, arrogant stallions, lynx on the prowl.

His fingers on her sleeve were as strong as bands of steel, and his tall body smelled of outdoor scents, like hay and horses and old leather. He wore jeans and a sheepskin coat with a red bandanna at the neck. His battered gray Stetson was much stained and discolored around the band.

Their eyes met again briefly, and the man's polite smile faded. His face took on a guarded expression— an animal on the alert for possible danger.

"There," he said quietly, letting her sleeve fall away and avoiding her eyes. "Just a little tear. Should be real easy to mend."

"Thank you," Kate said with distant courtesy. "It was kind of you to help."

Both of them, she realized, were deliberately scrambling to establish some space between themselves and that unsettling moment when their eyes had met. There had been far too much intimacy in that first glance, too much admiration.

Kate managed to keep her expression calm and polite, but her body was still talking to his, and she could feel his answering.

Well, hello, they were saying. Who are you? Where have you been? I've been looking such a long time for you. Come closer, I want to touch you. Come, let me see how good you feel....

This treacherous reaction of her body was unsettling, to say the least. Kate couldn't remember the last time she'd felt physically drawn to any man, including her husband. And this was certainly the worst possible time and place for such feelings to evidence themselves.

Finally taking a deep breath, she turned away from the man's watchful dark gaze to face the group of hostile women around the desk.

"Hello, again," she said. "I'm Kate Daniels."

The three women made no effort to hide their disapproval. Worse, Kate could feel an active dislike flowing from them, and it puzzled her.

Kate Daniels wasn't accustomed to being disliked. Usually, people were drawn to her. Even Mamie acknowledged this.

"You may not have much of anything else going for you," her mother had once commented rather tactlessly when Kate was a gangly, graceless teenager. "But you do seem to have a real knack for getting along with people, don't you, chickie?"

Until today, Kate thought. How could you make friends with women like these, who apparently disliked you without even knowing you?

While Kate was wrestling with this problem, the women got to their feet and began to file silently past her in the direction of the lobby. The last of them paused on the way out.

"I'm Agatha Krantz," the woman said. Kate recognized the voice as the one that had accused her of stealing Adam's money. "I'm an alderwoman on the town council."

Kate nodded and murmured a greeting. The woman ignored Kate's outstretched hand. "The town has something to say about what you're doing here," she said darkly. "You'll be hearing from us."

And with that ominous threat, Agatha Krantz left the office and marched through the lobby and into the coffee shop, clutching her handbag like a weapon.

CHAPTER TWO

KATE LOOKED AROUND at the empty office. Even the attractive man in the Stetson had left. She sighed and flipped through a few of the stained, flyblown notices on the bulletin board, then went next door to look at the room where she planned to sleep.

The windows appeared to be intact here, as well, and the room was dry, though chilly and not at all clean. A single bed covered with coarse gray blankets was pushed against one wall, and an old dresser stood next to it on three legs. A block of wood had been wedged under one corner to compensate for the missing leg.

Kate stored her suitcase in the bare alcove that served as a closet, then ventured down the hall to examine the adjoining room, which was completely empty. A musty smell hung in the air. The floor was littered with old beer cans, candy wrappers and some material that looked suspiciously like a mouse's nest.

Kate shuddered. She certainly couldn't remember the Realtor showing her this room when she'd told him her plan to create a pleasant main floor suite for herself.

In fact, he'd been warmly enthusiastic. He'd praised her creativity while dragging her around the building, pointing out the sturdiness of the walls and floor joists and the remarkable preservation of the nineteenth-century woodwork.

Kate brooded over the musty remnants of the mouse nest, then shook her head and went back into the hallway.

"Okay," she said aloud to a glowering portrait of a mustachioed early settler in an antique frame. "Okay, so it's going to take a little more work than I thought. That's no problem. I've still got lots of money, and all the time in the world."

But the pioneer looked unconvinced, and after her hasty tour of the rest of the hotel, Kate was more than ready to agree with him.

Some of the upper rooms had apparently housed vagrants over the winter, and were in an appalling state. Almost all the plumbing fixtures needed to be replaced. Many of the floors were stained and cracked from moisture seeping through broken windows, and a few of the ceilings on the lower stories had also suffered from water damage. Over everything lay the sad, musty scent of an abandoned building.

By the time Kate returned to the office, she was so depressed that she could hardly keep from bursting into tears. Adding to her misery was the knowledge that her comfortable bank account was beginning to look smaller by the moment.

Until now, Kate had been rather proud of the way she'd handled all the financial details of this transaction. With the Realtor's help, she'd added the purchase price, the renovation costs as estimated by the building contractor and living expenses until the hotel began to make a profit. The total had been a sum Kate felt she could manage with ease.

But she hadn't reckoned on the actual physical state of the Wolf Hill Hotel. Belatedly, Kate began to realize that perhaps she'd placed a little too much trust in the Realtor, who'd seemed like such a nice man.

She wandered into the coffee shop. The lunch crowd had dispersed and only a few people lingered at the plastic-covered tables. None of them, Kate saw after a hasty survey, were the women from the town council. The handsome cowboy had also vanished, much to Kate's relief.

She sat at a table and looked out the window at the bleak main street of Wolf Hill.

"Ready to order?" a voice said at her elbow.

She turned and saw a bulging red-and-white striped apron. Behind the apron was a small person who reminded Kate of a gingerbread lady. She was about sixty, short and fat, with little black-currant eyes, a round pink mouth and a frosting of curly silver hair.

"Hilda Fairweather," the woman said, beaming at her. "I guess you're my new landlady, ain't you?"

Kate smiled back, warmed by the woman's friendliness. "I suppose I am," she said. "I'm Kate Daniels."

She recalled the Realtor mentioning that a Hilda Fairweather ran the coffee shop, and telling Kate that the rental of the coffee shop provided her, as the hotel owner, with an immediate source of income.

"Just another bonus," he'd said happily, "in a real sweet deal."

"I got plans to discuss with you," Hilda was saying.

"Plans?" Kate forced her thoughts back to the present.

"Just a minute. I'll bring you something to eat, then tell you all about it. What do you want?"

"I guess..." Kate looked vaguely at the menu. "Just an egg salad sandwich and a pot of tea, please," she murmured.

"Brown bread?" Hilda asked. "You look like the brown-bread type."

"Please," Kate said with a smile.

She watched Hilda's brisk departure to the kitchen, then returned to her contemplation of the drab scene beyond the window.

Hilda reappeared almost immediately, carrying a tray with Kate's sandwich, a generous-size teapot and two white mugs. She settled herself, poured tea for both of them and watched in satisfaction as Kate began to devour her sandwich.

"It's delicious," Kate said when she was able to speak. "Just delicious."

"'Course it is," Hilda said amiably. "Wait till you taste my bilberry pie. Now, what I'm planning, Mrs. Daniels, is to expand."

"You want a bigger coffee shop?"

"No, I want to open a dinner-type place along with the coffee shop. Fine dining, you know."

Hilda sat back in triumph, waiting for Kate's reaction.

Kate looked at her cautiously. "Are you sure... do you think Wolf Hill is ready for fine dining?"

"Well, sure it is. Right now, lots of folks drive into the city for steaks and wine, and they could eat right here, instead. I was planning to move into the old dining room, which is only used right now to store Walter Hamill's frozen carcasses and taxidermy supplies. We could do it over real nice, say in a Spanish style," Hilda said enthusiastically, "with all them little archways and dark beams and stuff. Raymond says you can get them beams made out of plastic, look exactly like the real thing, you know."

Kate nodded, her head spinning. "Mrs. Fairweather," she began.

"Hilda."

"Yes, Hilda. Well, I wouldn't mind considering the idea of a restaurant in the hotel after I've had a chance to... to get settled in a bit more." She paused for a moment. "Actually, I was hoping to keep the place sort of historically authentic," Kate added. "If you know what I mean," she finished lamely.

"I'm not sure I do."

"I mean, any changes or improvements I make to the building, I'd like them to be in keeping with the hotel's appearance at the turn of the century when it was built."

Hilda looked dubious. "Well, now, near as I can figure from what my grandma said, back in them days, people ate buffalo stew and biscuits in the dining room and spit on the floor. I can bring in some old pictures."

Just then, a stolid-looking gray-haired man in coveralls and a plaid shirt entered the coffee shop and seated himself across the room. Hilda's face brightened. She inclined her curly head toward the newcomer. "That's Luther Barnes," Hilda said in a stage whisper. "He's crazy about me. Can't keep his eyes off me."

Kate peeked at the man while he unfolded a newspaper, put on a pair of reading glasses and began to read intently.

"Always after me to marry him." Hilda sighed, studying his shaggy bent head. "The man can't leave me alone."

"And you're not interested in him?" Kate ventured.

Hilda shrugged. "I'm a career woman," she said.

Kate smiled and finished her sandwich. "A man I met this morning in my office," she began hesitantly. "Tall and dark, wearing an old gray hat and cowboy boots..."

"Nathan Cameron," Hilda said, her voice softening. "My, he's a real sweetheart, that boy is. If I were thirty years younger, he wouldn't be running around loose, I can tell you that."

Kate nodded and stirred sugar into her tea.

"Although, come to think of it," Hilda added, "I don't s'pose a career woman would want to get tied up with Nathan."

"Why not?"

"Being his wife, that'd be a full-time job. I sure can't see any Cameron wife having a career besides. Helping to run that ranch of his would be enough of a job for any woman."

"Why? Is it such a big ranch?"

"Pretty big," Hilda said briefly. "Getting bigger all the time."

"He was talking with a group of women," Kate said, returning to her main concern. "They seemed very upset about something."

Hilda snorted. "Aggie and her bunch, they're *always* upset about something."

"But it seemed to be something to do with the hotel."

Hilda sipped her tea and looked fondly at Luther Barnes. As far as Kate could tell, the man hadn't once glanced in their direction since entering the room. "They don't want you to get the liquor license back," she said, turning to Kate.

"But... but the hotel isn't even close to being profitable without the liquor license," Kate floundered. "It's absolutely essential to have it."

"I *know* that," Hilda said impatiently. "But them women on the town council, they think their husbands will stay home more if they don't have a bar to go to at night. And," she added with a grin, "they're probably right. Think about it, Kate. Would you stay home with a person like Aggie if you could go down to a nice cozy bar and sit around talking with all your friends?"

Kate smiled in acknowledgment. Still, she was more than a little concerned by this unexpected source of opposition. Especially since the Realtor had once casually mentioned that the hotel owner could be denied a liquor license if sixty-five percent of the town voted against it.

"Not that such a thing is ever going to happen," he'd said airily. "Wolf Hill loves its hotel, Mrs. Daniels. Believe me, the whole town is anxious to have that place up and running again."

Kate felt another stab of annoyance with the Realtor.

"Butts," a hoarse voice said at her elbow. She looked up, startled.

A man stood near their table, small and wiry, with a sad wizened face and a bald head that gleamed in the light when he removed his cap and nodded expectantly at Kate.

"Butts," he repeated.

Kate regarded him blankly while Hilda vanished into the kitchen again.

"Raymond Butts, general contractor. Come to give the estimate."

"Oh! Mr. *Butts*," Kate said eagerly. She shook the little man's hand, then looked out the window at his truck, which had a covered box filled with tools and a ladder and wheelbarrow strapped to the roof.

Kate sighed in relief, then turned back to Mr. Butts with an emotion close to love.

Here was the answer to all her problems. In Raymond Butts's grimy hands—and in his truckful of tools—lay the solution to rotting floors, broken windows and useless plumbing.

Mr. Butts would fix everything.

"I'm so glad to see you," Kate told him warmly.

Raymond Butts gave her a noncommittal glance. "Maybe we better look around, okay?" he said. "I gotta do the estimate."

"But I already have the estimate," Kate said in surprise. "You gave it to the Realtor, and he passed it on to me."

"That was just the preliminary estimate. Now I gotta do the real one, all itemized and everything." The contractor whipped out a legal-size yellow pad and a ballpoint pen.

"But—"

"Mrs. Daniels, you want this place fixed up, or not? Because I'm a busy man, you know. I got lots of things to do."

"Oh, yes," Kate said humbly, terrified at the thought of Raymond Butts vanishing with all his tools. "I'm sorry, I just assumed the Realtor's estimate was final, that's all."

Her impression turned out to have been badly mistaken. Kate's spirits plummeted as she toured the hotel with Raymond and he pointed out problems she hadn't even thought to consider.

Walls were off line, requiring the removal of lath, plaster and studs, and the installation of new lumber. Cast-iron plumbing had to be ripped out to its source and replaced with expensive copper pipe. All the window frames had rotted and needed to be replaced before new windows could be installed.

"But," Kate ventured, examining an upstairs window frame, "this looks fine, Mr. Butts. It looks really solid to me."

"Termites," Raymond said.

"Termites?"

"Eat their way through from the bottom up. Can't tell they're even in there until the window falls apart. Terrible things, them termites."

"But I didn't think termites were a problem on the prairies. I thought the winters were too cold."

"Look, Mrs. Daniels," the contractor began, looking wounded, "if you don't want me to—"

"I'm sorry," Kate assured him, instantly contrite. "It's just that all this is going to be so much more expensive than I'd realized. I'm not sure how I'm going to…"

But Raymond wasn't listening. He was off again, clattering down the ornate curved staircase, heading for the basement.

"Stairs prob'ly need to be replaced, too," he called over his shoulder. "Solid oak risers and hand-turned spindles. Won't be cheap."

"Oh," Kate moaned, wringing her hands.

She followed him into the basement, a dreadful hole where a dark, many-armed monster, comprising the hotel's heating system, lurked behind cobwebs and scattered garbage.

Raymond Butts stood in gloomy silence, examining the boiler. "Ugly old sucker, ain't it?" he said at last. "This thing's been down here since the beginning, I reckon."

Kate paused beside him on the cracked concrete and regarded the boiler—the size of a couple of large automobiles—made of stained cast iron and dripping with tattered insulation.

"Prob'ly been through three conversions. Burnt coal in the old days," Raymond said. "Then oil, then natural gas. The whole thing needs to come out, and all them pipes, too. Likely come close to twenty thousand dollars."

This, at least, was an expense that Kate had planned on. "It'll be awfully hard to get this old boiler out of here, won't it?" she asked dubiously. "It must weigh tons."

"Gotta break it up with a sledgehammer and take it out in pieces. It'll take a whole crew," Raymond said. "That'll cost extra."

He turned his attention to the rest of the basement, squinting at the dusty ceiling with a speculative expression that Kate was beginning to dread. Her spirits sank even lower.

"Need to replace most of them beams," Raymond announced. "Otherwise, the whole building's gonna fall down."

Kate looked at the beams, which were about three feet thick and appeared to be as hard as concrete.

"They seem . . . really strong," she offered without much hope.

"Brittle," Raymond said briefly. "Wood like this here, it gets so old and dry, it just turns brittle. Them beams could snap at any time."

Kate stared at him in horror. "How much . . . how much will it cost to replace them?" she whispered.

He shrugged. "New beams, that's real expensive. See, the whole building needs to be jacked up while the old beams come out. And these big chunks of wood, they don't come cheap."

"But . . . how much?"

He shrugged again, making a note on his pad. "I gotta check it out. About ten, maybe fifteen thousand."

"Fifteen thousand!" Kate sagged against one of the old wooden uprights that supported the beams. "Mr. Butts, I can't possibly afford that. Not with all the other—"

"Some kind of problem here?" a voice inquired mildly, just above their heads. Kate looked up to see Nathan Cameron sitting on the basement steps, watching them with interest. He still had the gray Stetson tipped over his eyes, but he'd removed his sheepskin coat. He wore a faded blue denim shirt and a tooled leather belt with a big silver buckle.

Raymond gave the younger man a sullen glance and went on writing.

"Ray?" Nathan asked. "What's going on?"

"Mrs. Daniels and me are talking business," Raymond said coldly. "I'm the contractor on the job here."

"I see." Nathan Cameron turned to Kate.

Again she had the impression of contained masculine power, but his voice when he addressed her was surprisingly gentle. "Anything the matter, Mrs. Daniels?"

Kate hesitated, disarmed by his kindness. "I just... I had an estimate on the renovations," she said, her voice trembling. "But Mr. Butts says it's likely to cost so much more than the initial estimate, and I don't know how I'm ever going to afford it."

Raymond frowned at her in warning, but Kate barely noticed him. She was looking up at Nathan Cameron, who rubbed his jaw and nodded slowly.

"I see. What kind of extra expenses are you looking at, Mrs. Daniels?"

"Oh, all kinds of things," Kate said in despair. "All over the hotel. Like these beams," she added, ignoring Raymond's fierce glare. "Mr. Butts says they're brittle and need to be replaced, and it's going to cost fifteen thousand dollars. I can't possibly..."

She fell silent, unable to go on. Nathan Cameron turned his gaze on the contractor.

"*Brittle*, Ray?" he asked gently.

Raymond shifted nervously on his feet. "Maybe the beams are okay," he said after a moment, crossing an item off his list. "I guess they'll hold up for a while. Now, Mrs. Daniels," he added, deliberately turning his back to Nathan, who still sat on the stairs, "if I could get you to sign this..."

"You know," Nathan said, "it's been a long time since I looked at this old place. Maybe before Mrs. Daniels signs that, she wouldn't mind giving me a little tour. You might as well come along, Ray," he added with a winsome smile. "You can show me some of these problems that need fixing. I'm real interested in construction, since I'm having so much work done out at the ranch these days."

Raymond glared. "Look, Nathan, this here deal is between me and Mrs. Daniels. You got no right to interfere."

Nathan smiled at him again, then turned to Kate. "You said you had an estimate, ma'am?" he asked. "Now, where did that estimate come from?"

"The Realtor gave it to me before I bought the hotel," Kate said. "He told me it was Mr. Butts's estimate for doing the most necessary renovations, but it's—"

"And this Realtor," Nathan interrupted, looking interested. "What was his name, did you say?"

"Larry Miller."

"Ah." Nathan glanced at Raymond. "That's your wife's cousin's boy, isn't it, Ray? You know," he said, gazing into the depths of the littered basement, "I always thought Larry was a little slick. Come on, Raymond," he added, his voice hardening, "let's have us a look at the rest of this building."

Raymond's frown deepened as he climbed past the young rancher, stamping up the stairs to the lobby.

Kate climbed up a couple of steps and looked at Nathan, whose eyes glittered in the dusky light. The man was a confusing combination—part Superman, part Clark Kent.

"Thank you," she said, beginning to feel uncomfortable when he didn't move to make way for her. "I guess I must look awfully gullible, don't I?"

"You look pretty good to me," he said quietly. "Can I call you Kate?"

"Yes, of course."

"Kate," he murmured with satisfaction. "I've been wanting to say that all day. I've never met anybody whose name suited them better."

"What do you mean?" Kate asked.

"It's a real wholesome, nice kind of name."

Kate tensed, wondering if he was making fun of her. But his face was calm and sincere beneath the brim of the old Stetson. Suddenly, she remembered the scene that morning in her office, and realized there was something she badly wanted to tell him.

"I didn't, you know," Kate murmured shyly.

He raised an eyebrow.

"I didn't...cheat my husband out of all his money. Everybody around here seems to think I've got some kind of fortune, but it's not true."

Nathan's teeth flashed in the shadows. "I didn't think you did."

"You didn't?"

"I figure," he said, getting to his feet with a lithe motion, "that fleecing a man out of all his money would be a greedy, selfish thing to do. And this..." He gestured at the disaster area of the basement. "This doesn't exactly look to me like the kind of place where you'd find a greedy, selfish woman."

Their eyes met. Kate smiled and began to feel a great deal better, almost her old self.

Nathan stood aside courteously to let her precede him up the steps. Kate's cheeks warmed as he followed close behind, the sound of his boots clattering in the cavernous depths of the old basement.

This time, Kate's tour of the hotel was vastly more enjoyable. Raymond Butts discovered that many of the problems he'd been concerned about earlier didn't seem quite as serious on closer examination. His legal pad gradually filled with cross-outs and corrections, although his shoulders were stiff with resentment and his face remained sullen.

Nathan Cameron followed them around the building, through the hallways and up and down the stairs, looking impassively at the shabby rooms. He said almost nothing, but his quiet presence dominated. It was clear that Raymond was uncomfortably conscious of the younger man, as Nathan studied window frames, reached up to touch splintered woodwork, peered into closets and bathrooms. By the time they reached the lobby again, Kate felt so happy that she could barely contain herself. All the dreams that had been snatched away with such abruptness were back, shining like rainbows. It was all she could do not to bounce and cavort with excitement.

"So, what do you think?" she urged Raymond, who stood frowning at his yellow pad.

Nathan leaned against the newel post and smiled at the contractor. "Yeah, Ray," he murmured. "How's that estimate looking now?"

Raymond glared from under the brim of his cap. "It looks," he said stiffly, "like the job might come in at pretty close to the estimate Mrs. Daniels had when she bought the place. Provided she's content with a building that ain't really fixed up proper."

"Oh, I don't think she will be," Nathan said softly. "I think when Mrs. Daniels signs that estimate, Ray, she's going to expect a real good, tip-top job."

"I always do a good job," the contractor said with an injured look.

Nathan sighed. "I know you do. You may be a greedy little sucker, Ray, but you're a damned good builder."

Kate ignored most of this conversation. She was happily running figures through her head, adding and subtracting, weighing bank balances against cash outflow. After a moment, she turned to the contractor with a radiant smile.

"In that case," she said, "there's another job I'd like you to do, as well, Mr. Butts, if you wouldn't mind having a look at it." They trooped down the hall to the room Kate planned to occupy, and she explained how she wanted a couple of walls knocked out to make living quarters for herself.

"She never said nothing about this before," Raymond complained to Nathan, who was regarding him in watchful silence. "Not a word."

"I didn't think I could afford it," Kate told both men. "Not when all the other repairs were going to cost so much. But now I'm pretty sure I can have this done at the same time."

Nathan looked at the narrow bed and the wobbly dresser.

"So what were you planning?" he asked. "When you thought you couldn't afford to fix up some decent living quarters for yourself, I mean. Were you just going to have the other work done, and live forever in this little room?"

Kate nodded. "I didn't feel I had much choice," she said simply.

Nathan cast a cold look at the contractor. Again Kate saw a brief, knife-edged flash of the man's power and strength. Nathan Cameron, though mild and soft-spoken, certainly wasn't a man you'd want for an enemy, she thought with a shiver.

Evidently, Raymond Butts felt the same way. He turned to Kate with an ingratiating smile, then hurried to jot down some numbers on his yellow pad.

"Well, Mrs. Daniels," he said at last, "this here job is kind of a bonus. I can likely do it real cheap, since I'll have a crew here, anyway."

Kate inhaled deeply. "Really? How much?"

Raymond contemplated his page of figures. "Maybe three, four thousand. That includes knocking out all the walls, repairing the ceilings and floors and putting in new wiring and plumbing fixtures."

"Oh, wonderful!" Kate said, dazed with happiness. "Isn't that *wonderful?*"

She turned joyously to Nathan, who met her smile with startled silence. For the first time, Kate saw the man's composure slip. He shifted awkwardly in the doorway and turned away from her with such haste that she felt as though she were being dismissed.

His dark eyes moved over the room, examining Kate's suitcase in the shabby alcove, the torn wallpaper and stained ceiling, the rickety old dresser. Finally, he looked at the bed with its narrow mattress and prickly gray blankets.

To her horror, Kate found herself blushing like a schoolgirl. She hurried across the room, feeling shy and unaccountably embarrassed.

"This window, Mr. Butts," she said hastily. "I was thinking it would be nice to make it into a French door opening onto the garden. I'd like to restore the flagstone terrace out there eventually, and be able to sit outside with my coffee when I wake up in the morning."

Raymond's sallow face expressed his disapproval of such high-flown notions. Still, he crossed the room to study the window.

"Shouldn't be hard to do, but I'd have to rip all this out and install a new frame for the door." He gave a little experimental tug at the windowsill, which lifted and came away in his hand. Raymond looked at the piece of oak, then at Kate. "Just lifted smooth as butter," he commented in amazement. "I doubt that it was ever nailed in place."

He leaned over to peer into the wall cavity beneath the missing sill.

"Well, I'll be damned," he muttered.

"What is it?" Kate asked.

"Some kind of old book sitting on a ledge in here," Raymond said, reaching into the opening. "God knows how long it's been here."

He fished out a book about the size of his yellow pad. It looked like a thick ledger, with sturdy black covers.

"Just like new," Raymond marveled. "No water damage at all. Them walls and moldings must be sounder than I figured."

"May I see it?" Kate asked, peering over his shoulder. She took the book and opened it to the cover page.

To Ellen Livingston from her Loving Papa, the inscription read in a flowing copperplate hand. On the Occasion of her Twentieth Birthday.

The facing page was covered with slanting, vigorous handwriting, markedly different from that of the inscription. The ink had probably once been navy blue, but had faded to a shade of gray so pale that it was almost indecipherable in places. The first entry was dated August 22, 1904.

"It looks like a diary," Kate said, leafing reverently through the closely written pages. "And you know what?" she breathed. "It's almost a hundred years old."

Raymond cast another cautious glance at Nathan, his face registering both greed and fear. He cleared his throat and shuffled his heavy work boots. "Well, now, I reckon that book should prob'ly be mine," he said with elaborate casualness. "Seeing as I was the one who found it."

Nathan was silent a moment, looking at the contractor. Finally, he turned back to Kate. "I'd appreciate it if you'd let me have the diary, Kate," he said quietly. "My great-grandfather settled here about a hundred years ago, and my mother's always been interested in local history. I'm sure she'd love to read that book."

Kate looked at the two men in panic, her smile fading. She clutched the diary to her chest and felt a wholly uncharacteristic surge of defiance.

"No," she said firmly, surprising herself as well as the others. "It's *my* book. I own this hotel, and that includes everything in it."

Raymond shrugged in defeat and turned to leave the room. "Well, then, I'll just go in the coffee shop and work out this here estimate," he said over his shoulder. "And you can sign it, okay?"

"We'll be there in a minute," Nathan said. "Make sure you add real careful, Ray."

Alone with the man, Kate's newfound confidence began to falter. She looked at him nervously, conscious again of his penetrating eyes and the controlled grace of his body.

She was also beginning to realize, with a miserable sinking feeling, that her brief moment of assertiveness about the diary couldn't begin to compensate for her general ineptitude in her dealings with Raymond Butts.

What upset her more was the realization that she'd made almost no progress in her painful journey toward independence. Here she was again depending on somebody else to solve her problems and get her out of trouble, just as she always had. If Nathan Cameron hadn't come along when he did, she probably would have signed the contractor's inflated estimate and ruined any chance of making this hotel a pleasant and profitable venture.

Irrationally, Kate's anger with herself slowly hardened into resentment of the man who'd helped her. She looked at the floor, wishing he would go away.

As if reading her thoughts, Nathan gave her a gentle smile. "You'll learn to manage Ray," he said comfortably. "Folks around here are used to him, but I guess he can be pretty intimidating if you haven't known him all your life."

"That's no excuse for being as foolish as I was," Kate said. She turned away abruptly, still unwilling to meet his eyes, and put the diary in the back of one of the dresser drawers.

"I think you're being a little hard on yourself, Kate."

Kate ignored him. "Thank you very much for your help," she said in a neutral voice, moving past Nathan and into the hallway. "If you don't mind, I think I can deal with Mr. Butts from now on."

Her statement sounded cold and ungrateful, even to her own ears, but she didn't want any more of his quiet helpfulness. A person could so easily get to rely on that sort of thing, and Kate needed to stand on her own two feet.

A shadow passed over Nathan's face. He looked at her in silence for a moment, then nodded courteously and strode off through the hotel lobby and out the door into the prairie wind.

CHAPTER THREE

Monday, August 22, 1904

Here I am at the beginning of my saga. Papa gave me this beautiful book for my birthday in June, and since then I have been wild with impatience to begin recording the events of my life on these inviting blank pages. But I vowed that I would not set pen to paper until my Great Adventure had well and truly begun. And now it has!

In fact, I can hardly believe that I am writing these pages in the King Edward Hotel in Calgary. I suppose I could really have begun my diary during the train journey west, which was interminable. Already it seems like months since we left Ontario and began rolling across the prairie. I never dreamed there was so much land in all the world.

I felt reluctant to begin this book on the train because the vastness all around us made me feel far too insignificant to be doing something so trivial and self-centered as recording my life in a diary. And, if truth be told, I was also rather sad and homesick. I fear that I had moments when I thought Papa might be right, after all, and I am far too young and inexperienced to travel into the wilderness and take on the challenge of teaching school in a place that is not yet even an organized province.

But now that I have arrived in Calgary, I feel much better. This town, though rough and noisy, is not at all the wilderness outpost that I expected. There are some very smart carriages on the downtown streets, and many of the ladies are wearing the latest fashions. I must admit that some of them look more stylish than I do, although I *am* rather proud of the navy shirt-waist that Auntie Grace made for me before I left. It looks as nice as anything they are wearing in the hotel dining room.

But enough of that. I have resolved that I will not deal with such superficial things as clothes and hair-styles in my diary anymore, now that I am grown up and so far from home.

I was, as I said, relieved to find that Calgary is not some wilderness outpost filled with outlaws and herds of buffalo. But of course, I should have known better than to have those foolish fears. After all, the North-west Territories will be incorporated into two prov-inces in the coming year, and this area will be given the name Alberta.

What an exciting time that will be! My students and I will watch history being written. I feel such a thrill when I write "my students." I can hardly wait to reach Wolf Hill and see my school. And, very soon after that, I will begin to meet my students. The letter from the newly formed school board says that they expect twenty-four students this term, ranging in age from six to fourteen. And they have never had a school be-fore! I will be their first teacher, as they will be my first school. Wonderful, terrifying thought...

I was just interrupted by a disturbance in the street below me. A rough-looking group of men came careening down the street on horseback, dismounted and ran into a building across from my window. Soon afterward, they rushed out again, and I heard gunshots as they mounted their horses and galloped away. A few ladies screamed and people ducked hastily into doorways, but nobody seemed much alarmed, and after the disturbance, they went quietly on about their business. Perhaps the Northwest Territories are not quite as civilized as they appear in the lobby of the King Edward!

Well, I shall soon find out. In a very few days, I embark on the final part of my journey, to the town of Wolf Hill and my new life.

KATE SAT in her bed against a mound of lumpy pillows, covered by the cleanest of the blankets she'd been able to scrounge from other rooms in the hotel. She finished reading Ellen Livingston's first entry, then leafed through the hand-written pages, delighted to see that the schoolteacher hadn't lost interest and stopped recording events in her diary. The book was filled to within the last few pages with her vigorous slanted handwriting.

Thinking of the pleasure that awaited her within those pages, Kate sighed, then frowned when she recalled Raymond Butts laying claim to the diary, and Nathan asking for it, as well. At least she'd asserted herself and kept the book. Kate's cheeks still burned with embarrassment when she thought about her other dealings with the contractor, and how she'd only been saved from disaster by Nathan Cameron's quiet protectiveness.

The man must consider her a complete idiot....

She stiffened, listening to an ominous creaking noise out in the lobby. When she'd first climbed into bed, Kate had been too interested in the diary to be aware of anything else. But now she became conscious of the fact that she was the only living person in the building.

The coffee shop had closed an hour ago and Hilda had gone home, after pressing Kate to come with her for the night. Though strongly tempted, Kate had refused, explaining to Hilda that this was now her home and she had to get used to it sooner or later.

She held the diary in her arms and looked at the dingy chintz curtains that were drawn against the night. The darkness and solitude wouldn't have bothered Kate so much, but the old building was also alive with noises, creaks and moans and suspicious rustling, ominous thumps and clatters—probably from the ancient heating system.

In the darkness of the spring night, it wasn't hard to believe that the old hotel was haunted by ghosts from its colorful past. Kate shivered and opened the diary again, hoping that the struggle to decipher Ellen Livingston's faded handwriting would soon make her drowsy enough to fall asleep.

Wednesday, August 24, 1904

I have finally arrived. I can hardly believe it. This morning, bright and early, I was collected at the hotel in Calgary by a dour grizzled Scotsman named Angus McLean, who travels once a week to Wolf Hill with mail and supplies.

"Miss Livingston?" he said when I met him in the lobby.

"Yes," I said, delighted to see him. "And you must be Mr. McLean."

"Aye," he said, and marched out to the street where his wagon was waiting. I record this conversation because they were the only words he spoke to me during the entire thirty-mile drive. The man was like one of those cigar-store Indian figures carved out of wood that have become so popular back East. I simply could not get him to answer a question, or to volunteer any information at all. Throughout the trip, he ignored me as if I were a fly buzzing around his head, or some other minor source of annoyance.

The wagon was so loaded with sacks of flour and sugar, and crates of supplies for the general store in Wolf Hill that Mr. McLean could barely find room for my trunks and hatboxes. Under his disapproving glare, I felt like a rather frivolous creature to have burdened him with two trunks. And to think that Mama despaired for months of any lady transporting a proper wardrobe with less than *four!*

We stopped at a number of farms along the way to deliver the mail and rest the horses. It took until evening to reach Wolf Hill, and by then I was dusty, weary and very tired of the company of Mr. McLean.

But I was *not* tired of the prairie. This country seems so different when viewed from the seat of a wagon rather than from the window of a train. There is a lovely subtlety to the colors of land and sky, the depth of the horizon and the arch of the heavens. I have never felt so free and alive as I did on that journey. There were times when I wanted to leap down from the hard wooden seat and run into the wind with my arms outstretched, shouting like a child. It was all

I could do not to laugh aloud with joy, but Mr. Mc-
Lean already disapproved of me so heartily that I
hesitated to give him more frivolous behavior to frown
about. So I was very decorous, and thanked him po-
litely when we arrived at the Wolf Hill Hotel.

He grunted, dragged my trunks into the lobby and
vanished, leaving me alone to contemplate the place
that will be my home for at least a year.

The Wolf Hill Hotel is a rather impressive building, recently constructed and surprisingly elegant. The
lobby is done in rich wood paneling and dark green
wallpaper flocked with gold velvet. Lamps decorated
with gold fringes hang above the sofas and armchairs, and an intriguing frontier touch is added by
several strange-looking chairs made entirely of curly
buffalo horns, upholstered with steer hide, that are
placed near the reception desk.

While I waited for my trunks to be taken to my
room, I peeked into the dining room and saw a number of tables and a large fireplace in which a fire
crackled despite the warmth of the August night. It
seemed cozy but I was not at all hungry, having taken
my evening meal at a farm along the way. Mr. Mc-
Lean and I dined on beef stew with a weather-beaten
pioneer woman and her four silent children, who spent
the entire meal staring at my hat.

There was a baby, too, who wore a little nightshirt
and crawled about in an area marked off with kegs and
floored with an old quilt to protect him from splinters. He was a lovely baby, clean and happy despite the
roughness of the cabin. When I took him on my knee
after dinner and played with him, the other children
softened and began to talk with me.

Not even the eldest knows his letters, and they are not in the Wolf Hill district, so they cannot attend my school in the coming term. My heart aches for them. I wish I could educate every child in this territory. But, of course, that is not possible. Papa says I always try to do too much, and I suppose he is right. I must be content with my school and my job, small though it may be.

Anyway, back to Wolf Hill. I want to finish writing this before I fall asleep, but I am so tired. While I was waiting in the lobby, a door opened to another part of the hotel. I fear that this other room must be a beer parlor as I heard a lot of rowdy men's voices and some music, and caught a whiff of a stale and rather exciting smell.

A man came out into the lobby and looked at me with such intensity, almost insolence, that I still feel troubled at the memory. He was tall, dressed in ragged buckskin pants, knee-high leather moccasins and a coarse linen shirt laced with a rawhide thong. His face was dark and hawklike, very handsome in a rugged kind of way, and his eyes were black and piercing.

He looked at me for an unpleasantly long time, then smiled. His teeth were white against his skin, which was tanned as dark as chestnut. "You must be the new schoolteacher," he said, holding out his hand as if I were a man.

I shook his hand, trying to maintain a look of grave dignity but wondering what to do next, as Mama would faint if I addressed a man in a hotel before we were properly introduced.

"I'm Joshua Cameron," he said. "I live west of town."

KATE CLOSED the book, switched off her reading lamp and lay staring into the darkness, her mind whirling with dates and numbers.

Almost a hundred years ago, she thought. What would the man be? Nathan's great-grandfather? Or would it be...

She rolled over and snuggled against the pillows, thinking how surprised Nathan Cameron would be if she showed him the description of his handsome frontier ancestor. But as soon as the thought entered her mind, Kate dismissed it.

The diary was Kate's treasure, and hers alone. She certainly didn't want Nathan's family laying claim to the book just because it mentioned some long-dead forebear of theirs. The schoolteacher and the frontiersman would have to remain her secret, at least for a while, until she learned how the story ended.

Or if there was a story at all.

Kate felt comforted by the courageous spirit of Ellen Livingston, a girl who had braved hardship and solitude in a time when women were supposed to be frail creatures. Ellen wouldn't have allowed herself to be intimidated by the darkness and the creepy noises, Kate told herself firmly.

Wearied by her long and eventful day, she fell asleep, her mind filled with confused thoughts about Ellen Livingston's first night in the Wolf Hill Hotel, Raymond Butts's yellow pad, Hilda Fairweather's plump figure in the striped apron... and Nathan Cameron's dark handsome face.

In her dreams, Nathan wore buckskin and moccasins, and a coarse homespun shirt tied with a rawhide thong.

NATHAN RODE among his placid Hereford cows, enjoying the warmth of the April sunshine. Spring had finally arrived, and the cows searched hungrily for the tender shoots of green grass that pressed up from beneath the dried winter growth. The rolling prairie was starred with crocuses and tiny mayflowers, sparkling like jewels on the hillsides.

Nathan ran a watchful eye over the grazing cows. A few of them already had calves, frisking and leaping awkwardly in the sunshine. Hundreds more were due to arrive over the coming weeks. The calving season required much of his attention.

As he rode, Nathan looked around his domain, a sprawling thirty-square-mile tract of land that had been in his family for almost a century. The rolling hills faded in the distance to bright gold, lit by the afternoon sun, and the sky was an incredible blue, shadowing into turquoise where it dipped toward the wide horizon. Like her hair and eyes, Nathan thought dreamily. And her cheeks when she blushed were the color of the wild roses that filled the coulees in June....

He drew himself erect in the saddle and gripped the reins, embarrassed by his flight of poetic fancy.

"What do you think, Scout?" he asked his big piebald gelding. "Have I gone clear out of my mind, or what?"

The horse twitched his ears and sidestepped as a horned lark flew up from the sagebrush and flitted away on the breeze. A pair of antelope crested a ridge and stood watching the rider pass, their dainty bodies silhouetted against the sky.

Nathan sighed and tried to stop thinking about the shy blue-eyed woman, dealing so ineptly with Raymond Butts in the basement of her big old hotel. He turned his horse around and headed for home, settling into an easy rocking canter that covered the miles with ease.

He approached the sprawl of buildings and trotted up the long driveway flanked with cottonwoods that had been planted by his great-grandfather, Joshua, the first Cameron to occupy this land. The old tree branches, entwined above Nathan's head, were still bare and delicate against the sky.

Nathan passed through the arch of trees and rode into the barn. He dismounted, loosened the cinches and stripped off the saddle and the steaming blanket, heaving them onto a rack near the box stalls. Finally, he led the horse outside, brushed and watered him and turned him loose in a small pasture near the barn, then started toward the house. At the sound of a vehicle churning up the driveway, Nathan looked around, frowning briefly when he recognized his visitor. A rusty compact car rocked to a halt near the house, and Aggie Krantz got out and approached him.

"Hi, Aggie," Nathan said, his spirits sinking rapidly. "How are you on this nice spring afternoon?"

Aggie sighed. "Oh, 'bout as well as can be expected, I guess."

Nathan suppressed a chuckle. As long as he could remember, Aggie had been saying exactly the same thing.

"It's warming up a little," she conceded, gripping her handbag against her jacket front and looking at the rolling prairie. "You finished calving, Nathan?"

"Not for a couple of weeks," Nathan said, waiting patiently for the woman to get around to the purpose of her visit. He knew that, like most prairie people, Aggie would take a while to get down to business. First she'd deal with the social niceties, inquire about his family and perhaps discuss the neighbors for a while.

"How are your folks?" Aggie asked.

"They're fine. Real good, in fact."

"You know, I just can't understand them moving away from all this." Aggie looked at the big, pillared ranch house beyond the circular driveway.

"My mother was happy to get to the city after being out here all those years. And after Dad's heart attack, he had to move away from the work and the worry."

"But a *condo!*" Aggie shuddered. "I truly can't imagine Josh and Marian Cameron living in some little condominium."

"It's a pretty nice place," Nathan said mildly, thinking about the luxurious multilevel town house his parents had recently bought in Calgary. "They love it. There are hot tubs and tennis courts and a big swimming pool, all kinds of amenities. Besides," he added, "they spend a lot of time traveling. They just got back from Australia, and they're going on an Alaskan cruise in a few weeks."

"Must be nice," Aggie said stiffly.

Nathan smiled at her, knowing how she always hated to hear about other people enjoying themselves. "Can I help you with something, Aggie?" he asked.

"We're organizing a town meeting next month in the United Church hall," Aggie said, getting down to business at last. "I want to make sure you're there, Nathan."

"What's going on?" Nathan asked, though he already knew the answer.

"We want to talk about the hotel. We're getting together a petition to stop that woman from opening the bar."

Nathan sighed. "Why can't you just leave the poor woman alone? She's not hurting anybody."

"Not *yet*," Aggie said darkly. "And she won't, neither. Not if we all pull together and protect our town."

Nathan looked at the woman's cold gray eyes behind her steel-framed glasses. "You know, Aggie," he murmured, "not everybody feels the same way you do. There are a lot of people in town who'd like to see the bar opened again and the hotel all fixed up and lively like it was in the old days."

"Then they don't have to sign the petition. All we need is sixty-five percent of the names, and I'm pretty sure we've got them already. That's why we're having the meeting, so we can file an intent to petition. Then she can't get a liquor license until we proceed."

"If she can't get a license, she can't make a living," Nathan said quietly.

"Make a living!" Aggie jeered. "As if that woman needs to make a living! She's got millions of dollars. Her husband is world famous."

"Ex-husband," Nathan said. "And if she's so rich, Aggie, what's she doing in a run-down old dump like the Wolf Hill Hotel?"

Aggie shrugged. "Who knows? Maybe she just wants... publicity, or something. Those movie-star types, there's no telling what they'll do."

Nathan thought about Kate Daniels's radiant smile, her endearing, awkward manner and her obvious stress when she was being bullied by the contractor. He wondered if anybody in the world could be considered less of a "movie-star type."

But there was another aspect to consider. Making the old hotel into a profitable operation would be a daunting task, even for someone a lot more experienced in business than she appeared to be. Maybe they really would be doing her a favor to discourage her early, before she invested a lot of her time, money and energy.

"All right," Nathan said at last. "I'll come to your meeting. Next month, you said?"

"That's right. The evening of the fourth, in the church hall." Aggie nodded with satisfaction. "Thanks, Nathan. We've got to stop this woman."

"Are you inviting Mrs. Daniels to the meeting?"

"Of course not! We're making real sure she doesn't find out about it."

"Don't you think you should let her know about your petition before she starts the renovations?"

Aggie shook her head. "She's already bought the place, Nathan. The shape it's in, nobody's going to take it off her hands, not in a million years. But if she gets Ray to fix it up a bit, she's got a better chance to sell it at a profit. Everybody thinks so. We're not doing her any harm by letting her go ahead with the renovations, and lots of people in town will get some work out of it."

Nathan hesitated, torn by indecision. He could see the sense in Aggie's reasoning, but the general underhandedness of the whole operation was disturbing to him.

Finally, he turned aside, gesturing toward the house. "Would you like a cup of coffee?" he asked courteously. "I think Bessie was making bread this afternoon."

"No, I can't stop. I still need to get to six more ranches before dark." Aggie turned and marched back to her car.

Nathan watched her head off down the lane of poplars. At last, with a shake of his head, he started up the flagstone walkway and through the back door of the big ranch house, where the cook had filled the kitchen with the rich smell of fresh-baked bread.

AFTER TWO WEEKS of renovations, the Wolf Hill Hotel was already vastly changed. Kate realized that Nathan had been right when he said that Raymond was a good builder. Nevertheless, life with Raymond Butts was a daily struggle, and Kate already wore a number of battle scars.

There were times, especially when the costs edged upward or unforeseen "problems" developed, when she was sorely tempted to invite Nathan Cameron around for a casual visit.

But she resisted the urge. It was too much like begging for help in dealing with the school bully. Still,

Kate was frequently dismayed by the contractor's stubbornness and his sly greed.

On a pleasant morning in late April, she stood with Raymond and Hilda in the lobby of the hotel, where a couple of burly young men with ponytails were installing new hardwood flooring, and a woman on a scaffold painted the stamped metal ceiling tiles with a long-handled brush.

The lobby was hardly recognizable as the same place Kate had entered a couple of weeks earlier. The front door had been replaced, and sunlight streamed through sparkling new windows, glimmering softly on the old oak woodwork that Raymond had repaired himself, then sanded and refinished with such professional skill that it glowed like satin.

Kate, who planned to spend the day painting bedrooms, wore blue jeans, a stained T-shirt and a red cotton bandanna tied around her head. She sighed with pleasure as she surveyed the progress of her renovations, then turned to Hilda who had just arrived, clutching an old photograph album.

"I found them pictures I told you about in my grandma's album," Hilda said. "They don't have dates, but I think they must be from about 1910. Before the war, anyhow, because the ladies are still wearing long dresses."

"Oh, wonderful!" Kate said. "May I see them?"

Hilda moved across the room, avoiding the stacks of hardwood flooring, and opened the album on the reception desk. Kate and Raymond pressed closer to examine the old sepia photographs.

"Look at this one," Kate breathed. "Here's the hotel lobby, almost the same as it is now."

Raymond squinted at the photograph. "What's them funny chairs?"

"They were made of buffalo horns and covered with tanned steer hide," Kate murmured, entranced. The other two looked at her in surprise, and she shifted uncomfortably. "I...I think I must have read that somewhere, about those chairs."

"Ugly-looking things," Raymond commented. "Look, Kate. There used to be a brass rail all along the desk here. I could get a brass rail for you," he added thoughtfully. "But it wouldn't be cheap."

Kate nodded gloomily. Raymond probably had a second cousin who ran an ornamental brass-and-ironworks. Sometimes Kate felt that Raymond had a thousand relatives in the area, and every one of them had a pipeline into her bank account.

"I don't think we need the brass rail right now, Raymond. But," she added, studying the photograph again, "I'd really love to restore those old lamps. Aren't they wonderful? Look at that fringe."

Raymond rubbed his jaw reflectively. "I'll see what I can do."

"Thanks," Kate said dryly.

"No problem. 'Course, them special antique lamps, they'd likely be real expensive," he added, looking pleased.

Kate sighed and turned to the other woman. "Look at that old flocked wallpaper, Hilda. Isn't it grand? I'd like to find some exactly like it for the lobby. The same color, and everything."

"Can't tell what color it was," Hilda said, frowning at the picture. "I'll bet it was red," she added. "They used a lot of red back then."

"I believe it was green," Kate said with a faraway smile. "Dark green, flocked with gold velvet. Wouldn't that look beautiful against the oak?"

Hilda nodded without enthusiasm. "I s'pose. Actually, what I looked up my grandma's album for," she went on, "was to see if I could find any pictures of the dining room, since you want it to look like it did back in the old days. But there aren't any."

Raymond glanced at them with sudden alertness. "Hilda, you still thinking about doing the dining room over and opening a restaurant?"

"Kate thinks it's a good idea," Hilda told him. "But she says we gotta make it look old-fashioned."

"Yeah? Won't be cheap, restoring that place," Raymond observed with obvious satisfaction.

Kate felt a growing panic. "Let's all go have a look at the dining room, all right?" she said. "Raymond, do you still have the key I gave you?"

The contractor produced a jangling key ring and selected a heavy old skeleton key, which he fitted into the double oak door that led to the unused dining room.

The three of them trooped inside and stood looking around. Kate shivered in her thin T-shirt. She hugged herself, depressed by the musty room.

Except for the blackened, empty hearth, there was no sign of the cozy dining area that Ellen Livingston had described. This place had been abandoned years ago, and was now used only by Walter Hamill who ran a taxidermy shop out of his garage and stored most of his supplies in the hotel dining room.

Two big freezers stood along one wall. Kate looked at the freezers apprehensively, knowing they were filled with hooves, heads and other gruesome animal parts. The floor was littered with stacks of hides, wooden and plastic forms of bird and animal bodies and cardboard boxes heaped with feathers, antlers, glass eyeballs and other unsavory items.

"Poor Walter," Hilda said without sympathy. "What's he gonna do with all this taxidermy stuff? He'll have to part with a bit of his cash and build himself a storage shed."

"I'll be glad to have it out of here," Kate said. "Sometimes, I lie in bed at night thinking about all those hooves and eyeballs and I can't fall asleep."

Hilda chuckled. "I truly can't imagine you sleeping here alone every night, Kate. All the folks in town think you're real brave to do that."

"They do?" Kate looked at the other woman in surprise.

Nobody had ever considered her brave. The idea startled yet pleased her.

Raymond was strolling around the room, tapping the walls and surveying the warped flooring. He returned to Kate, looking increasingly happy. "Likely it'll need to be—"

"No new walls," Kate said firmly. "*Or* ceilings. And the floor can probably be fixed just by shaving and replacing some of the boards, like you did in the office."

Raymond looked injured. "I wasn't even thinking about ceilings or floors," he told her with dignity. "But I reckon you'd still want the woodwork to match the lobby, wouldn't you? That means installing all new oak panels and making them look like the old ones.

Likely, it's gonna cost a pretty penny," he added, rubbing his hands together.

"But I..." Kate hesitated, looking from Raymond to Hilda, who stood gazing at the big room with a smile of rapture.

"Oh, Kate," Hilda breathed. "I'd *love* to have a nice dining room in here. I truly would. It'd be the talk of the countryside. We could even have the menu like it was in the old days," she added with a wily glance at Kate. "We could look up my grandma's recipes, and some of them old articles in the newspaper where they always described the specials at the hotel dining room."

Kate was painfully tempted. In her mind's eye, she could see the dining room restored to its original elegance, serving the same food that Ellen Livingston would have eaten each night after her day of teaching. That image was hard to resist.

But she hadn't reckoned on such a major expenditure, at least not at this point. And, with Raymond's steady inroads on her bank account, her funds were getting dangerously low....

"Kate?" Hilda asked.

Kate shook herself out of her musings and tried to smile. "I think it's a good idea. I'm just getting a little worried about money, that's all. I wish I could get the liquor license," she added with a frown. "I thought I'd have it by now, and be making a profit from the bar. Then I'd have no worries at all. But yesterday, when I went up to Calgary, they told me there was going to be some kind of delay."

Hilda and Raymond exchanged a glance. "You'll get the license," Hilda said with forced heartiness, turning back to Kate. "Just wait and see."

"I hope you're right." Kate watched while Raymond examined the plywood sheets that covered the broken windows.

"Maybe we should get some of them leaded-glass windows in here," he said. "Like the ones in the office. That'd look real nice."

"But they're...so expensive," Kate faltered. "And we don't even know if they were here in the first place. I want the restoration to be as authentic as possible, Raymond."

"I believe I remember my grandpa saying once that they had fancy glass windows in the hotel dining room," Raymond told her earnestly. "Don't you, Hilda? They were made special in a glass shop down East, and shipped out by train."

"What were?" a voice inquired from the doorway.

Kate turned to see Nathan Cameron leaning casually against the wall. She'd spoken with the young rancher a couple of times since her arrival, but she was always astonished by his dark good looks.

Kate wondered if Ellen had suffered the same reaction to Nathan's handsome ancestor. Did Ellen's heart pound like this, and her mouth go dry, and her body feel all soft and moist with confused yearnings, the way Kate's did?

Probably not, Kate decided. The young schoolteacher had clearly been made of sterner stuff. In fact, Ellen had encountered Joshua Cameron once again,

this time at a church picnic held just before the school
term was due to begin, and had put him firmly in his
place....

There was a huge crate wrapped in burlap sacking under a tree. It was obviously the most exciting thing at
the picnic, and I could understand why when I learned
that it contained ice cream. What a thrill for these
frontier children, many of whom have never tasted
such a delicious confection!

Mr. Cameron came by while Mrs. Oates and I were
looking at the crate. He looked rather more civilized—but still exceedingly handsome!—in tweed
jacket and flannel pants instead of his customary
buckskin. He told me he would get me an ice-cream
cone.

"We can sit together and eat, and get to know each
other better," he said with a smile designed to melt
stone.

"Thank you, but I don't care for any ice cream," I
told him, annoyed by his arrogance.

He just smiled again and went off, shouldering his
way through the crowd and returning almost immediately with two ice-cream cones.

"Mr. Cameron, I told you I did not care to have any
ice cream," I said with admirable loftiness. And then
I swept away to the music tent, leaving him standing
with ice cream dripping over his hands and the most
comical look of consternation on his face. Mrs. Oates
was quite scandalized. She says that no woman has
ever treated Mr. Joshua Cameron in such a fashion in
all his life....

KATE SMILED at Nathan. "We're talking about restoring the dining room along with the rest of the hotel. Hilda wants to open a fancy restaurant."

"She does?" Nathan looked at the plump woman with warm affection. "I'd be your best customer, Hilda."

"Now, Nathan," Hilda objected, beaming. "Bessie would get jealous if you ate in my dining room."

Kate had recently learned that Nathan's elderly housekeeper was Hilda's sister, and a bitter rivalry flourished between the two of them over who was the best cook.

"She'd just have to get used to it," Nathan said. "Anyhow, Bessie knows I love her." He turned to Kate. "You think you'll restore the dining room, Kate?"

"I'm not sure," Kate said. "I hate to go to all that expense until I can be sure the work is historically accurate. There are government grants available," she added, "if you remodel a heritage building but keep it true to the period. I want to be sure we qualify, because I'd hate to miss out on that kind of assistance. I need all the help I can get."

"You know, my mother's quite an amateur historian," Nathan said casually. "She's got all kinds of pictures and information about Wolf Hill in the old days. Would you like to talk with her about the hotel, Kate?"

"Oh..." Kate looked at him, wide-eyed. "That would be really wonderful! If it's not a lot of trouble," she added hastily.

"No trouble," Nathan said. "Matter of fact, I'm driving into Calgary tomorrow on business, and stopping off to visit my folks. You can ride along and spend time with my mother if you like.''

"I'd like that very much," Kate told him. "Thank you, Nathan."

"I'll pick you up at one o'clock," he said, looking at her for a long moment before he turned away and strolled across the lobby.

"Well, well," Hilda said, watching his erect figure as he vanished into the coffee shop. She gave Kate a meaningful grin. "Well, well, *well!*"

"Oh, for goodness' sake," Kate muttered, her cheeks warming uncomfortably as she marched out into the lobby and began to collect her painting supplies.

CHAPTER FOUR

"WHAT ARE those fluffy yellow flowers called?" Kate asked, peering out the truck window at the prairie rolling by. "They're so pretty."

Nathan glanced at the fields near the road, dotted with wildflowers and grazing cattle. He turned to her with a smile.

"Buffalo beans," he said. "They always bloom in the spring, before the wild roses."

Kate leaned forward to study the carpet of golden flowers. "I've never heard of them."

She tried to remember if Ellen had ever mentioned buffalo beans in her diary. But then, Kate reminded herself, Ellen had arrived on the prairie in late summer, not springtime....

"Folks say Native women used them as a form of contraceptive."

Kate stared at him, fascinated. "Really? Did they eat them, or make them into tea, or what?"

"I'm not sure. You'd have to ask my father. He's always been interested in that kind of thing. He has a lot of books on local plants and flowers."

Kate looked at the flowers again. "Did it work?" she asked shyly. "Was it an effective method of birth control, I mean?"

Nathan grinned. "I'm not sure. It probably did, because they knew a whole lot about the medicinal value of plants. Native people were using willow bark as a source of aspirin, you know, thousands of years before anybody else thought of it."

Kate fell silent, looking cautiously over at his handsome profile as he drove. He seemed very near to her within the cab of the truck, so close that she could have touched him if she wanted to. And there was no denying that she wanted to touch this man. From the first time she'd met Nathan Cameron, Kate had felt a disturbing physical pull toward him that seemed to overwhelm reason and sense.

She knew that she had no time for a relationship now. She was fully absorbed in the greatest challenge of her life. She needed to get the hotel restored and operating on a profitable footing. Nothing else really mattered.

Besides, Kate had lived without male company for such a long time, she should have learned to be content by now. During the years of her marriage, love had brought her nothing but pain and loneliness, and sex was something she'd mostly learned to get along without. It was better that way.

But a treacherous hidden part of her still yearned to touch Nathan's arm and fondle the bulge of his arm under the smooth leather of his jacket, or rest her hand on the leg that looked so hard and muscular in worn denim jeans....

"So, how's it going?" he asked in a casual tone, startling her.

"I beg your pardon?"

"The hotel. Is your renovation going along pretty well?"

"Well, mostly." Kate hesitated, longing to tell him about her daily conflicts with Raymond and her worries over the liquor license, which seemed mysteriously difficult to obtain.

"Any major problems?" Nathan asked, giving her a keen glance.

Kate drew a deep breath and shook her head firmly. "None at all. I can't believe how well things are turning out. We should be ready for the grand opening by early summer if the work keeps going like this."

"That's good," Nathan said, sounding somewhat unconvinced. "I'm glad to hear it, Kate. Are you really planning to let Hilda go ahead with this dining room thing?" he asked after a moment's silence.

Kate watched a couple of mule deer daintily picking their way down the edge of a coulee, then turned back to him. "I guess so. Hilda is so excited about the whole idea. And it really would be nice to make a complete restoration and have the hotel running the way it used to."

"But all this is going to be a lot more expensive at start-up than you'd planned, isn't it?"

Kate sighed. "Everything's more expensive than I'd planned," she said, then turned deliberately to look out the window again so she could avoid his thoughtful glance.

She fingered a pile of fabric swatches and wallpaper samples that she was taking to show to Marian Cameron. It really would be nice to have some help, she thought wistfully, hoping that Nathan's mother turned out to be as nice as she sounded. Although

Kate loved the hotel more every day, and was fully absorbed in the project she'd undertaken, there were times when she felt lonely and frightened.

Just like Ellen Livingston, who'd begun her teaching job early in September and was finding it considerably more daunting than she'd ever expected.

Kate stole another surreptitious glance at the dark-haired man beside her, wondering if Ellen could have been Nathan's great-grandmother, and if he looked at all like her.

The diary, though it contained much vivid detail of life in Wolf Hill at the turn of the century, gave few hints about Ellen's own appearance. By now, Kate felt as close to the young woman as a sister, but she still didn't know if Ellen had been fair or dark, tall or short, pretty or plain.

She must have been attractive, Kate thought, because Joshua Cameron was so obviously smitten with her, right from the start.

"Your family's lived here a long time, haven't they?" she asked, searching for a way to get Nathan talking about his ancestors.

Kate wished sometimes that she could just show him the diary and ask him to satisfy her curiosity about Ellen and the handsome frontiersman. But her fear of losing the old book had certainly not been eased by the knowledge that Nathan's mother was an avid historian. Nathan hadn't mentioned the diary since that first day, and Kate hoped that he'd forgotten all about it.

"Just shy of a hundred years," Nathan said, glancing at her with a smile and then looking down the highway again.

"How did they happen to settle here?"

"My great-grandfather volunteered for a couple of terms in the North West Mounted Police, the forerunner of the R.C.M.P., which was a pretty rugged assignment back in those days. Their first mission was to stop the illegal whiskey trade between the Canadian prairies and the western states. It was lonely, dangerous work. After his service, they rewarded him with a tract of land here in the wilderness, late in the 1890s. The family's been adding to it ever since," Nathan said in a matter-of-fact tone. "My grandfather bought out a lot of the local farmers who went broke during the thirties, and expanded the property quite a bit."

"What was his name?"

"My grandfather?"

"No, your great-grandfather," Kate said, trying to sound casual.

"Joshua Cameron," Nathan said briefly. "The same as my father, and his father was Nathan, like me. The family doesn't have much imagination," he added with a grin. "They just sort of alternate those two names through the generations, for the eldest son."

"Did you ever know him?" Kate asked, struggling with the dates that whirled through her mind. "I mean, did he live long enough to... no, I don't suppose..."

"Old Joshua? He died long before I was born. My father remembers him a little," Nathan said, his face clouding briefly. "But not with any great fondness, I guess."

"Didn't your father like him?"

There was a brief, awkward silence. "He was a bitter old man, my great-grandfather," Nathan said at last. "Not very nice to anybody in the family, I guess."

Kate glanced at him, startled. She thought about the handsome young man at that long-ago church picnic, looking at the pretty schoolteacher with comical surprise while ice cream melted over his hands.

She sighed, feeling baffled, and looked out the window again at the flowing sweep of green land, fading to a misty shade of purple where grass and sky met far in the distance.

"What about your family?" Nathan asked.

"My family?" Kate smiled, thinking about Mamie and her new boyfriend.

Mamie had reported with satisfaction that the major was falling nicely into line, though he was still "stiff as a board."

"Where do they live, and what do your parents think about this hotel project of yours?"

"There's just my mother," Kate said. "She's in Vancouver. I never saw much of my father while I was growing up," she added. "They divorced when I was really young, and Mom and I moved around a lot. I went to a new school every year."

Nathan looked at her in sympathy. "That must have been hard. I had such a stable childhood out on the ranch."

"Mine was stable, too, in a crazy kind of way," Kate said. "I mean, we lived in lots of different places and I never knew what was happening next, but I could always trust my mother to look after me."

"What's she like?"

"She's..." Kate floundered, searching for words to describe her mother. "She's glamorous, and exciting, and really pretty..."

Nathan grinned. "In other words, she's just like you. Right?"

"Yeah, right," Kate agreed dryly. "Glamorous and exciting, that's me."

"These things are entirely a matter of opinion," Nathan said, looking solemnly down the highway.

There was a brief silence while Kate thought about his words.

"How long were you married?" Nathan asked as they approached the outskirts of the sprawling prairie city.

"A little over ten years." Kate paused, then turned to look at him. "How about you? Have you ever been married?"

He shook his head. "I just can't seem to find any woman who's ready to cope with the loneliness of living on my ranch."

"Surely it's not as isolated as it was a hundred years ago," Kate said. "I mean, it's not as if weeks go by without your encountering your neighbors, is it?"

He smiled. "You're right, Kate. The problem isn't really the isolation, so much as the..."

Kate waited as he searched for the right words, looking over at him with growing curiosity. "I guess," Nathan said finally, "it's just the sheer scope of the whole operation. It can be a little overwhelming."

"Hilda said once that being a Cameron woman was a full-time job," Kate said, then felt awkward and embarrassed when she heard the implication of her own words.

But Nathan merely nodded. "Hilda's right. You know, I think it's partly my mother's fault," he said unexpectedly. "My mother's very... dynastic," he added with a wry smile.

"What do you mean?"

"Well, she tends to take the whole Cameron-ranch thing very, very seriously. You'll see when you meet her."

Kate subsided, feeling vaguely uneasy, and gazed out the window at the rolling fields.

"What was it like for you, being married to somebody so famous?" Nathan asked.

"I learned what *real* loneliness was," Kate said. "Somehow, I was far more lonely in the middle of big cities surrounded by people, than I feel now when I walk all alone on the prairie."

"That's probably because none of those people really understood you," Nathan said quietly.

Kate was surprised and warmed once again by his perception. Although they'd only met a few weeks earlier, she had the absurd feeling that this man genuinely understood the way she felt about many things.

"Do you ever see him?" Nathan asked, looking intently at the streams of traffic.

"My husband?"

"Yeah. Do you still have contact with him?"

"Sometimes. He calls from Paris or Singapore occasionally to see how I'm getting along. He thinks it's so hilarious," Kate added with an involuntary touch of defensiveness. "What I'm doing, I mean. Trying to fix up this old hotel and make a success of it."

"Why?"

"I don't know," she said after a moment's thought. "Probably because it's not the sort of thing I've ever done. Everybody... I mean, my mother and Adam and the people who manage his affairs, they've always considered me sort of inept, I guess. Kind of a nice but muddleheaded person who needs to be helped and looked after."

"Then it's lucky you got away from all of them," Nathan said calmly. "We're often shaped by the perceptions of the people close to us. If they all expect you to mess up and fail, that's probably what you'll do."

"Self-fulfilling prophecy," Kate said.

"That's right." Nathan turned to her with a smile that made his eyes glow and lit up his dark face with boyish warmth.

Kate smiled back, suddenly feeling weak and shaky, and was relieved when he pulled into the parking lot of a town house development on the banks of the Bow River. "Well, here we are," Nathan announced. "My mother's going to be so happy to meet you. I've told her all about you."

Kate followed him along the flagstone walkway, shaded by trees dusted with a lacy mist of new green leaves. She felt nervous, as she always did before meeting new people.

Nathan's mother was tall and regal, with upswept silvery hair, high cheekbones and a slender elegant figure in tailored slacks and cream-colored silk blouse. Josh Cameron was equally imposing, a big sturdy man in jeans and a cardigan. Kate caught her breath as she looked at his dark hair graying at the temples and his keen, hawklike profile. Josh Cameron was precisely what Nathan would be in thirty years' time. Kate could hardly take her eyes off him.

Their living room was big and luxurious, tastefully furnished and decorated with treasures and works of art collected from around the world. Nathan led the way into the room and made the introductions while his father took Kate's hand in a hearty grip, his eyes crinkling as he smiled at her.

Kate smiled back, finding it hard to believe that this tall rancher, with his callused hands and weathered skin, was also a collector of pressed flowers and a student of local horticulture.

Marian took the fabric and wallpaper samples from Kate and graciously invited her to a seat on one of the leather couches. Despite Kate's nervousness, the two women soon became absorbed in a conversation on the decorating of heritage buildings while Nathan and his father sat nearby with their coffee, discussing the progress of spring calving.

After a while, Marian excused herself and disappeared into an adjoining room. Moments later, she emerged with a stack of photograph albums and boxes containing artifacts and information from the early days of Wolf Hill. Fascinated, Kate leafed through the brittle old newspapers, pausing whenever she came across an article or advertisement dealing with the Wolf Hill Hotel.

"This is wonderful," she breathed. "Just marvelous. I've been dying to get my hands on some material like this."

Marian sat next to her, pointing out items of interest as they discussed the restoration of the dining room. Kate was so preoccupied that she barely noticed when Nathan got up to leave, saying that he had some business to look after and would be back in a couple of hours.

"Is that all right with you, Kate?" he asked. "Do you mind if I leave you here until, say... four o'clock or so?"

Kate glanced at her watch, feeling a tug of alarm. "No, that's... that'll be fine. It's going to take me at least two hours to look at all this. As long as your parents don't mind having me around," she added hastily.

"We'd be delighted," Marian Cameron said.

"Good." Nathan waved a casual farewell at the group in the room, then left the building and strode across the parking lot to his truck.

Kate smiled as her host got up to refill her coffee mug and offered more carrot cake. "Thank you," she murmured, helping herself to another of the iced squares. "This is so delicious, Marian. I'll have to get the recipe."

"Jealously guarded family secret, I'm afraid," Josh said comfortably, moving toward the door. "My wife doesn't give up her recipes without a fight."

Marian watched calmly as Kate nibbled on the rich confection.

"If you'll both excuse me," Josh said, "I have a few things I need to finish."

He vanished into another room, while Marian turned to Kate with a rueful look.

"They talk about men having a hard time filling their days after they retire," she said. "But that certainly doesn't apply to Josh. He has so many interests. He's busy all day long."

"It must be a very different life for him now, leaving ranch life behind after so many years."

Marian's eyebrows raised. "We certainly haven't left the ranch behind," she said with sudden coolness. "We no longer live there, but the ranch is still very much a part of our lives."

"I see," Kate said, her cheeks warming.

"The Cameron ranch is extremely important to the Wolf Hill community, and to the history of southern Alberta," Marian went on. "I don't know how much Nathan has told you about our history, but it's not something that the family takes lightly."

Kate had an unpleasant sense of being scolded and warned at the same time. She looked at the album in her lap, searching for a way to change the subject.

"These are such wonderful old photographs," she murmured, squinting at the faded brown prints. "Look, here's a group of tepees pitched at the edge of town. That's exactly where the school is now, isn't it?"

"That's right," Marian said, leaning over to study the album. "The modern composite school was built in 1960. Before that, there was a big two-story brick schoolhouse on the same site. But you know, we have the bell tower from the very first school in a storage room here in the city," she added. "We're negotiating to have it moved to the museum grounds."

"We?"

"The Wolf Hill Historical Society. You might like to join, Kate. We meet once a month in the town library."

Kate thought about Aggie Krantz and her cohorts, and made a wry face. "I'm not at all sure the townspeople want me to be a part of anything they're do-ing."

"It often takes a considerable amount of time for the townspeople to warm to newcomers," Marian agreed, folding her hands calmly in her lap.

Kate nodded gloomily as she examined the page of old photographs. "What's this?" she whispered, her breath catching suddenly in her throat.

"That's the one I told you about...the very first school in the Wolf Hill district. See, there's our bell tower. I don't have a date for the picture, but it must be sometime around 1910. The earliest school was a couple of miles outside town in a location that was convenient for most of the settlers."

"I know," Kate murmured, examining the sturdy little building. "In fact," she added, hardly aware of what she was saying, "it was right on the edge of the original Cameron ranch property, wasn't it? Your husband's grandfather had to donate a small piece of land for the school grounds."

Marian looked at her with sudden interest. "Now, where did you learn all that?"

Kate flushed and bit her lip. "Just...I don't know," she said. "I guess it must have been something Hilda said, or maybe Raymond."

Marian smiled. "Everybody in Wolf Hill is a his-tory buff," she said. "Even Ray Butts. Look, Kate," she added, turning a page. "This is the very first school class in the history of Wolf Hill. It was taken late in September of 1904. Aren't those little boys precious? Just look at their homemade overalls, and their solemn expressions."

"Oh," Kate breathed, leaning forward to study the photograph.

She recognized the school building from the previous photograph, but she would have known it anyway from Ellen's description. It was a small wooden structure with wide front steps and a whimsical bell tower, making it look like a little church. Just visible at the rear of the building were the outhouse and a barn where the children who rode to school stabled their ponies.

The school building looked new and shiny in this picture, its shutters and trim neatly outlined against a coat of fresh white paint. But the relentless prairie wind had evidently been blowing even while the picture was being taken. Some of the little girls' long skirts whipped against their legs, and tumbleweeds massed along the side of the building.

The students were positioned on the steps of the school, with the largest boys squatting on the dusty ground in front and the smaller children packed in a dense group behind them. At the top of the steps stood a young woman. She was slender and trim in a high-necked white blouse and dark skirt, no taller than many of the older girls around her.

Still, this young woman was clearly the person in charge. Her carriage and poise, the quiet lift of her head and the set of her mouth, all gave her a look of calm confidence. But Kate, staring wide-eyed at the picture, knew the young teacher hadn't felt confident at all.

Oh, Ellen, she thought, almost in tears. Ellen, you were so brave....

She studied the young woman hungrily, unable to concentrate on anyone else in the picture. Ellen Livingston had abundant dark hair rolled into a loose knot on top of her head, and a pale complexion that contrasted with the sun-browned faces of the children. Her face surprised Kate, who had somehow not expected her to be so beautiful. Perhaps because the young teacher's diary entries were often wry and self-deprecating, Kate had expected her to be a sort of homely intellectual, a real bluestocking.

But Ellen's face was sweetly oval in shape, her eyes wide and serene. Her mouth, though solemn for the picture-taking, had an engaging tilt that made her look as if she might be about to burst into laughter. Kate found herself smiling mistily as she studied this girl from the past.

"Most of the students were the children of immigrants," Marian was saying. "The early register looks like a United Nations roll call. It must have been hard for all those poor young teachers. They usually came out from the East, you know, without much idea of what they were getting into."

"Oh, yes," Kate breathed. "Yes, it was terribly hard."

Oblivious to Marian's curious glance, she reached out gently to touch the edge of the old photograph, her mind filled with the memory of one of Ellen's recent diary entries.

Monday, September 19, 1904

I cannot possibly do this! I wish I were as small as little Herman Mueller, my youngest student. Then, like Herman, I could hide in the barn, pull my shirt over my head and howl. Papa was right, after all. This job is far too hard. In fact, it is impossible. The only thing that has kept me from submitting my letter of resignation is the thought of all those smug faces back home, the sour old biddies who will nod to one another with pursed lips and say, "We knew she could never do it. She has always been such a silly thing with all her high-and-mighty notions."

All right. A few moments have passed and I feel somewhat better, having gotten all that cowardly whining out of my system. Of course, I will never resign. I might die at my desk, but I will never resign. What would Papa think, and the poor struggling members of the school board of Wolf Hill, who are trying so hard to provide a better life for their children? What would Joshua Cameron think? Would he laugh at my weakness?

But that man is another of the things I must avoid thinking of, if I am ever to make a success of this nightmare. First of all, let me try to explain why my job is so difficult. This is one of the few moments I have been able to spare for my diary since the school term began, and there is so much to tell.

To begin with, the school board was wrong in its calculations, which apparently were made early in the spring. There are not twenty-four students. There are thirty-seven, the youngest aged four. That, of course, is little Herman, whose mother died a few months ago in childbirth, so Herman is forced to accompany his older siblings to school while his father works in the fields.

My oldest student is Luke Grossman, aged seventeen, a sullen, hulking young brute about a foot taller than I, whose mother has ambitions for his future. There are times when Luke eyes me from the back of the room with a look that suggests he, too, has ambitions—of a quite different sort than his mother's! But then, perhaps I am overestimating my attractiveness. It is possible that Luke merely longs to be elsewhere, and sees me as the obstacle blocking his path.

Of my thirty-seven students, there are fourteen... *fourteen!*... who speak not a single word of English. The seven Mueller children, as well as the Karpajians and the Gobels, do not speak English in the home. They sit at their desks, hands quietly folded, watching me with blank, unreadable faces, and I despair of them. Where to begin? *How* to begin, when there are so many others who must be kept occupied at the same time?

Strangely, it is not during lessons but at lunchtime that I feel the most isolated. I sit at my desk, buried under mounds of slates and crudely lettered papers, trying to work while I nibble at the lunch packed for me each morning by Mrs. Goldman in the hotel kitchen. My lunches are dainty and nourishing—cucumber sandwiches, rolls of ham spiced with cloves, neatly wrapped pieces of cake and a shiny red apple, with a jar of milk encased in damp burlap to keep it fresh.

And out there on the steps, the little Muellers and Gobels and Hellmans are eating strange things like headcheese and knockwurst, huge uneven chunks of black bread and onion and sour pickles. Even the smallest of the children carry earthenware crocks filled not with milk, but with strong, black coffee.

I feel so lonely, as if I have ventured onto some alien planet where the languages and customs are utterly different from anything I am accustomed to. Whenever I pass, the older girls watch me with cool faces in which I detect hints of mockery.

It seems that they are years older than I, these young female students of mine, and I can understand why. Many of the bigger girls, even the fourteen- and fifteen-year-olds, are simply filling in the year and will be married next spring. By the time they reach my age in five or six years, they will be long-married women with two or three babies. No wonder they regard me with contempt. They think that I have failed as a woman.

Perhaps they are right, because I have had only one ambition for as long as I can remember, and that was to be a schoolteacher. And now I fear that I am failing in my dream.

I have begun to sniffle in cowardly fashion so that my words mist and blur in front of my eyes. I am sorely tempted to curl on my bed and have a good cry, but I must compose myself. Mrs. Goldman is calling me from the hotel lobby, and I must go and see what she wants....

Half an hour later. The strangest thing has happened! Before going out to answer Mrs. Goldman, I concealed this pitiful, incriminating diary in its hiding place, a perfectly dry and hollow cavity that I have discovered under the windowsill in my room. Then I smoothed my skirts, wiped away any humiliating sign of tears and approached the front desk to see what was required of me this time.

Although it is early in my term, I have already dealt with an angry parent who felt his son was unfairly

singled out for punishment. That young lout butch-
ered a pair of gophers on the school grounds, in full
view of the smallest girls who were traumatized by the
little animals' suffering! I was so angry, I fell upon the
boy in a rage and thrashed his shoulders with my long
ruler. When his father came to the hotel to ask stiffly
whether I considered that punishment appropriate, I
must confess that I snapped, "No. It certainly was
not. I should have used the buggy whip!" and
marched back to my room.

I have also been called upon by a school board
member who questioned the wisdom of my allowing
boys and girls to sit near one another in the classroom. "Miss Livingston, there is great evil in the
hearts of young people," he said darkly.

And in the hearts of school board members, I
thought, but was wise enough for once to hold my
tongue as Papa has always advised me. Instead, I told
the gentleman earnestly that heterogeneous group-
ings within the classroom are the newest teaching style,
and have been proven more effective at controlling
discipline problems and producing academic excel-
lence. He looked utterly baffled, which of course had
been my intention, and went away without further argument.

But tonight I was not summoned to deal with any
visitor. Instead, a bulky package awaited me at the
front desk, wrapped in coarse brown paper and neatly
tied with string.

Mrs. Goldman looked as excited as I have ever seen
her. "Jimmy Cracker brought it," she said. "He left
it on the desk and said it was for the teacher."

"Oh, dear." I looked rather dubiously at the package. "I do hope Jimmy isn't going to start bringing me presents."

Jimmy Cracker is a gentle young man in his late twenties with a sweet vacant expression and shambling walk. He was kicked in the head by a horse when he was a little boy, and has never been the same since. When his parents moved on from Wolf Hill, they left Jimmy behind, rather like an unwanted pet, but the townspeople feel great affection for him and he is always cared for.

"This package isn't from Jimmy," Mrs. Goldman said. "I'd bet on it. Open it, Ellen, and let's see what's inside."

Feeling somewhat cheered after the dismal moments in my room, I unwrapped the brown paper and then paused in astonishment. Within the coarse wrappings was a woven basket of incredible intricacy, tan colored with lovely black geometric designs worked around the edges. The basket was filled with shining dark berries, similar to blueberries but plumper and slightly more reddish in color.

"They're saskatoon berries," Mrs. Goldman commented, running her fingers appreciatively though the shining mass. "And beautiful ones, too. I wonder where he found them."

Her words were confirmed by the folded note that I lifted from among the berries. The handwriting was black and powerful, and I immediately shivered with recognition. I have never seen that hand before, yet I would have known it anywhere. The note read:

A small gift for you. Mrs. Goldman will bake you
a saskatoon-berry pie to make you believe in
heaven. The basket, by the way, was made by a
friend of mine, a lady almost ninety years old
who lives on the Piegan reserve. Perhaps some-
day I'll take you to meet her.

I looked up from the note to the graceful woven
basket, torn as always between appreciation of his gift
and annoyance at his presumption. But when I read
the final sentence, I was wholly undone. "They tell me
you are doing a fine job in your first weeks of teaching," the note continued. "We are all very proud of
you." It was simply signed with the initials "J.N.C."

Doing a fine job...

I clutched the woven basket to my chest and fled to
my room before utterly disgracing myself. Nothing the
man could have said would ever have touched me as
deeply as those simple words of praise.

This is what I have needed to hear, longed for with
all my being! How could he possibly have known that?

I retrieved my diary from its hiding place and am
now sitting cross-legged on my bed with my skirts
tucked up in a manner that would scandalize Mama.
But Mama is thousands of miles away and her careful
admonitions grow fainter all the time. And I am running my fingers through the rich mass of berries and
writing these words while tears flow down my cheeks.

A fine job...

He thinks I am doing a fine job, in spite of all my
muddles and doubts and despair. Thank you, bless
you, Joshua Cameron, for those kind words! Thank
you from the bottom of my heart.

I lift one of the berries and pop it into my mouth, and am astonished by its burst of rich sweetness. Do kisses taste like this? I wonder. The same rush of sweetness that satisfies yet leaves one hungry for more? I suppose they do, but they would have to come from the right mouth or they would never be sweet enough.

The right mouth... I wonder...

Ellen Livingston, that is *quite enough!* You will put this diary away at once, and you will return to the work of making tomorrow's lesson plans, and there will be no more silly talk of kisses!

CHAPTER FIVE

WITH AN EFFORT, Kate dragged herself back to the present, and to Marian Cameron who was watching her with concern.

"Are you all right, Kate? You're looking a little pale."

"I'm fine. I just..." Kate glanced into the woman's questioning face. "Sometimes I go off on flights of fancy, you know? I guess I'm a dreamer."

Marian continued to watch her with interest. "I must confess, I've never been much of a daydreamer, myself," she said. "Josh always teases me about being too busy to dream. I guess I'm more of a doer." She smiled and looked a little less severe. "What were you thinking about just now?"

Kate gazed down at the old photograph, and Ellen standing among her students trying to look calm and authoritative.

"I guess...just the things you were saying about these young teachers, and how hard it was for them. All at once, I got such a vivid picture of what it must have been like in a strange place, so far from home."

"Oh, Lord!" Marian said, laughing. "The location wasn't the half of it. It was truly a dreadful job, you know. Those poor young things had to chop wood and get the fire going on freezing winter mornings before the children arrived. They had to dry out all the wet clothes on clotheslines strung across the back of the schoolroom, keep the water barrel filled, do emergency first aid, teach basic hygiene and intervene to stop fights. And they were allowed virtually no social life, partly because they were supposed to set a moral example, but mainly because as soon as a young teacher got married, the school lost her and had to go looking for a new one. They weren't even supposed to talk to a man on the street, or go anywhere at all without a chaperon."

Kate studied Ellen's face in the picture, wondering why Marian just didn't come out and say the young woman was an ancestor. Surely Ellen had gone on to marry Joshua Cameron after a year or two of teaching at Wolf Hill. It already seemed clear that they were smitten with each other. And Joshua had lived to be an old man, nothing had happened to him....

Perhaps Marian simply didn't know. Maybe Ellen's teaching career had been so brief that the family had forgotten about it in later generations, and they didn't associate this quiet young woman pictured on the school steps with their great-grandmother. Kate steeled herself to ask.

"I've been wondering... Oh, thank you," she said as Marian got up to refill her coffee mug and pass the sugar bowl.

"About what?"

"About Joshua Cameron. Not your husband," Kate added hastily. "The first one, his grandfather."

"Now, why on earth would you be thinking about old Joshua?"

"I guess...just because I started thinking about his having donated the land for the first school. Nathan told me that his great-grandfather served in the earliest version of the R.C.M.P.," she added nervously when Marian didn't answer. "That must have been a really exciting life, don't you think?"

"I think it was probably just hard and monotonous work," Marian said dryly. She paused, then squared her shoulders and turned to Kate. "Nathan tells me you've found some kind of old diary in the hotel."

Kate tensed, gripping the handle of her cup in sudden alarm. "Yes," she said. "That's true, I did. It was hidden inside the windowsill in my room."

"Would you mind telling me about it? I'd be very interested in something like that."

Kate's mind whirled. She felt as if she were treading on thin ice. Suddenly, this elegant woman in her beautiful home and the kind of power that her family—Nathan's family—represented, increased Kate's sense of isolation.

"I've just started reading the diary," she said, forcing her voice to remain calm. "Actually, it was written by one of those young schoolteachers you were talking about. I guess that's why I was so intrigued when I saw the pictures."

"Really? That's fascinating, Kate. I do wish you'd bring it around sometime for me to look at."

Kate thought protectively of Ellen, of her courage and her despair, her girlish fancies and touching struggle to seem mature and confident. And then she thought of Joshua, who'd founded the Cameron family dynasty that Marian was so proud of. She took a deep breath and smiled at her hostess. "In a little while, all right?" she said. "When I've finished reading the diary, Marian, I'll be happy to let you see it."

Marian looked at her a moment longer in silence, then glanced at her watch. "My goodness, Nathan will be back soon to collect you, and we haven't made any decisions about this wallpaper," she said with forced brightness. "Let's look in the catalog and see what goes best with oak paneling, shall we?"

Kate allowed herself to be drawn back to the problems of interior decoration. But she was quiet and thoughtful for the rest of the visit, and during all of the drive home to Wolf Hill with Nathan.

ABOUT A WEEK later, on an evening rich with the scent of apple blossoms and damp new grass, Nathan drove his truck past the rolling fields to the town of Wolf Hill where most of the residents were gathered in the church hall.

He moved through the crowded room to an empty seat near the front, murmuring greetings to friends and neighbors as he passed.

"Hi, Lute," he said, sinking into a chair next to the sturdy form of Luther Barnes, who nodded his head gravely.

"Evening, Nathan. Calving all finished?"

"Pretty much. We just lost six, and a couple of heifers. How about you?"

Wistfully, Luther examined his pack of hand-rolled cigarettes. He sighed, put his cigarettes back in his pocket and turned to Nathan. "I been cutting down my herd the last couple years. I got only fifty cows left, and they calved out fine this year."

"Does it feel pretty good to be retired?" Nathan asked with a smile, trying to fit his long legs under the chair in front of him.

Luther looked at Hilda Fairweather's curly silver head a couple of rows in front of them. "It feels lonely," he said.

"I know," Nathan said quietly, gazing into the distance. "I know, Lute."

Aggie, seated at a table at the front of the hall, rapped a gavel smartly and glared at the latecomers who were still searching for chairs. Nathan watched her in fascination, wondering where she'd found a real gavel.

Only Aggie, he thought, would do something so pretentious.

"I'm calling this meeting to order. Jennie will take the minutes," she said, gesturing at the plump woman beside her who blushed and shifted importantly in her chair.

"A lot of the men aren't here, Aggie," a woman complained from somewhere near the back. "My Harold and a bunch of others went to the livestock auction over at Silver Springs and didn't get back yet."

"Prob'ly they got unavoidably delayed in the Silver Springs bar," a man called, and the crowd laughed.

Aggie's eyes glittered behind her glasses. "No doubt that's exactly what happened," she said coldly. "And it's just another reason why we don't want a drinking place right here in our town. Isn't it, ladies?"

There was a murmur of assent from some of the women in the audience, while the men remained silent. Nathan and Luther exchanged a glance, then looked up as Aggie rapped the gavel again and inclined her head graciously at a woman sitting in the audience.

"Myra Jones is going to read us a few statistics," she announced, "outlining the increased incidence of serious traffic accidents in towns that have licensed drinking premises."

"Oh, come on, Aggie," Hilda protested. "We don't even *have* a set of traffic lights in Wolf Hill. In fact, we've never had a serious traffic accident that I can remember."

"How about that time George Mueller's axle broke and he lost a whole load of chickens right on Main Street?" somebody asked.

Hilda grinned. "Well, that was a mess, all right," she agreed. "But liquor had nothing to do with it. It was the pothole in front of the general store that the town council never got around to fixing."

Aggie's cheeks reddened. She pounded her gavel furiously. "*Myra* has the floor," she said. "If you want to contribute anything, Hilda, you'll have your chance when we open the meeting for questions."

Nathan exchanged another thoughtful look with Luther Barnes and settled back to listen. Myra's voice droned on and on, citing traffic statistics that had no relevance at all to the citizens of Wolf Hill. She was followed by Lydia Humphreys, who read a long government document on the relationship between alcohol abuse and family violence.

Nathan folded his arms and frowned, thinking about Kate. She seemed to be in his thoughts all the time these days. While he rode through his herd, delivered calves and hauled feed and stacked hay bales, he saw her shy radiant smile and her wide blue eyes. He even heard her gentle voice in the whistling spring wind.

But it was in the evenings that she haunted him the most. When the day's work was done, whether Nathan was sitting at his kitchen table doing paperwork, or lounging in the luxury of his big ranch house listening to music on the stereo, he hungered for her presence. He longed to talk with her. He wanted to tell her about his day and enjoy the play of emotions on her face as she listened and responded to him....

"... ready to take a vote?" Aggie was saying, and Nathan was jolted abruptly from his reverie.

"Vote on what?" he asked.

"On whether we want to go ahead and submit the petition to keep this woman from opening a drinking place in Wolf Hill," Aggie told him with exaggerated patience. "That *is* the topic of discussion, Nathan."

He tensed and looked around the room, wondering what to do. Nathan had half intended to vote for the petition, believing that it would probably be in Kate's best interests in the long run. Running the Wolf Hill Hotel would be a daunting task even for some hard-bitten career woman, let alone someone as gentle and inexperienced in business as Kate Daniels.

And he knew, as well, that there was no way to convince her to give up, short of this kind of intervention. Aggie's petition was, he had believed, the gentlest way to block Kate's efforts and ease her out of an impossible situation.

But now, Nathan wasn't so sure. Kate was determined to succeed. She would be so hurt. Besides, this secret meeting of Aggie's had the flavor of a lynching. He wanted no part of it.

"We can't vote," he said, turning his attention to Aggie. "Most of the men still aren't here."

"Well, that's their problem, isn't it?" Aggie said coldly. "They knew about the meeting."

Nathan suspected Aggie's meeting had been deliberately scheduled to coincide with the livestock auction in Silver Springs, which many of the local men attended every month.

"You can't fight her, Nathan," Luther murmured beside him. "She'll just get her back up and act nastier than ever. She's been that way since she was in diapers."

Nathan subsided, watching in growing helplessness as the vote was taken and counted. When Aggie turned to him, he voted firmly against the petition and was surprised how good it felt. After Nathan lodged his vote, a few of the women were also emboldened to oppose Aggie, but their numbers were not enough to defeat her campaign.

"Fifty-six people voting," she announced. "Thirty-seven in favor of the petition, nineteen opposed. That's..." She paused, her fingers punching a small calculator on the table in front of her. "Sixty-six percent in favor," she announced triumphantly. "We'll submit the petition, and she won't get her license. Meeting adjourned. Jennie and Myra will serve refreshments at the back."

She rapped the gavel a final time and the townspeople got to their feet, looking a little dazed. Hilda paused near Luther and Nathan on the way to the door, her round face pink with anger.

"That woman's a menace," she said furiously. "Poor Kate, how's she supposed to make a decent living if she can't open the bar? And who's going to tell her?"

Luther was silent, and Nathan realized with sympathy that his friend was unable to speak when Hilda was so close to him. Both of them looked at the woman in helpless concern.

"Somebody's got to tell Kate," Nathan said. "She can't pour any more money into that old place if it's going to be a complete loss."

"*I'm* sure not telling her," Hilda said with another dark glare at the front of the room. "For one thing, I'm not done fighting with Aggie yet. Besides, I don't want Kate to give up while there's still a chance. I want my dining room."

"Well, I doubt that Ray's going to tell her," Nathan said dryly. "He's making far too much money off those renovations."

He watched in silence as Hilda stamped away, angrily refusing an offer of coffee and cake from the ladies at the back of the hall.

Luther watched her, as well, sighing. "You know what I wish, Nathan?" he said plaintively. "Times like this, I wish there was someplace in this town a man could go for a drink."

Nathan smiled in spite of himself and moved toward the door with his companion, wondering how he could help Kate Daniels out of this dilemma.

KATE STOOD in the basement of the hotel, brushing absently at a long cobweb hanging from one of the beams. She wore grubby blue jeans, an old plaid shirt and a blue bandanna tied around her head, and her mood was as dark as her surroundings.

Raymond had finally brought in a crew during the week to break up the old boiler. Its grimy carcass was now scattered all over the basement, hacked into chunks of various sizes, while a tangle of pipes and insulation littered the corners. Meanwhile, the sleek new boiler, still in its wooden packing crate, was stored in a shed behind the hotel.

It seemed that Kate's new boiler would remain in the crate forever. Apparently, Raymond was experiencing labor difficulties. "The crew wants another four dollars an hour," he'd told Kate the previous day. "Each."

"Or else what?"

"Or else they won't clean up the basement and we can't install the new boiler."

"But there are *five* of them," Kate said in disbelief. "That's another twenty dollars an hour, just to get rid of the scrap iron! And they work so slowly, they're like turtles crawling around down there. It'll take them days to finish."

"Terrible, ain't it?" Raymond commented with satisfaction.

As the general contractor, Raymond got a percentage of everybody's pay, all of which came out of Kate's pocket. Labor problems didn't bother him at all.

But Kate's control had finally snapped. "Fire them," she said.

"*Fire* them?"

"Yes. Tell them I'll clean the place up myself."

And so she was laboring and sweating in the musty depths as she hauled heavy chunks of scrap up the outside steps, through the bulkhead and into the backyard. Her shoulders ached, her face was smeared with dirt and grease, and sweat trickled down her back under the shirt. But at least, she thought grimly, Raymond wasn't going to win this round.

Kate frowned and gathered a few lengths of pipe into her arms, still thinking about the contractor. Raymond was behaving rather oddly these days, looking at her with cautious speculation when he thought she wasn't watching. Hilda, too, had an awkward, constrained manner that made Kate feel uneasy. Something was going on. She could sense it all around her, and she was growing increasingly nervous.

In fact, she jumped in alarm when a shadow fell across the basement floor and a tall figure clattered down the steps. "Oh!" she gasped, dropping a length of pipe to the floor.

"Sorry," Nathan apologized, coming over to lean against one of the wooden uprights. "I didn't mean to scare you. My God!" he added when his eyes adjusted to the dim light. "Kate, what are you doing?"

"What does it look like?" she asked with some irritation, tossing smaller chunks of scrap onto an old wheelbarrow.

"It looks awful. Can I help?"

"No. You're too clean."

Nathan wore faded jeans, a baseball cap and a white T-shirt that displayed the breadth of his chest and shoulders. Miserably conscious of her own grimy, disheveled state, Kate tried not to look at that broad chest. But to her distress, she found herself battling a cowardly urge to fling herself against him, cobwebs and all, and burst into tears.

"Why can't Ray do this?" Nathan asked, frowning.

"Because Raymond doesn't do actual *work*, except for carpentry. He merely supervises. And his crew demanded a raise of four dollars an hour each or they wouldn't clean up the basement."

"So you sent them packing," Nathan said with a grin.

He began to toss pieces of scrap iron onto the pile, then hefted the wheelbarrow and rolled it toward the outside steps, his muscles bulging and straining under the soft cotton of his shirt. "Look, you don't have to do this," Kate said. "It's hard, filthy work, and it's my job. I can do it on my own."

"Yeah?" He looked down at her, his eyes bright beneath the peak of his cap. "Can you lift this wheelbarrow?"

"Of course not," she said coldly. "I can only load it half that full. It takes me twice as long, but I'll get it done eventually."

"Oh, Kate..." Nathan paused by the wheelbarrow, his face so full of sympathy and tenderness that she was almost overcome once more. "Kate, this is all so damned hard. Why don't you—"

He fell abruptly silent, but his words hung in the air, unspoken.

"Give up," Kate said flatly. "That's what you're wondering, isn't it, Nathan? Why don't I just give up and go back to the city?"

"I didn't say that."

"You didn't have to," Kate said, her anger mounting. Suddenly, she was so tired and miserable that she couldn't control herself anymore. All the frustration of the last few weeks grew and pounded inside her head.

"I know what you're thinking, all of you. Raymond and Hilda and everybody else. You all think I'm an idiot for trying to make a success of this. Even the Realtor..."

"What about the Realtor?" Nathan asked when she stopped and turned away. "Kate?"

Her anger faded as quickly as it had come, leaving her with a weary, helpless feeling. "He came by this morning and said he'd had an offer on the hotel. I could get out of the deal with my initial investment, and most of the money I've spent on renovations. Not *all* of it, mind you. Just most of it."

Nathan set the wheelbarrow carefully in place and looked at her. "I see. And what do you think about that? Are you going to sell?"

"I don't know. I suppose I should," she muttered bitterly. "After all, I'm far too inept to take on a challenge like this and make a success of it, right? I can't even handle Raymond Butts. How can I possibly run a hotel?"

"Kate, you shouldn't look on this as a failure. There are some things that nobody could make a success of, you know. Maybe you should just chalk it up to experience, and..."

"Go back to the city," Kate concluded when he paused. "Isn't that right, Nathan? I should just get out of your town and quit upsetting everybody."

"I never said that. The last thing I want is for you to leave."

"Why?" she asked furiously. "Because it's so much fun to watch me floundering and messing up?"

He made a brief impatient gesture. "No, dammit! Because if you leave, this town's going to seem like a sad, empty place, that's why. Because you're the most interesting woman I've ever..."

He paused. Kate stared at him, her mouth dropping open in surprise. After an awkward moment, she turned away, feeling hot and confused.

"Kate," he whispered, putting his hands on her shoulders and drawing her into his arms.

She struggled briefly. "Nathan, please don't. I'm such a mess...."

"You're beautiful," he murmured, bending his head toward her. "No matter what you're doing or how you're dressed, you're always beautiful."

Kate sagged in his arms, overcome by his powerful masculinity. His lips were cool and soft against hers, and his arms felt so good.

She'd never known a kiss like this. The sweetness of his mouth was overwhelming. Kate felt herself drowning in passion and a confused image of fresh-picked berries, ripe and bursting with flavor...

Oh, Ellen, it's really true, she thought, shivering in his arms. When it's the right mouth that kisses you, it's wonderful. It's so wonderful.

Shocked by her thoughts, Kate took herself hastily in hand and pulled away from him. She avoided his eyes, bending to pick up a few pieces of scrap and toss them aimlessly into the wheelbarrow.

Nathan watched her in silence. "What are you going to tell the Realtor?" he asked after a moment.

"I'm going to tell him I don't want to sell," Kate said, looking down at her gloved hands. "Maybe I'm crazy, but I want to keep trying for a while. If I can just get the liquor license soon, I'll be making enough of a profit to finish the renovations. It can't take much longer, no matter how much red tape is involved."

She glanced up at Nathan, whose eyes were dark and unfathomable beneath his cap. "Look, there's something we need to talk about," he said abruptly.

"What?" Kate tugged at a piece of scrap iron wedged beneath the stairs. "What do we need to talk about?"

Nathan reached down to gently restrain her. "Not now. We'll talk later, all right? Leave this mess, Kate. Go back to your painting and wallpapering. I'll come by tomorrow morning and clean this up for you."

"You can't do all that work for nothing. I'll have to pay you."

"Of course," he said, so calmly that Kate gave him a suspicious glance.

"You'll let me pay you?"

"We'll work something out," Nathan said.

"Oh, yes? Like what?"

"Well, for one thing, I want you to come visit me at my ranch this weekend and see my house. No visit, no cleanup."

In spite of herself, Kate felt a smile tugging at the corners of her mouth. "You drive a pretty hard bargain, don't you? Maybe I'll just go ahead and finish this job myself."

"No, you won't," he said comfortably, smiling back at her. "You'll go up and have a nice hot bath and forget all about this mess. And on Saturday afternoon, you'll be waiting for me around one o'clock. That's the deal."

Kate knew she was foolish to give in. If she let him help, she'd sink deeper into his debt, even further from her goal of rigid self-sufficiency. And now the situation was complicated by the memory of that delicious, passionate kiss. But the thought of a hot bath was so tempting...

"All right," she said at last.

"Saturday afternoon," he repeated, watching her intently. "One o'clock."

"Yes," Kate said in defeat.

"Good. I'll see you then." He reached out and touched her face, slowly rubbing his thumb over a smear of grease on her cheek. After a long, charged moment, she pulled away, ran up the stairs and hurried through the lobby before he could say anything more.

THAT NIGHT, Kate brewed a mug of tea on the hot plate in her cluttered, half-finished bedroom. She put a dressing gown over her fleecy pajamas and picked her way through stray bits of drywall and building materials to retrieve Ellen's diary from its hiding place.

As she removed the old book, she thought about Ellen's description of the loose windowsill. For the first time, Kate had a powerful sense of physical closeness to the young schoolteacher. Ellen Livingston had touched this same piece of oak, had actually slept in this very room, all those years ago. The thought gave Kate a warm comforting feeling, as if she had a friend nearby.

She curled into a shabby blanket-covered armchair with the book and her tea, and opened the yellowed pages to her bookmark.

Thursday, October 20, 1904

Autumn on the prairie is a lovely season, with warm golden afternoons and crisp starry evenings. A huge red harvest moon slips above the horizon at night, so beautiful and melancholy that I sometimes watch it from my hotel window and find myself crying.

My job continues to be terribly difficult. I am embarrassed to confess that my only consolation thus far has been poor attendance! Harvest was very late this year, and all of my students have been absent in turn over the past month as they helped their parents with the haying and threshing. Luke Grossman and two of the oldest girls have been "working out," hiring themselves to one farmer and then another, and have not come to school at all since the first week, much to my relief. I have no idea how I shall manage when the weather turns colder and all thirty-seven of my students come back to school at the same time.

One of my few triumphs has been the Mueller twins, Gunter and Elsa, aged eight. They are both learning English with astonishing speed. At first, their progress made me quite giddy with my success as a teacher, but gradually I came to realize that the twins are so bright, they would learn no matter how they were taught.

I grow so weary of seeing rows of suspicious faces looking at me each day. Many of the children seem sullen and unwilling to participate, particularly the boys. Perhaps here on the frontier, it is considered unmanly to have scholarly aspirations. Or perhaps they are just members of such a tightly knit community that I, as a newcomer, am not to be trusted.

Yesterday, though, we had a small breakthrough, and from a most unlikely source. When I went outside at noon, I saw a disturbance across the school yard and went over to investigate. The excitement centered around our new outhouse, and for good reason.

I have spent some weeks requesting—perhaps "demanding" would be more accurate—that the school board install a second outhouse so the girls and I may have some modicum of privacy. After much tedious delay, Mr. McLean finally arrived yesterday with the little building on his wagon. Taciturn as ever, he set about digging the hole and installing the facility. There it sat, its fresh-cut lumber glistening in the sunshine, but when Leisel Gobel opened the door, she found that it was not empty. A large rattlesnake had already taken up residence!

Apparently, the loathsome creature had crawled in through a crack at the side of the building during the morning, and had slithered down into the hollow cavity beneath the wooden seat. The boys now had it cornered inside, where it rattled furiously at intervals, practically shaking the little building with its outrage.

The girls were terrified—as was their teacher, I must confess. They huddled together on the school steps, while the boys ranged themselves in a group near the outhouse and watched me with impassive faces.

"Won't it come out if we all go away?" I ventured.

They were silent. Finally, Charles Oates spoke up. Charles is the son of the school board president, and his mother is my friend and mentor. I fear that he often suffers from divided loyalties at school, but this time he decided to help me. "Winter's coming," he explained briefly. "Snakes are looking for dens."

"But it cannot possibly spend the winter in our outhouse!" I exclaimed in horror.

Gunter, who is a fat, happy little boy, gave me a cherubic smile. "Ven da girls sit down, dat schnake vill bite dem on—"

"Gunter!" I said sharply, while the other boys hooted with laughter.

I stood for a moment looking at them, battling my own instincts. I have always rather prided myself on my abilities as a problem solver. But on this occasion, I felt utterly helpless, and I was forced to admit it.

"Well, I have no idea what to do," I told my ragged group of urchins. "I am completely at a loss, and I am also terrified of snakes. Unless you fellows are able to help me, I am defeated."

Clearly, this was the right thing to say. They scattered into the brush-filled ravine near the school and emerged brandishing an array of forked sticks. While I watched from a careful distance, wringing my hands anxiously, they swarmed into the outhouse and teased the snake until it crawled outside, where they killed it with skill and dispatch.

I praised all of them with proper feminine adulation, and they seemed much gratified. Since then, though I am almost afraid to say it for fear of a relapse, the atmosphere in school has been noticeably more pleasant and cooperative. Two of the older boys have actually offered to take part in the play we are presenting next month, and several of the little ones helped me to fill the water barrel this morning.

As a result, I feel quite overcome with well-being this evening, although I know that my job will still be a difficult one.

I am ashamed of myself. Honesty compels me to admit that my current optimism is not entirely due to my small success at school. I also have quite an interesting engagement to look forward to on the weekend!

When I came home from school today, Mrs. Oates was waiting for me in the lobby. She tells me that she and I, along with several other local ladies, have been invited for tea on Sunday afternoon at...guess where? Joshua Cameron's house!

Mrs. Oates teased me a little, saying that she believed Mr. Cameron would have preferred to have just one guest, but propriety compels him to make a party of the occasion. I was careful not to give her the satisfaction of a response, and pretended to be very nonchalant about the whole idea, but I must confess that I can hardly wait to see his house...and him....

ELLEN HAD CROSSED OUT the last two words, but Kate was still able to make them out beneath the lines of faded gray ink. She smiled, marveling at the coincidence. She, too, was looking forward to seeing the Cameron house on the weekend. And like Ellen, she was looking forward to seeing Nathan even more.

The only difference, Kate thought, was that back in those proper and carefully chaperoned days, Ellen had

not yet felt Joshua's arms around her, or the sweet
thrill of his lips on hers. Kate shivered and turned to
the diary again.

Sunday, October 23, 1904

What a strange and rather disturbing afternoon!
Mrs. Oates called for me at three o'clock in her pony
cart, and we bowled off jauntily through the mellow
autumn countryside. I blush to admit that I was
wearing my navy shirtwaist, which I have always intended to save for special occasions like Christmas and
school recitals. But none of the other things I tried on
seemed right for the occasion, and the dark color is, I
believe, quite flattering.

When we arrived, I was glad that I felt confident in
my outfit, because Amy Lord was one of the guests.
Amy is the mayor's daughter. She is a dainty, pretty,
simpering young woman, the sort who is cool and
snappish while in feminine company, but sweet as a
kitten when men are nearby. I have never liked her, but
I came to dislike her intensely when I saw how she
clung to Joshua Cameron, flattering him outland-
ishly and batting her eyelashes at him with a propri-
etary air.

To his credit, I must admit that he did not respond
to her or give her any encouragement at all, but still I
found her behavior annoying.

I must quit thinking about her, as it makes me feel
angry and uncharitable. Instead, I will describe Mr.
Cameron's house. He insists that I must learn to call
him Joshua, but it is difficult. He lives in a three-room
cabin built with his own hands, and quite civilized by
Wolf Hill standards. Clearly, his ranch is doing well,

as he has bought some rather nice china and comfortable furnishings for his home, but his ambitions range much further.

"I plan to build a new house on this property in a few years," he told us over tea and cakes, which Mrs. Goldman helped him to serve. "Painted white with green shutters. A two-story house with a deep veranda all around, just like the home I grew up in back East."

Amy edged closer to him, clearly delighted at this prospect, and began to bounce on her chair with a girlish display of enthusiasm. How I dislike the woman!

"What do you think of that, Miss Livingston?" he asked me.

"I like this cabin," I told him calmly, sipping from my teacup. "It must be very warm and cozy in here on a cold winter night."

His eyes rested on me with such a look of interest that I grew warm all over. I swear that my remark was utterly innocent, but as soon as he looked at me, I could see the little cabin bathed in lamplight, and the two of us sharing that big leather armchair, snug and cozy while the wind howled outside the windows. Worst of all, I suspected that he harbored a similar thought!

Amy regarded me with cold blue eyes. "How silly you are, Ellen," she said in her high, childlike voice. "Who could possibly prefer this little cabin to a wonderful mansion like the one Joshua is going to build?"

"Obviously, no woman with a shred of common sense," I muttered, concentrating on my piece of seed cake while the others looked at me curiously.

The conversation went on, dealing mostly with building and improvements, a topic that seems to obsess everybody here on the frontier. After a while, Joshua addressed himself to me again.

"I gather that you aren't overly enthusiastic about big houses, Miss Livingston," he said with a smile. "But are there any other improvements you could suggest for my property?"

I thought for a moment. "Trees," I said at last.

"Indeed? Where?" He watched me closely, seemingly oblivious to the other women in the room.

"I would plant cottonwood trees along the drive leading to the house," I told him. "Two rows, in fact, one on each side of the drive. Then, in time, the branches would grow and entwine overhead, and make a shady green tunnel. Without at least some trees, I fear that I would find life here on the prairie almost intolerable."

"That's ridiculous!" Amy scoffed. "Ellen has no idea how difficult it is to grow trees here. Poor Joshua would need to haul thousands of gallons of water if he wanted them to survive."

But Joshua ignored her. Possibly he did not even hear her, because he was concentrating so intently on me.

"That's a fine idea. Next spring," he told me softly, "as soon as the frost is out of the ground and the cows have finished calving, I'll begin planting your row of trees, Miss Livingston."

Was it just my imagination, or did his voice and eyes hold a promise of something beyond trees? I tremble and hug myself when I think of it, feeling warm and cold by turns. It is clearly time to put my diary away and try to sleep. Tomorrow will be another hard day at school and there is no time for me to be thinking about Joshua Cameron!

CHAPTER SIX

ONCE AGAIN, Kate found herself sitting next to Nathan Cameron in his big pickup truck, looking at the sweep of the landscape. But this time, they were heading out of town in a westerly direction, toward his property. And Kate was even more apprehensive about spending an afternoon alone with him than she'd been a couple of weeks earlier at the prospect of meeting his parents.

"It's so *green*," she murmured, watching the carpet of grass as it rolled all the way up into a sapphire sky. "I always thought the prairie was a dull kind of yellow-brown."

He smiled, his teeth flashing white against his tanned skin. "It will be, as soon as the sun gets higher and hotter. But this is May, and there's been a lot of rain this spring. We'll have green grass for a few weeks yet."

Kate nodded and looked out the window again, thinking about the diary. She felt so close to Ellen these days, more and more intrigued by the similarities in their two situations. But Ellen's adventure had begun in the fall, while Kate found herself journeying through a country springtime so glorious that it was almost intoxicating.

"By the way, I didn't have a chance to thank you," she said at last, turning to Nathan. "I was in the city all day yesterday, shopping for a good deal on mattresses."

"Thank me? What for?"

"For cleaning up the hotel basement. It was so nice of you, Nathan."

He waved his hand casually. "I picked up Luther Barnes and got him to help. It only took us six or seven hours, and part of that time we were having a big meal up in the coffee shop."

Kate smiled. "Is Luther really in love with Hilda?"

"Yeah, I think he is. Poor guy."

"Why feel sorry for him? Hilda's a nice person."

"Sure she is," Nathan said. "But she's never going to give up all the fun of running her own business for something as dull and ordinary as a man."

He cast Kate a significant glance that she chose to ignore. "Who owns all this land?" she asked, peering out the window again.

"My family," Nathan said briefly. "Matter of fact, we've been driving through Cameron property for quite a while now."

Kate looked at him in surprise. "Really? How big is your ranch?"

"About thirty square miles," Nathan said calmly, examining a small herd of cows near the road.

Kate fell silent, trying to imagine what it would be like to own thirty square miles of this rich countryside.

"Those are the ranch buildings," Nathan said, pointing with one hand. "You can see them now, off to the west."

Kate peered though the truck window, where a sprawl of barns, stables, sheds and corrals filled most of the valley. She could see a small airstrip at the side of the road, where a couple of aluminum hangars glistened in the sunlight. "Hilda says that when you have your branding out here, people fly in from all over the place in their private jets," Kate said. "She told me some federal politicians were here this year, and a couple of movie stars."

"That's true. I never pay them much attention. All those VIPs just get in the way. My mother likes to come out and play hostess, but I'm usually too busy to talk to them."

"Too busy for movie stars?" Kate teased. "What on earth would you be doing?"

He shrugged. "Gathering cattle, roping and wrestling calves, doing the vaccinating, that sort of thing. Calf branding's a real busy time around here."

"But don't you have ranch hands to do all that?"

"I like to be involved," Nathan said briefly. "Cattle ranching's my business, Kate. You can't run a ranch properly if you're not down in the corrals where things are happening."

Kate nodded and looked out the window again, a little intimidated by what she observed. The ranch was dominated by a stately old house on small rise of land. Large and square, white with dark green shutters, it loomed above the other buildings. Gleaming white pillars supported the roof of a deep veranda that ran the width of the front and disappeared around the sides of the house.

They pulled into a long driveway of cottonwoods that flanked both sides of the approach road. The trees were tall and sturdy, covered with fresh new leaves that formed a rustling green roof above their heads. Kate's mouth curved into an involuntary smile. "Who planted all these trees?" she asked with deliberate casualness.

"My great-grandfather," Nathan said. "Joshua Cameron. They've been here for fifty years."

Kate studied the green archway, her smile gradually fading. "But...Nathan, aren't you mistaken? These trees have to be a lot more than fifty years old."

Nathan glanced at her in surprise. "What makes you think so?"

"Well, they were planted..." Kate paused in confusion, then went on. "If your great-grandfather planted these trees, that would have been back around the turn of the century, wouldn't it? Around...say, 1905, or so?"

"I don't know what you're reading in that old diary you found, Kate, or who wrote it," he said with a teasing smile, "but they've got a few things wrong. These trees date back to the early forties. Apparently, it was just about the last thing my great-grandfather did before he died, planting this double row of trees."

Kate tried to grasp what he was saying. She felt a growing bewilderment and a vague chill, as if a cloud had passed over the sun. "But I don't understand," she murmured. "I thought... Nathan, are you *sure* the trees were planted then?"

"Positive," he said cheerfully. "My father was born in 1936, Kate. He was just a little boy when old Joshua planted these cottonwoods, probably about eight years old or so. He still remembers being forced to help, and how much he hated it."

"Why?"

Nathan's mouth tightened. "From all accounts, the old man was bad enough in his prime. By the time he was over seventy and crippled with arthritis, he was pure hell to be with. Especially for a little kid as quiet and sensitive as my father. Dad doesn't have any fond memories of his grandfather, Kate. I think he was really glad to move to the city and get away from this damned double row of trees, even all these years later."

Kate gripped her hands nervously in her lap, staring blindly at the green tunnel until they drove out into the sunshine again and parked by the big triple garage next to the house.

She was thinking about a young girl in her best dress, and a man's handsome dark face, his warm smile as he made her a promise.

"Next spring," he'd said to Ellen.

Had Joshua Cameron been all talk and swagger, a man who made promises to attract the woman he wanted and then casually ignored her?

Maybe that explained the family's coldness toward the memory of Joshua Cameron. Perhaps he'd married Ellen and then slowly broken her heart by refusing to take care of her, or pay any heed to the things that mattered to her so passionately.

Like her yearning for shady green trees on the barren loneliness of the prairie....

Kate frowned, thinking about the young woman who was obviously falling deeper in love on every page of her diary. She couldn't bear to think of Ellen being unhappy or neglected in her marriage.

She glanced at the man beside her, wondering for the first time if perhaps he, too, was not as warm and charming as he appeared to be. There was something almost overpowering about this place, its obvious wealth and the weight of family history that Marian Cameron had recounted with such pride.

Kate twisted her hands in her lap, gazing out the truck window. She knew, all too well, what it was like to move in the orbit of wealthy and powerful men like the one sitting next to her. A woman could easily find herself being swallowed up, all her dreams and aspirations lost in the glare of a man's success.

"Is something the matter, Kate?" Nathan asked. "You look a little sad, all of a sudden."

"I'm fine," Kate said briefly, opening her door and climbing out of the truck. "Is your housekeeper here today?"

"Bessie's always here. I think she's going into town this afternoon for groceries, but not before she gets a look at you," Nathan said cheerfully, unlatching a gate in the picket fence and holding it open for Kate.

"Is she like Hilda?"

"Well, they look quite a bit alike, but Bessie's a different kind of person. Much less driven by ambition. Hilda's a real career woman, as she's no doubt told you."

He grinned at Kate, his eyes slowly darkening with concern when she didn't smile back.

"Kate," he said gently, taking her arm. "Are you sure you're all right? You seem worried about something."

"I'm fine," Kate said again, struck again by his quick perception. This time she didn't like the feeling that Nathan Cameron was able to read her mind with such ease. "I'm just fine." She shook his hand away and started up the walkway ahead of him, wishing the afternoon was already over so she could go home.

But as the day went on, she found it more and more difficult to resist Nathan's charm. To her dismay, after so many weeks of living in her shabby hotel, she also found herself beguiled by the comfort and richness of his life.

The ranch house was even more luxurious than she'd expected. Marian and Josh Cameron had many beautiful possessions in their city condo, but they'd obviously left a lot of things behind, too. Looking around the gracious, high-ceilinged rooms, Kate was awed to realize just what a prosperous operation this ranch must be.

When she'd first met Nathan, he'd been so casual and unassuming that she'd formed an entirely wrong impression. Despite Hilda's comments about the ranch, she'd somehow pictured the man living in a rustic bunkhouse, rather like Joshua's cabin, with his boots on a shelf nearby and his horse tied up outside the door.

But Nathan Cameron lived amid beauty and luxury, surrounded by fine artwork, good music and some of the best food Kate had ever tasted.

"Oh, Bessie." She sighed, sitting in the kitchen and helping herself to more peach cobbler and whipped cream while Nathan watched from across the table. "This is *so* delicious."

Bessie smiled placidly. "Be sure you let Hilda know about it, then. That girl thinks she's the only one in the family who can cook."

Kate looked meaningfully at Nathan, who turned to his housekeeper with a smile. "Now, Bessie, don't you two get Kate involved in your family warfare. I sure don't want her killed in the cross fire."

Bessie snorted, removed her apron and took a set of keys from a rack near the door. "I'm off to do some shopping in town. I'll be back in a few hours," she announced. "There are some stuffed game hens in the oven, but it's set to come on automatically. Dinner's at six." She stood at the door looking at them expectantly.

"We'll be here," Nathan promised.

Kate looked at him in alarm. "For *dinner?* Nathan, I don't think I should be—"

"A deal's a deal," he said, leaning back comfortably in his chair. "I cleaned up your basement, so I get you for the rest of the day."

"But—"

"And Bessie's gone to a lot of trouble over this meal. Haven't you, Bessie?"

"I sure have. Anyway, see you both in a few hours. Nice to meet you, Kate." The housekeeper smiled and left them alone. She marched down the walkway to the garage while Kate watched her through the window, feeling increasingly alarmed.

A COUPLE OF HOURS LATER, after an extensive tour of the ranch, a brief horseback ride out to see the new calves and a lot of talk and laughter, Kate's mood had mellowed considerably. She sat next to Nathan on the porch swing, sipping a frosty glass of ice tea and touching her foot to the veranda floor occasionally to keep the swing moving.

He lounged back against the cushions with his hat tipped low over his eyes and a glass resting on a patio table beside him.

"Ah." He sighed from beneath his hat, reaching out to stroke her arm, then take her free hand in his. "A glass of tea, the fragrance of roasting chickens, and thou, my love. The essence of happiness."

Kate considered this. "They're not chickens," she said at last, pushing energetically with her toe. "They're Cornish game hens."

"Whatever. Quit rocking the boat, okay? I'm getting seasick."

"Let go of my hand, and I will."

He chuckled and sat up, tossing his hat onto the floor. "Let go, you say?"

Kate ignored him, squinting at a row of neat bungalows among the ranch buildings. "Nathan, how many people work here?"

"Don't change the subject. Here, give me your glass before I spill it."

"Why would you spill my tea?" Kate asked as he moved closer.

He grinned at her, his eyes sparkling. "Because I'm about to ravish you," he explained, "and if we don't get rid of that glass, it could be messy."

"I don't want to be ravished," Kate said. She sipped her tea calmly, though her heart was beginning to pound with pleasurable excitement. "And you have to be considerate of my wishes."

"Yeah? Why?"

"Because you're the host. The etiquette books are very specific about this. A proper host never ravishes his guests if they don't choose to be."

"Who said I was a proper host?"

Kate glanced at him, smiling in spite of herself. "Aren't you?"

"Not at all. Matter of fact, I'm a big black spider and you're a juicy little fly I've finally enticed into my parlor. Now, my dear, I'm about to have my way with you."

Suiting actions to words, he took Kate's glass and set it next to his on the patio table, then fell on her with lusty energy. He swept her into his arms, kissing her face and neck, holding her so tightly that they collapsed against the soft cushions and wriggled together, laughing.

"Damn spiders," Kate muttered against his neck. "Where's that bug spray when a girl needs it?"

Nathan chuckled and drew her closer, moving his long body until he lay almost on top of her. To her embarrassment, Kate found herself responding eagerly, almost hungrily. It had been such a long time since she'd lain with a man like this, warm and close in his arms, lips pressed against his. Kate wrapped her arms around his neck and returned his kisses with rising passion.

But when his hands began to roam over her body, stroking her hips and thighs, then pulled her shirt out of her jeans and slipped underneath to cup her breasts, Kate shivered and tried to pull away.

"Nathan," she whispered, "don't do this. Please don't."

His hands stilled at once, but he continued to hold her. "Why not?" he muttered against her cheek.

"Because I don't..."

I don't trust you, Kate wanted to say. Maybe you're not as nice as you seem. But most of all, I'm so afraid of getting caught up in a man's life all over again.

"I don't think I'm ready," she said aloud. "I just got out of a long-term relationship, Nathan. I think it's too soon for me to get involved with someone."

"Get involved?" he echoed, his face still hidden against her hair. Kate could feel the hard tension of his body, and hear his ragged breathing. "Is that what we're doing here, Kate? Getting involved?"

"Isn't it?"

He lifted his face and looked down at her soberly, still lying close to her. "I don't know. I thought maybe we were falling in love, or something old-fashioned like that," he said. "I didn't realize we were just getting involved."

Kate watched as he moved away and sat up, reaching for his glass of tea.

"Nathan," she began, then stopped.

"Do you still love him?" he asked, squinting at the distant horizon.

"Who?" Kate asked in confusion.

"Your husband. Is that the problem, Kate? Do you still have feelings for him?"

"Adam? I'm still fond of him," she said after a moment's thought. "I think it's probably been a long time since I've loved him, but he's always been a likable person. Adam may be rich and famous, but he's really just a little boy who's never grown up."

"Doesn't a woman get tired of having a little boy around all the time? Wouldn't you rather have a man, Kate?"

Kate didn't answer, but her mind was reeling. Yes! she thought in anguish, looking at the hard line of his cheek and jaw. Yes, I want a man. I want you, Nathan, but I'm so afraid...

He helped her to sit up, then waited while she tucked her shirt into her jeans and ran a trembling hand over her hair.

"Look, Kate," he said after an awkward silence, handing her the glass of tea, "there's something I have to tell you. I guess I should have told you some time ago, but I was afraid to."

Kate tensed, wondering if her own fears were about to be confirmed. Probably the man already had a wife and children somewhere, or some other dark secret in his past. But his next words astonished her so much that she almost spilled her drink.

"It's about your liquor license," he said.

"My—my *liquor license?*" She looked at him blankly. "What about it?"

"You're probably not going to get it," Nathan said quietly. "I'm sorry, Kate."

"Not going to *get* it?" Kate continued to stare at him, holding the glass tightly in her hands. "What do you mean? How do you know?"

"The town had a meeting," he told her in that same quiet tone. "It was organized by Aggie and her crew. They met to organize a petition against your license, and got enough votes to file an intent. That's going to hold up your license until after their petition circulates, and then they'll probably defeat it."

Kate's hands began to shake. She put her drink down hastily before it spilled. "Nathan," she whispered, feeling stricken. "That's... that's just *terrible*.

I need that liquor license! If I can't open the bar pretty soon, there's no way the hotel will be able to survive."

"Oh, Kate..." He looked at her with concern and reached out as if to take her in his arms again, then let his hands drop. "Maybe you should take that offer you were telling me about," he said at last. "Sell the hotel while you've got a chance, before you lose any more money."

"No!" Kate said abruptly. She got to her feet and moved away from him to the veranda railing, where she stood hugging her arms and gazing at the rustling archway of trees.

Nathan followed and stood behind her, putting his hands gently on her shoulders. "Kate, I told you before, you're not a failure. You've already done a wonderful job on that old place. Everybody thinks so. But unless you've got unlimited funds, honey, you may have to cut your losses and get out. It's a simple business decision."

"Please don't lecture me," Kate said quietly. "I don't want your business lessons, Nathan. I just want to make a success of my hotel, and there's no reason I shouldn't. I'm working so hard, paying my own way, not hurting anyone... Why should I be forced to give up now?"

"Why does it matter so much, Kate?" he asked. "Why is it so impossible to give this up?"

"Because it's the first time I've ever really set out to do something all on my own!" Kate said passionately. "Because everybody predicted I'd make a mess of it. Adam's agent and managers, my mother...even my lawyer. They all thought it was such a dumb idea, but I went ahead anyhow."

"And now you're going to keep throwing good money after bad, just trying to prove they were wrong?"

Kate shook her head wearily. "It's not that simple. It's more like trying to prove something to myself. If I fail at this, Nathan," she went on, turning to face him, "then I'll know they were right. I'll be just another inept, helpless woman who can't do anything without the help of some man."

"It's not necessarily weakness to accept someone's help, Kate."

"I know it isn't. But I really need to do this on my own."

"So what will you do about Aggie?"

"I don't know," Kate said miserably. "I just don't know." She had a sudden thought, and looked up at him suspiciously. "Nathan, you said that you should have told me earlier. How long have you known about this?"

"About Aggie's petition? Almost a month, I guess. Everybody knows about it. Ray and Hilda were both at the meeting."

"Well, I can understand why *they* didn't want to tell me," Kate said with some bitterness. "They both stand to gain by my insanity, after all. But what about you, Nathan? Why didn't you let me know there was going to be a problem as soon as you heard about it? I thought we were friends."

He shifted awkwardly. "I guess," he said at last, "I was being just as selfish as Ray and Hilda. I didn't want you to give up and leave. I still don't, but I can't keep putting my interests ahead of yours if it's going to hurt you."

"So you really think I should sell the place and go back to the city?"

"No," he said softly. "I think you should sell the place and stay here."

"If I sold the hotel, where would I live?"

"Here," Nathan said, waving his hand at the sprawl of ranch buildings. "With me."

Kate looked at him in disbelief. "In this house, you mean? You're suggesting that I move in with you?"

"Don't look so horrified, Kate. People do it all the time, don't they?"

"Nathan, we hardly know each other."

"We knew each other the first time we met. I felt it, and I know you did, too. I could see it in your eyes."

Kate turned away. "That was just some kind of...physical attraction," she said in a low tone. "Hardly enough to build a permanent relationship on."

"Maybe it was, back then. But it's more than that now. God knows, I'm attracted to you sexually," Nathan said. "I'm dying for you. But there's a lot more to this feeling. I love talking with you and watching you think. I love the way you laugh and get tickled by little things, and the way you've taken on the challenge of that big old building and wrestled it into shape. I even like watching you fight with Ray Butts," he added with a fleeting grin.

Kate didn't smile back. "If you really like my fighting spirit, why are you so anxious for me to give up?"

"Because you can't fight city hall, honey. Those women are dragons. There's no reasoning with Aggie Krantz, and I don't want to see you get crushed."

"I'm not going to be crushed," Kate said with a good deal more confidence than she felt. "I'm going to win. I'm very sorry to disappoint you, Nathan, but I have absolutely no intention of quitting when I've come this far."

"Kate..."

"I'll find some way to solve this," Kate went on. "And I'm afraid I'll have to refuse your offer of board and shelter, kind as it is."

Nathan was on the point of responding when Bessie drove up and parked near the picket fence.

"Come help me carry these groceries," she called to the two on the porch. "There are about a dozen bags in here. The frozen goods are starting to melt."

Kate and Nathan hurried out to the car, and their argument over Kate's uncertain future was suspended for the rest of the evening.

THE MEAL, served to them by Bessie in the dining room, was delicious.

"This is what I'd like my hotel dining room to be like," Kate said, gazing admiringly at the ornate wallpaper and antique crystal chandelier, the costly oil paintings and heavy oak sideboard. "I love this atmosphere, Nathan. It feels like there's a whole century of tradition in this house."

She studied the heavy old pieces of china and silverware, wondering if Ellen had chosen them for her new home. Perhaps Ellen had held this very spoon, gripping it in silence while Joshua bullied her or one of their children....

"Want to see my arrowhead collection?" Nathan asked, watching her over the rim of his coffee cup. "Go for a walk in the moonlight? Make popcorn and watch a movie? I'm at your disposal for the rest of the evening. Whatever you want, just ask."

Kate shook her head. "Those things all sound lovely, but I really should be getting home. The plumber will be coming at seven in the morning to install new fixtures in my bathroom, and I have to be up before six and out of his way."

"What a woman. Are you working tomorrow, too?"

Kate nodded. "I have four upstairs bedrooms left to paint. And I told Raymond I'd help the plumber, too, because it saves paying somebody else about fifteen dollars an hour."

"Come on," Nathan said, grinning. "What can you do to help the plumber?"

"Lots of things," Kate told him with dignity. "I can run errands, hold wrenches for him, carry pipes around, turn the water on and off. Stuff like that."

His grin faded as he watched her across the table with sudden intensity. "I love you, Kate," he murmured softly.

She gazed back at him, startled and confused. "Nathan," she whispered, "I'm not—"

"Never mind," he said, getting briskly to his feet and striding around the table to hold her chair. "If the plumber's helper has to be up at six, we'd better get on the road. Where did we put your jacket?"

Kate followed him, still feeling dazed. Nathan took her jacket from the closet by the door and waited while she thanked Bessie for the meal, with many solemn assurances that Hilda would be told all about it. Then they left the house in silence and walked toward his truck.

When they drove into the archway of trees, Kate looked out at the darkening tunnel around them and felt a little irrational shiver of fear.

"Are you okay?" Nathan asked in concern, seeing her tremble. "Not getting too chilly?"

"I'm fine. I guess somebody was . . . walking across my grave," Kate said, trying to smile.

Nathan looked at her a moment longer, then stared straight ahead as he drove her back toward Wolf Hill.

"Looks like you've got your first customers already," he commented when they arrived at the hotel and parked behind a dusty silver Mercedes-Benz with an out-of-province license plate. "Do you recognize that car, Kate?"

She peered at the car, feeling another clutch of dread. "I've never seen it before," she murmured. "But I wonder if . . ."

Her fears were confirmed at that very moment when the lobby door burst open and a bright figure came running across the veranda.

Kate sighed, gave Nathan a stricken glance and climbed out of the truck to embrace her visitor.

"Hi, Mom," she said wearily.

CHAPTER SEVEN

MAMIE HUGGED her daughter joyously, then stood back to pat Kate's cheek and give her a delighted smile. "Katie, it's so wonderful to see you! Tell me, sweetie, are you surprised?"

"Yes, Mom," Kate said dryly. "I'm really surprised."

Her dismay at her mother's unexpected appearance made her feel disloyal, especially when she realized how happy Mamie was to see her.

The problem, Kate thought with despair, was that a person only had so much energy.

"I had no idea, Kate!" Mamie said, bouncing happily on the veranda of the hotel. "This old place is simply *darling.*"

"It's darling?" Kate echoed blankly, looking up at the shabby brick building, then back at her mother. Mamie wore gold sandals, tights of hot-pink spandex and a long yellow T-shirt printed with pink pineapples and dusted with gold. On any other woman of Mamie's age, the outfit would probably have been ridiculous. On Mamie, though, it looked dashing and sophisticated, like everything she wore.

Mamie suddenly seemed to become aware of Nathan, who stood quietly by his truck. She looked from him to Kate with bright speculation.

Kate gave her mother a pleading glance that begged her not to say anything embarrassing. As usual, Mamie serenely ignored her. "My, my. And who, pray tell, are you?" she asked Nathan with a dazzling smile.

"I'm Nathan Cameron," he said courteously, coming up the steps to offer his hand.

"And I'm Kate's mother, since she obviously isn't going to introduce us. My name's Mamie Hodges." She continued to examine Nathan with lively appreciation. "Katie, honey, you never told me the natives were so impressive."

Kate gave her mother another warning glance.

"Kate doesn't think I'm impressive," Nathan said cheerfully. "She usually just thinks I'm annoying."

"Well," Mamie said with a cozy smile, taking Kate's arm in both her hands, "that opinion will have to change, won't it? A mother should have some influence. Don't you think so, Nathan?"

"Absolutely," Nathan agreed.

Kate stood between them in silence. As often happened in Mamie's company, the conversation was slipping beyond her control. It was a relief when the lobby door opened again and a man stepped out onto the veranda, then marched over to stand beside Mamie.

He was of medium height, spare and erect, with thinning gray hair and a neatly trimmed mustache. In fact, the most impressive thing about him, Kate thought, was his impeccable neatness. He wore a crisp white shirt and blue cardigan, both expensive and well fitting, and a pair of gray slacks with knife-edge creases. Just the sight of him made Kate feel hot and rumpled, uncomfortably conscious of the greenish stain on her jacket sleeve where Nathan's horse had nuzzled her with sloppy affection.

"This is Major Reeves," Mamie said, clutching his arm and giving him another of her radiant smiles. "And this handsome young man is Nathan Cameron, and this is my own sweetie, Kate."

"Call me Tom," the major announced, reaching out to give Nathan a firm handshake. "Retired, you know," he added, smiling rather shyly beneath the mustache. "Mamie likes to call me Major. Just a quirk of hers. No need at all."

Kate began to like the man. She knew from long experience what it was like to have Mamie steamroller one's requests and objections.

"Hello, Tom." Kate shook his proffered hand. "What brings the two of you all the way out to the prairies?" she asked.

"Mamie insisted," the major said. "Getting anxious to see the place. Wanted to help," he added, "if at all possible."

Kate's heart sank even further.

"Now, why the long face, chickie?" Mamie asked, reaching out to hug her. "Aren't you happy to see us?"

Kate shifted uncomfortably on the floorboards of the veranda, conscious of her mother, the major and Nathan, all looking at her with concern.

She managed a smile and looked from one face to another. "Of course I am, Mom. I'm just really... surprised, that's all."

Nathan looked at her over the heads of the other two, his eyes warm with sympathy. Kate cast him a glance of rueful appeal, though of course there was nothing he could do to rescue her. He held Kate's gaze for a moment longer, then turned and clattered down the steps to his truck.

"I have to be up at five to check the calves," he told the three on the porch. "Don't keep Kate up too late, Mamie. She's rising at the crack of dawn to start work as a plumber's helper."

"Plumber's helper!" Mamie echoed in horror. She waved to Nathan as he pulled away from the curb and headed out of town, then turned back to Kate. "What's this nonsense about a plumber? Was he just teasing?"

"No, Mom," Kate said. "He wasn't teasing." She walked into the lobby, flanked by her mother and the major. "I spend a lot of time helping the workmen. It saves paying extra wages."

Mamie stopped and grasped one of Kate's hands, studying it in appalled silence. "Oh, Tom," she muttered, moving aside to give him a better view, "look at this poor girl's hands. Just look at those cracked nails and calluses! Is that not a crime? I'm willing to bet she hasn't had a decent manicure for... for weeks!"

Kate and Tom exchanged a glance so full of humor and understanding that Kate almost burst into laughter. She bit her lip and looked away quickly, then patted her mother's shoulder with a gentle hand.

"It's okay, Mom," she murmured. "Really it is. I love the work I'm doing here. Wait till you see the rooms now that I've finished most of the painting and wallpapering."

"Looked at several of them," Tom offered in his clipped fashion. "Found two that were habitable, second floor. Have to share a bathroom."

"Oh, now, Major, is that so terrible?" Mamie asked him coyly. "He's afraid I'll tie up the bathroom for hours on end, and he won't have time to shave," she told Kate. "Isn't that silly? I never monopolize the bathroom, do I, Katie? I'm in and out like a flash. Right?"

Kate, who'd spent much of her girlhood waiting for her mother outside closed bathroom doors, murmured something noncommittal. Gradually, the import of their conversation dawned on her and she felt her uneasiness grow into genuine alarm.

"How...how long are you planning to stay, Mom?" she asked, removing dust sheets from two of the new velvet couches in the lobby and gesturing for her visitors to seat themselves.

"We're not sure," Mamie said, running an appreciative hand over the rich fabric. "The major and I are both at loose ends just now, so to speak. We thought we'd just stay around as long as you needed help. A few little things will have to be tended to, of course," she added darkly.

"Like what?" Kate asked.

"Well, that woman in the coffee shop doesn't have a very helpful attitude, does she? She hadn't a scrap of fresh grapefruit for my lunch, and didn't seem to have the slightest idea how to obtain any. And when the major and I requested Darjeeling tea, she looked at us as if we'd asked for ground rhino horn."

Kate suppressed a wan smile. There was no doubt that Hilda and her mother would have some major battles if they had to cross paths very often.

"Actually, Mom," she began, trying to be as tactful and gentle as possible, "everything's really upside

down these days, you know. We're not exactly
equipped to make guests comfortable just yet. Hilda's working twelve hours a day on the new dining
room and the expansion to her kitchen, and I'm trying hard to get the decorating finished so we can open
in July. And," she added, frowning, "we're having
such a lot of trouble with the new boiler."

"Trouble?" the major asked, looking suddenly
alert, like a gray terrier sniffing the breeze for suspicious scents.

"Actually, it's the contractor," Kate told him. "His
name is Raymond Butts, and he's caused me no end of
problems, right from the beginning."

"What sort of problems?" the major asked.

Grateful for a sympathetic audience, Kate relaxed
among the cushions and allowed herself the luxury of
recounting her dealings with Raymond. She told it all,
from the brittle beams and termites to the conflict over
the new boiler, which Raymond now refused to install unless he received a hefty commission on the
purchase price.

"Man's a complete scoundrel," the major growled,
looking ominous. "Needs to have his buttons polished straightaway."

"Oh, now, Tom," Kate said anxiously, "I don't
know if we should. After all, he's the only—"

"I intend to speak to the man first thing in the
morning," the major interrupted. "Quite outra-
geous. Simply cannot be allowed to continue."

Mamie smiled adoringly at her military man. "The
major will sort this . . . this Butts person out."

With increasing alarm, Kate pictured the possible outcome of a confrontation between Raymond and the major.

"Now, sweetie, why do you look so tired and anxious?" Mamie asked gently. "I believe you told me after the divorce that this whole silly project was your dream come true. Has it gone and turned into a nightmare?"

Kate looked up at her mother in surprise. Despite Mamie's quirks and apparent shallowness, she'd always had this uncanny ability to understand whatever her daughter was feeling.

"There, there, sweetums," Mamie crooned, wrapping her arms around her tall daughter. "Tell Mummy all about it. What's the matter?"

Kate bit her lip and moved out of Mamie's grasp.

"It's just . . . hard," she said, toying with the fringe on one of the cushions. "Everything's a lot harder and more complicated than I thought it would be. And it costs so much money. Especially when Raymond's always finding things that exceed his original estimate."

"Man's a disgrace," the major grumbled. "Ought to be horsewhipped."

"Please, Tom," Kate said, "I don't want any more problems with Raymond, not when we're so close to finishing the job. If he'll just install the boiler and do the paneling in the dining room, I can—"

"A good soldier is never intimidated," the major quoted, sounding like a military training manual. "A good soldier knows that he has right on his side. Therefore, he is invincible."

"A good soldier's never run up against Raymond Butts," Kate said with a wry smile. "Actually, though, I just found out today that I've got an even bigger problem than Raymond."

"What's that, chickie?" Mamie asked, holding one of Kate's hand in her own well-manicured fingers and examining it with a sorrowful frown.

"It's the liquor license. Apparently," Kate said, "a group of ladies in town oppose my plan to reopen the bar. If they're successful, I'll never be able to make a living. I need the revenue from the bar just to make the books balance."

"But how can they stop you, dear?" Mamie asked.

Kate took a deep breath and repeated what Nathan had told her earlier in the day about Aggie Krantz's secret meeting and petitions.

"Weren't you made aware in advance there could be a problem?" the major inquired shrewdly.

Kate shook her head. "Nobody told me anything about the bar. Well, that's not quite true," she added. "The Realtor said the bar was a really popular place, sort of the town's social center, and everybody was anxious to see it opened again."

"Ah." The major rubbed his jaw slowly. "Do we know the Realtor?"

"He's...actually, he's the son of Raymond's wife's cousin," Kate confessed.

"Ah," the Major said again, his eyes beginning to glint like cold blue ice.

"Oh, forget this Butts person," Mamie said briskly. "I'm more interested in Aggie Krantz. Was that her name, sweetie?"

"That's her name."

"Do you think it might help if I talked to her?"

Kate looked in alarm at her mother's artfully painted face, her curly golden hair and sandals, her hot-pink tights. "I don't think so, Mom. Please don't get involved. I'm going to talk to her myself, as soon as I get my thoughts organized."

Mamie gazed thoughtfully into the distance and didn't answer.

"Mom? Promise me you won't talk to anybody about the liquor license. Please promise."

"Not to worry," the major said, reaching out to pat Kate's hand. "Your mother will be discreet."

Kate wondered if the man honestly believed what he was saying. Over the years, a number of men had unsuccessfully tried to control Mamie, but perhaps the major was made of sterner stuff.

"Thanks, Tom," Kate said, giving him a brief smile.

"All these worries and troubles of yours, Kate," her mother said, "they're just about money? Or, more precisely, the lack of money?"

"I guess so," Kate admitted. "If I had unlimited funds, I wouldn't be so concerned about all of Raymond's demands, or about getting the bar opened as soon as possible. But my budget is pretty tight."

"And why is that?" Mamie said triumphantly. "It's because you refused to get enough money out of Adam in your divorce settlement. I *told* you, Kate, but you were so stubborn about it."

"Adam and I made a fair deal," Kate said. "I don't think we need to—"

"Well, what about that gorgeous cowboy type who brought you home just now?" Mamie said. "Where does he live, sweetie?"

Kate stared at her mother in horror. "Mom," she warned, "don't you dare. Just don't."

"Don't what, darling?" Mamie asked with wide-eyed innocence.

"You know what," Kate said darkly. "I'm thirty-one years old, Mom. I don't want you to start pushing me at the first eligible male who wanders onto the scene, the way you always used to."

"All I asked," Mamie said, giving the major an injured look, "is where the man lives, for heaven's sake."

Kate thought about Nathan's luxurious home, and what Mamie's reaction would be if she knew about the Cameron family's wealth. "He lives on a ranch just outside of town," she said. "He's... kind of a ranch hand, Mom. He works all day roping cows, and... and feeding bulls, and that sort of thing. He has a... a bunkhouse at the ranch."

"Oh, dear," Mamie said regretfully. "I don't suppose that would pay very much, would it?"

"Not much," Kate agreed, crossing her fingers.

"What a pity. He's so gorgeous. Well, then, how about the rest of the town?" she asked brightly. "Are there any nice doctors or lawyers running around?"

"Mom!"

"I was just asking," Mamie said, pouting.

"Come, my dear," the major told her briskly. "Early to bed, early to rise, you know."

Mamie, who liked to go to bed in the small hours and rise at noon, gave him a rebellious glance. "Can't

I stay up and have a nice long visit with Katie? I
haven't seen her for months."

"Kate's tired," the major said firmly. "Has to get
up at six. Tomorrow's another day."

"Oh, all right."

Kate watched in openmouthed astonishment as her
mother obediently got to her feet and followed the
major's erect figure up the curving staircase.

She smiled, giving devout silent thanks to all her
guardian angels for the unexpected arrival of Major
Tom Reeves in her mother's life. The man was truly a
godsend.

Kate wandered through the quiet hotel lobby to her
own cluttered room. Her mind was troubled not only
by the presence of her upstairs guests, but by scattered memories of Nathan's beautiful house and rolling green acres, his strong arms and handsome face,
his kisses and laughter...

She turned off the light and moved slowly through
the moonlit room to get Ellen's diary from under the
windowsill, thinking that she would have to find a new
hiding place next week when Raymond finally installed her patio door. Kate took the book and climbed
into bed, propped her pillows comfortably and
switched on her lamp, then turned to the last entry
she'd been reading.

Lucky Ellen, she thought wistfully, looking at the
pages of faded handwriting. The young schoolteacher had plenty of things to worry about, but at
least she didn't have parents dropping in on her unexpectedly. The only way for Ellen's parents to visit
would have been by means of an arduous two-week
train journey.

Ellen was safe from that problem, at least.

Kate smiled wryly, shifted against the pillows and began to read.

Wednesday, November 23, 1904

Another strange and turbulent day! I begin to wonder if any other kind of day exists. We are fully immersed in our lessons now, but we also spend an hour or so each day rehearsing for the Christmas concert, which I am determined will be a fine and splendid event, a credit to my students and the town of Wolf Hill, as well.

But my little actors and actresses do not make this easy. Though they certainly provide in enthusiasm what they do not have in experience, their histrionic skills are sadly lacking. None of these frontier children has ever appeared on a stage to recite the simplest verse. Most of them have never worn costumes or memorized parts, or even seen a play performed by others. I sadly fear that if we do manage somehow to get our pageant organized, stage fright will be a dreadful problem when the big night finally arrives.

Nevertheless, I am forging ahead. Fortunately, the older students are fully caught up in the excitement of the project, and are very helpful in organizing the smaller ones. Some of these—especially little Herman—become so agitated during our practices that they occasionally succumb to the calls of nature before they are able to reach the outhouse, and add greatly to the general confusion.

Speaking of the outhouse, today there was another traumatic scene in that building which seems to be so fraught with drama!

Snow has been falling heavily all week, piling around the edges of the schoolhouse and drifting across the playground, so I allowed the students to stay indoors over the noon hour and practice their singing. Karen Mueller, a sweet-faced girl of fourteen who is the oldest of the Mueller children, was helping me with the angel chorus. It's made up of a lively group of six- to eight-year-olds, who will all have lovely silk wings for the pageant if I am able to get them stitched in time.

After a while, I turned away from the piano—recently donated to the school, incidentally, by Mr. Joshua Cameron—to a considerable uproar at the back of the room near the stove. I soon realized that the angels were without supervision and quite out of control.

"Where is Karen?" I asked them.

"Outhouse," Gunter said briefly. "Long time," he added.

Elsa, his twin, nodded earnestly and echoed his words as she often does. "*Long* time," she said.

I spoke sternly to the angels and went back to my playing, but kept one eye on the clock. When another five minutes had elapsed and Karen had not yet returned, I put on my galoshes and overcoat, wrapped a shawl around my head and stepped outside into a wind so fierce that it almost swept me off my feet.

"Karen!" I called as I struggled through the drifts toward the outhouse. "Are you all right?"

There was no response from the little wooden structure.

"Karen?" I asked, knocking on the locked door. "Are you in here?"

I leaned close to the boards and heard a muffled sobbing.

"Karen, this is Miss Livingston," I said. "Open the door!"

After a moment, the door swung open, caught by the wind so that it nearly tore from its hinges. I gripped it, hesitated and stepped hastily inside, closing the door behind me to shut out the wind. Karen was huddled on the cold wooden seat, her face ghastly pale and wet with tears.

"Karen," I whispered, putting my hands on her shoulders and peering down at her. "My dear, whatever is the matter?"

"I am dying, miss," the poor girl said in her heavy accent, sobbing inconsolably. "I will soon be dead, and then who will help Papa with the little ones? Who will look after Herman?"

"Dying?" I said blankly, feeling chilled and uncertain. "What makes you think that? Do you not feel well?"

She swallowed hard and looked at me in agony. "I am...bleeding," she whispered. "Bleeding, just like...like Mama when she died."

"Oh, my dear girl..." It was all I could do not to give way to tears myself. While the melancholy frontier wind howled outside and snow hissed against the walls of the building, I took the poor motherless girl into my arms and began to talk.

Putting aside all modesty and reticence, I told her frankly about the wonders of motherhood and the female body, about the ancient rhythms and mysteries of nature. She listened in amazement, the color gradually returning to her face.

"Every month?" she asked when I fell silent.

"Just like clockwork," I assured her. "A dreadful nuisance, really, but one does grow accustomed to it."

"You, too, miss?" she asked, flushing scarlet in her embarrassment.

"Oh, most assuredly," I told her. "And every other woman that you know. One of us should have told you earlier. In fact, I blame myself terribly for not thinking of it."

She shook her head, still contemplating the astonishing things I had just told her. "What do I do now?" she asked finally, her practical motherly nature beginning to assert itself.

"Well, we must get you equipped with some supplies," I told her. "Tomorrow, I will bring some of my own to school, and show you what to do. But for now..."

I looked around the little building, feeling helpless, but once again Karen showed common sense far beyond her years.

"My petticoat is very old," she volunteered, lifting her skirts to display a cotton garment that was, indeed, limp and much darned. "Ready to be rags."

"Karen, that will be ideal," I said in considerable relief.

Working together, we tore strips from the petticoat and fashioned a makeshift bandage for her. I waited outside while she fitted it in place.

She emerged from the outhouse and walked silently beside me into the school, removing her coat and taking her place among the rowdy group of little angels with her usual gentle calm. But when her eyes met mine during the singing practice, there was a look of new maturity and shining gratitude in her expression that brought a lump to my throat.

Strangely, for perhaps the first time since my arrival on the prairie, I feel like a real teacher. I find that I relish the sensation!

But my day's adventures were far from ended. Later in the afternoon when school was dismissed, I went to the door with my students to contemplate the weather. Until now, I have tended to stay an hour or so later than the children, marking lessons and planning for the next day. It is almost a two-mile walk into town, which takes me about half an hour if I stride briskly, and up to an hour if I dawdle and daydream. During the lovely autumn days, the walk back to the hotel was one of my very favorite times.

But since the days have grown shorter and snow has begun to fall, I often accept a ride with one of the parents who arrive by wagon or sleigh to take groups of children home. Today Mr. Oates came, hauling a load of fresh straw for his pigs. He gathered up all the children who needed a ride in the direction of Wolf Hill. About a dozen of my students plunged immediately into the mounded straw, squealing and laughing, such a merry group that I was strongly tempted to join them.

But the wind had stilled and the afternoon was crisp and pleasant, so I decided to stay for a while and then

walk home. I gave my regrets to Mr. Oates, who tried
to convince me to change my mind, then departed for
town with his boisterous cargo.

Time slipped away from me, however. By the time
I finished copying out verses for the pageant, tended
the stove and left the building, it was almost five. The
sun was long gone and night was beginning to gather.
A gentle snowfall drifted like a soft curtain over the
darkening plains.

I quickened my steps, trudging along the snowy
rutted tracks and looking around at the deserted
countryside. Off to the north, a pack of coyotes began to howl, their melancholy cries sending a shiver
down my spine. I was relieved when a sled came
skimming up and stopped beside me with a cheery
tinkling of bells.

But when I recognized the man on the driver's seat,
I began to shiver again. It was Joshua Cameron,
wearing a bulky sheepskin coat and hat that made him
look more than ever like some dark-eyed warrior king.

"Thank you," I said with as much dignity as I could
muster, accepting his helping hand as I climbed into
the little sled and settled gratefully beneath the buffalo robe. "It really becomes quite cold after the sun
goes down."

"Yes, it does," he said in his arrogant fashion.
"And you're certainly not going to tramp down this
road in the dark anymore, my girl."

Although I had just reached the same conclusion, I
was not at all pleased to hear Joshua Cameron voice
this sentiment in such a high-handed manner. But I did
greatly appreciate the ride, so I decided not to take

offense. Instead, I began to tell him about the preparations for our Christmas pageant.

He laughed heartily when I told him about the naughty angels, and for the first time, I began to relax and feel quite comfortable with him.

"Is little Herman Mueller going to be in the pageant?" he asked.

"Do you know Herman?" I asked in surprise.

"I know all the Mueller kids," he told me. "They're my closest neighbors. But Herman is my favorite."

I smiled. "Herman will be a Christmas cherub. He is to be dressed in a little robe of white, with wings and a golden halo. He will greet the audience as the curtain opens and tell them that he brings good tidings of great joy."

Joshua chuckled, a warm and masculine sound in the chill of the winter night. "I can hardly wait."

I relaxed beneath the soft carriage robe, suddenly very conscious of his nearness. The seat was narrow, and we were sitting disturbingly close. I found myself overcome by a distressing rush of emotion, accompanied by a most unladylike urge to nestle against him! Fortunately, we arrived in town at that moment and skimmed up to the stable, where Mr. Cameron reined in his horse and turned to me.

"If you don't mind," he said, "I'd prefer to leave the horse here and walk you over to the hotel."

"That will be fine," I told him.

I stood in the fragrant, lamp-lit warmth of the stable, watching as he gave the boy instructions for the horse's care and the storage of his sleigh. For the first time, I noticed that this vehicle, which was a pretty little red cutter with gold trim, was very new and dashing. I commented upon it to Mr. Cameron.

"It looks like a little painted walnut shell," I said, enchanted. "Like something the fairies would ride in, pulled by white mice in scarlet livery."

"You are adorable, Miss Livingston," he said in a low tone, startling me so badly that I had no idea what to do with myself. But after that brief lapse—perhaps I imagined it!—he was all business again. He began to instruct me on the management of the horse, and what to do if the sled runners did not track evenly.

"Why are you telling me this?" I asked, puzzled.

"Because it's your sled, and your horse. You'll stable him here at night, and in the barn at school during the daytime. There's also a little pony cart to use when the snow is gone."

"But I . . . I cannot possibly—"

"I told you, I won't have you walking down that road in the dark. Not with winter coming on."

"Mr. Cameron," I began, struggling for some semblance of dignity.

"Joshua," he said with a flashing smile.

"Joshua, I cannot possibly accept a gift like this from you."

"Why not? You were happy to get the piano, weren't you?"

"That was for the school," I told him with some heat, waving my hand at the dainty red-and-gold sled. "This is . . ."

"For the schoolteacher," he finished calmly, taking my arm and leading me in the direction of the hotel. "If you insist, the horse can be designated as school property, and left behind for the use of the next teacher. But I'm afraid you'll still have to get used to this."

"To what?" I asked.

"To receiving gifts from me," he said in a husky voice, leaning toward me as we walked through the snow. "I intend to be giving you gifts for the rest of your life, Ellen," he murmured softly into my ear. "Starting with that row of cottonwood trees next spring."

Mercifully, by then we had arrived at the hotel steps. He said good-night in a formal manner and strode off with his usual abruptness, leaving me so flushed and agitated that I required a few moments to compose myself before I was able to enter the lobby.

Even now, when I think of his voice in my ear, whispering my name with such intimacy and making that astounding promise, I find that I am hardly able to contain myself. A proper lady would be shocked and insulted, but I am not. I want to run and sing and turn somersaults like a child, and at the same time I am troubled by yearnings and hungers that I cannot begin to comprehend.

Am I, perhaps, falling in love?

Nonsense! I cannot be distracted by these silly girlish fancies. I have such a difficult, important job to do here in Wolf Hill, and I intend to perform it with all my strength.

I refuse to think about Joshua Cameron. Instead, I am giving serious thought to the problem of naming the school's new horse. He is a pretty dapple gray with a snow-white mane and tail. I have decided he shall be called Mouse, and I plan to buy him another set of bells so people will hear me coming from miles away!

CHAPTER EIGHT

KATE WOKE just in time to get her clothes on and her bed made before the plumber was ushered into her room by Raymond, who looked especially sulky.

"Carl Mueller," Raymond announced curtly, indicating a burly graying man in a plaid jacket and denim overalls, carrying a pipe wrench. "You said you'd help him."

Kate smiled at the plumber. "Hello, Mr. Mueller. I'm so excited about getting my new bathroom."

The plumber nodded and vanished, reappearing almost at once with a greasy metal toolbox.

Kate turned to Raymond, who still hovered near the door. "Raymond, about the boiler..."

"I'm not doing it," Raymond said, glaring at her. "I'm not even talking about it until he's gone."

"Mr. Mueller?" Kate asked in confusion.

"No, not Mr. Mueller," the contractor said with heavy sarcasm. "That creepy soldier guy. You'd better keep him away from me."

"Major Reeves?" Kate asked, a light beginning to dawn.

"Whatever," Raymond snapped.

"Have you and Major Reeves had an argument about something?"

"Just keep him away from me," Raymond repeated darkly. "I'm warning you. I don't have to take this. I got lots of other jobs I could be doing, making more money than you're paying me." With this familiar threat, the contractor turned and stamped off through the lobby, leaving Kate watching him in distress.

"Mean little guy, Raymond is," Mr. Mueller commented unexpectedly, taking out a soldering iron. "He's always been that way. Back in school, we were all scared of him, even though he was pretty much the smallest kid in the class."

Kate tried and failed to picture Raymond as a child.

"What can I do to help you?" she asked finally, turning to the plumber, who had crossed the room and was examining the ancient bathroom fixtures with a gloomy expression.

But when he looked at Kate, his stubbled face was illuminated by a surprisingly gentle smile. "Well, first off, you can go down to the coffee shop and have some breakfast. I don't want nobody working for me who's all cranky and hungry."

Kate smiled back gratefully, wondering if one of the motherless little Mueller boys in Ellen's school had been Carl's ancestor.

Maybe it was Gunter, she thought, picturing that engaging red-cheeked urchin.

"Thank you," she said. "I'll hurry, all right?"

"No rush," the plumber told her. "I got to get all this old junk ripped out of here, likely take an hour or so before I can even get started. I won't be needing you till then."

Kate left him at his job and went through the sunny lobby to the coffee shop, where the morning crowd of locals was out in force. She walked among them to the staff table, painfully conscious of what Nathan had told her the day before.

How many of these men, with their bluff manner and cheerful smiles, had voted against her at Aggie Krantz's meeting? How many had already signed the petition that would doom her efforts to failure?

Probably not too many, Kate decided.

Nathan had told her that the community was sharply divided over the issue, with most of the men in favor of the bar's reopening and many of the women opposed to it. She frowned, wondering what she could do to win these women over, as she seated herself at the empty table near the kitchen.

Hilda appeared at once, order pad in hand. Kate gave the cook a timid glance, hoping that Hilda hadn't also been offended by Tom and Mamie's unexpected arrival.

But Hilda looked placid and unruffled, as plump and rosy as ever in her pink uniform and candy-striped apron.

"Hi, Kate. Aren't you s'posed to be helping Carl with the plumbing today?"

"He gave me a breakfast break. Hilda, sit down with me for a minute, okay?"

Hilda lowered herself into the opposite chair and gave Kate a curious glance. "What's up?"

"I'm really sorry if my mother and her friend were...a bother to you yesterday. I honestly had no idea they were going to turn up. I know how busy you are, and I don't—"

"No problem," Hilda said placidly. "I like your mother."

"You do?" Kate stared at her. "But she... I understand they made a big fuss about grapefruit, and some kind of special tea they wanted."

Hilda grinned. "They can fuss all they like. Don't bother me. Hello, Luther," she added, nodding to Luther Barnes who seated himself near the window after giving her a shy smile.

"Poor man. Can't bear to be away from me," Hilda told Kate in a loud whisper, beaming with pleasure.

"You should marry him, Hilda. You really should."

"I might," Hilda said thoughtfully. "But first, I plan to get my dining room up and running. Trisha!" she bellowed into the kitchen. "Bring Kate some breakfast, on the double! Coffee, orange juice and two poached eggs on whole wheat."

Kate smiled gratefully at the cook. "You're a treasure, Hilda. You're a genuine treasure."

"'Course I am," Hilda agreed, pouring coffee for both of them from a pot delivered by her pert, red-haired waitress.

"I went to visit Nathan's ranch yesterday," Kate said, trying to keep her voice casual.

"I know. News travels fast in this town. What did Bessie feed you?"

"Cornish game hens and fresh peach cobbler. I'm supposed to tell you it was absolutely delicious."

Hilda gave her a withering look. "Bessie thinks she's such a great cook. The woman never has learned to make a jelly roll that doesn't stick to the pan and fall apart. Were the mashed potatoes lumpy?"

"No, they were perfect." Kate smiled at Trisha who set a plate of toast and eggs in front of her.

"Well, I'll bet her poultry stuffing wasn't as good as mine," Hilda said darkly.

Kate thought it over, sprinkling salt and pepper on her eggs. "Maybe not *quite*. But that's hardly a fair comparison. Your stuffing is the best in the whole world, Hilda."

The cook nodded, apparently mollified. "Did you have a nice visit with Nathan?" she asked, giving Kate a meaningful glance.

Kate remembered his kisses, the feel of his arms around her.

"It was all right," she said briefly, studying the gingham place mat. "Nathan told me about this petition Aggie Krantz is circulating."

Hilda's plump face clouded. "Damn that woman! I didn't want you bothered with this. It's all such a bunch of nonsense."

"But I have to deal with it, Hilda. You know I need the revenue from the bar."

"I know," Hilda said, brooding over her coffee mug. "I just can't believe the whole town is dumb enough to let Aggie push them around. I keep hoping nothing's going to come of it."

"I'm afraid something's come of it already," Kate said. "They've managed to block my license so far. Now I understand what's been causing all these delays." She looked up at Hilda. "When are they submitting the petition, do you know?"

Hilda shrugged. "A couple of weeks, I guess. At the end of June. They wanted at least a month to get hold of the new voter's list and sign up as many names as they could."

Kate gave her friend a rueful grin. "My mother suggested she should go and talk with Aggie. Mom thinks she can persuade her to drop the petition."

Hilda threw back her curly head and gave a rich, booming laugh, causing Luther Barnes to turn and smile at her wistfully. "Now, *that* would be a sight to behold," she said, choking back her laughter and wiping her eyes. "Your mother talking with Aggie Krantz. I hope she wears them tight little pink pants of hers."

"Hilda, you're not helping, you know," Kate said severely.

But her own mouth was twitching with amusement, and she felt a good deal better when she eventually returned to her room and Carl Mueller, who had ripped out the bathtub plumbing and was starting on the sink. "I'm back," Kate announced. "Is there anything I can do to help?"

"Hand me that other wrench. The long one with the marks on the handle."

Kate obeyed, hurrying to hand him the wrench and peering under the shelf to watch as Carl opened the drain.

He heaved himself out from the cramped space and squatted by his toolbox, examining a pile of threaded couplings.

"How long has your family lived here, Carl?" Kate asked him.

The plumber gave her another of his gentle smiles. "Forever, I guess. My great-grandfather was one of the early settlers, and my grandfather went to the first school in Wolf Hill.''

"Really? What was your grandfather's name?"

"Herman Mueller."

Kate smiled with private delight, thinking about the Christmas cherub in his white robe and halo. She felt a wistful desire to ask about the others, too, and learn what happened to Karen and Gunter and Elsa. But she was reluctant to discuss Ellen's diary with anyone.

Maybe one day she would be able to part with the old book, but not yet. Not while Ellen felt more close and real to her with every passing day, and her story remained unfinished.

"JUST HOLD that wrench tight," Carl instructed a couple of hours later. "Keep a steady pressure on the handle while I drop the solder in place, okay?"

Kate nodded, squatting on the floor and frowning in concentration. The plumber stiffened suddenly and gazed up over her shoulder with a look of amazement.

"Don't let me bother you." Mamie's voice came sweetly from somewhere behind them. "I just wanted to talk with Katie for a minute."

Kate swiveled to look up at her mother, who was indeed a sight to behold. She wore tightly fitted white stirrup pants, high-heeled gold sandals, a sweater of fluffy pink angora and a wealth of glittering gold jewelry.

Mamie's hair and makeup were meticulous. Kate smiled, picturing poor Major Reeves with his razor and toothpaste, waiting outside the bathroom door while Mamie primped.

"Hi, Mom," she said, wondering if the old Wolf Hill Hotel had ever seen anything quite as exotic as Mamie Hodges.

Judging from Carl's expression, it wasn't likely.

"This is Carl Mueller," Kate said. "Carl, this is my mother, Mrs. Hodges."

"Hi, Carl," Mamie said breezily. "Don't listen to Kate. Call me Mamie."

Carl nodded in dazed fashion and gripped his soldering iron.

"Kate, sweetie," Mamie went on, "I need to talk to you."

"In a minute, Mom, okay? Carl's going to be finished installing the shutoffs pretty soon. Then he can connect the sink and my new shower stall."

Mamie picked her way daintily through the clutter to examine the new bathroom fixtures, still partly crated, that stood along one wall.

"It should be a nice room," she said. "Which wall are you knocking out?"

"That one. The room next door will be a sitting room, and this will be my bedroom and bath. And I'm getting Raymond to make that window into a French door opening onto the terrace. He should be doing the wall and door in the next day or so."

"Maybe," Mamie said in a cryptic tone that made Kate give her a quick look of concern.

"Mom?" she asked.

Mamie turned to smile at her. "Nothing, dear," she said airily. "The major and your Mr. Butts are having a little disagreement, that's all. I'm sure they'll work it out."

Kate looked at Carl in alarm. "Oh, no," she murmured, turning back to her mother. "Where are they, Mom?"

"I'm not sure. It's some horrible room filled with cow's hooves and glass eyeballs."

"Carl," Kate began nervously, "maybe I should go and..."

"Okay." The plumber took the wrench from her. "I can finish this now. You go on about your business, and when you come back in a few hours, you'll have a nice new bathroom."

Kate smiled gratefully and got to her feet, brushing plaster dust from the knees of her jeans.

Mamie went with Kate into the hallway, then put a hand on her arm. "Before we get involved in the men's arguments," she said with sudden firmness, "there's something I need to speak to you about, my girl. And I want some honest answers."

Kate looked at her mother in surprise and led the way into the office, which was one of the first rooms Raymond had completed. Despite her concern over a possibly disastrous confrontation between Raymond and the major, to say nothing of her mother's puzzling behavior, Kate still felt the same rush of pleasure she always enjoyed when she entered her office.

The woodwork was beautifully restored, gleaming softly in the morning light. The leaded-glass windows shone with rainbow prisms, and the hardwood floor was like oiled silk. Kate had found a charming old rosewood desk in the city, and Raymond had recently installed one of her greatest treasures, an antique message board with little cubicles corresponding to each room. Somebody, probably Hilda, had placed an earthenware crock filled with white lilacs on the desk, and the sweet perfume was heavy in the morning stillness. Kate looked around with a blissful sigh, almost able to believe that she was really about to become the manager of a successful hotel.

She seated herself behind the desk and watched while Mamie perched on the edge of one of the leather armchairs, looking purposeful.

"I had breakfast with Hilda," Mamie said. "I like that woman."

Kate nodded cautiously. "Hilda's a really nice person. She's been a wonderful help to me."

"She seems to know everybody in town." Mamie leaned forward to rearrange a spray of lilac.

"She certainly does," Kate agreed, increasingly puzzled.

"Like your Mr. Nathan Cameron, for instance," Mamie said, pausing to examine a long glossy fingernail. "Hilda's known him since he was a little boy. Can you imagine that?"

Kate's heart sank. "Mom," she pleaded, "don't do this. Please, Mom. I really, really don't want you to—"

"A *ranch* hand!" Mamie scoffed, glaring at her daughter. "Roping cows and living in a bunkhouse!"

"Well, it's true," Kate said. "Sort of," she added lamely. "Except for the bunkhouse, I guess."

"Hilda says the man is worth a fortune. She says his place is one of the finest ranches in the province, and he's very wealthy."

"I really wouldn't know," Kate said stiffly. "I never asked to see his bankbook."

"Katie, don't be an idiot," Mamie said sharply. "Hilda says the man is crazy about you. And she says everybody knows it."

"They do?" Kate's heart began to pound. She gripped her hands tightly in her lap and concentrated on the mass of white flowers.

"Yes, they do. And I want to know why you're being so stubborn."

Kate looked up in astonishment. "Who says I'm being stubborn? In what way?"

Mamie gave her daughter a shrewd glance. "I know you, my girl. Don't think I don't. You've got some bee in your bonnet about making a success of this place on your own, and you're not going to take help from anybody. Am I right?"

"Everybody succeeds or fails on their own," Kate said quietly. "Don't they?"

"Oh, nonsense!" Mamie snapped. "I saw the way that man looked at you last night. If you so much as batted your eyelashes, he'd be there in a second with his pen and a checkbook, solving all your problems so you could sleep at night."

Kate stared at her mother in disbelief. "Look, Mom," she began, "maybe *you* think it's all right to 'bat your eyelashes' and get men to write checks and solve all your problems. But I happen to feel that a woman should—"

"You know what I think?" Mamie asked, ignoring her.

"No, Mom," Kate said wearily. "I don't know. What do you think?"

"I think it's Adam," Mamie said. "I think you still love him. That's why you won't even consider a perfectly wonderful catch like this Nathan Cameron."

"For one thing," Kate began furiously, "I absolutely detest hearing men referred to as 'catches.' What are we, lobster fishermen? And for another thing, it's so ridiculous to say that I—"

"Adam's willing to adopt a baby, you know, if that's what you want."

Kate's mouth fell open. She stared at her mother, groping for words. "When . . . how did you . . ."

Mamie waved her hand casually. Her rings glittered in the morning light. "Adam and I talk quite frequently. He really misses you, Katie. He called last week from Paris and said if he'd known a baby meant that much to you, he'd have agreed to adoption long ago. He just didn't want to be tied down, that's all."

"Tied down!" Kate echoed. "Why do men like Adam always think having a baby would tie them down?"

"So," Mamie said as if Kate hadn't spoken, "if Adam agreed to adopt, would you go back to him?"

"Mom, this is really none of your business, you know. But the fact is, there were a lot of things wrong with our relationship besides the argument over wanting a family. I honestly don't think you have any right to—"

"Because otherwise," Mamie went on, "I can't understand why you wouldn't show any interest in this nice, rich rancher friend of yours."

"I don't think getting together with Nathan Cameron would be such a great idea," Kate said quietly. "I met his mother a while ago, you know. She acts like they're the Western version of the Kennedy family, or something. Like being one of the Camerons is a really high and noble calling."

"Does he feel that way?"

Kate frowned. "I'm not sure. I don't think Nathan's as intense about the family dynasty thing as his mother is, but I really doubt that he'd approve of his wife earning her living on her own. I think he'd want her to be involved full-time as mistress of the ranch."

"But he's nice?"

"Yes," Kate said briefly. "He's a very nice man."

"So what's the problem?" Mamie asked, genuinely puzzled.

Kate sighed. "You don't understand, Mom. I spent over ten years married to Adam, trailing around in his shadow and being looked after. I'm just beginning to discover who I am, and what I'm capable of. I don't want to be submerged in another rich man's life. Not now."

"So, let me get this straight. You don't want this man because he's rich? Because his family is powerful and impressive?"

"Mom . . ."

"I don't believe a word of it," Mamie said flatly. "In fact, I think next time I talk with Adam, I'll just let him know, ever so tactfully, that I believe you still have feelings for him and you'd like to try again."

"Is this some kind of blackmail?" Kate asked in disbelief. "Either I give some encouragement to Nathan, or you'll start meddling and pull Adam back into my life?"

"You know I always have your best interests at heart, darling," Mamie told her with a sweet smile, reaching across the desk to pat her daughter's grease-stained hand. "I really do."

Kate was spared the necessity of a reply by a sudden alarming crash from the direction of the lobby, followed by a bloodcurdling scream.

She rushed out of her office and ran across the lobby, followed by Mamie who moved with surprising speed despite her high heels. They burst into the partly restored dining room and were greeted by an astonishing sight.

Raymond Butts was having a tantrum. He stood by the window, wrenching skulls and animal forms from cardboard boxes and throwing them onto the floor where they clattered noisily. The source of the original crash was a wooden keg of glass eyeballs that had apparently been flung across the room. The eyes lay everywhere, winking brightly in the morning sunlight.

Major Reeves sat on another upturned keg with a notepad on his knee and a pair of reading glasses perched on his nose. He eyed Raymond's contorted features with calm appraisal and consulted his notes.

"Original estimate for the boiler installation," he read, "nineteen thousand two hundred and thirty-seven dollars. Total costs to date..."

"There were extra expenses!" Raymond shrieked, dancing from one foot to the other in his rage. "Don't you understand what an expense is, you damn fool?"

"I certainly do. Overhead and expenses are calculated into the original estimate, which cannot legally be altered without mutual agreement between the contractor and the client. For instance, the estimate for woodwork restoration in the lobby was—" Tom turned a couple of pages "—twelve hundred and fifty-five dollars, all-inclusive. Actual money charged..."

The major was a lot braver than she was, Kate realized. If she'd known her mother's boyfriend planned to make this kind of use of the information, she'd never have supplied him with the figures on the hotel restoration when he'd come down to ask for them the previous evening. The last thing she needed was Raymond Butts to quit.

Raymond caught sight of Kate in the doorway. He paused on the verge of ripping apart a stuffed pheasant with his bare hands.

"Stop him!" Raymond shouted. "Get this maniac out of my business! I'm warning you, Kate, if he doesn't get out right now, I'm gone. You can find someone else to do your damn renovations!"

"Oh, I don't think so," the major said, unruffled. "Defaulting on contracted work is an actionable offense. If this work is unfinished for any reason, you'll be subject to immediate legal action, Mr. Butts. Now, according to the agreement, the boiler is to be installed before the fifteenth of June. That gives you..." Tom paused to consult his watch. "Two days."

After all the weeks of Raymond's bullying, Kate wouldn't have been human if she hadn't taken some small pleasure in his discomfort. Still, her natural instinct as a peacemaker began to assert itself. Besides, Raymond's face was so scarlet with rage that she really feared for his health.

"Raymond," she said in a soothing tone, "if that's too rushed for you, I don't mind if you take until the end of the month to finish the boiler. I really don't."

Hilda arrived on the scene as Kate was speaking, followed by Luther who stood behind her and surveyed the scattered eyeballs and animal parts with a disbelieving expression.

"Now, Kate, don't you start knuckling under again," Hilda said. "Make him toe the mark. If the work order says two days, it means two days." She turned to the major, who was still calmly leafing through his notebook. "Did you tell him about the dining room furniture, Tom? Did you tell him it's supposed to be finished by the end of the month and he's already at least a thousand dollars over budget?"

At this new evidence of treachery, Raymond seemed to lose the last vestiges of his control. He charged around the cluttered dining room, shouting incoherently and skidding on the shiny glass eyes while Luther and Mamie tried to restrain him.

To her alarm, Kate found herself starting to giggle. Involuntary laughter bubbled from her. When she caught Hilda's eye and saw that Hilda, too, was grinning, she lost control altogether. The two women fell against each other as Luther captured and held on to Raymond's flailing body. Mamie followed them, teetering on her high heels, talking earnestly to the contractor while Tom continued to sit on the keg and study his notes.

"Well," a voice said behind them, icy with disapproval. "This is a pretty sight, I must say."

Moaning, Kate wiped her eyes, then stopped laughing abruptly.

Aggie Krantz stood in the doorway, gripping her handbag as she surveyed the scene. She turned back to

Kate. "I wanted to speak with you, Mrs. Daniels, but I can see that you're... busy at the moment."

Immediately, Kate felt hot with embarrassment. "Mrs. Krantz," she said anxiously, "I'm really sorry if you... I mean, we were just..."

"We're just throwing out some moldy old fossils, Aggie," Hilda said, reckless with hilarity. "If you hang around, you might be next." Apparently overcome by her own wit, she collapsed in another gale of laughter.

Aggie's eyes widened in outrage behind her steel-framed glasses. "Well!" she said. "I can see that nobody here is interested in having a decent conversation. Mrs. Daniels, I'll send you a letter telling you what the town council proposes."

"Oh, Mrs. Krantz," Kate said desperately, hurrying behind the woman out into the lobby. "Hilda didn't mean that. She was just teasing. Please, I'd like to talk with you. In fact, I've been meaning to..."

But Aggie was clearly in no mood to be appeased. She stalked through the lobby and out the front door, letting it slam behind her with a resounding crash. Kate looked bleakly at the door for a moment, then went slowly back into the dining room.

Luther stood next to Hilda, clearly alarmed, pounding the cook's back while she choked and hiccuped with laughter. After a moment, the older woman caught her breath and smiled at him, then turned to Kate.

"Sorry, Kate," she said, looking abashed but distinctly unrepentant. "I just don't know what got into me."

Luther took Hilda's arm protectively and led her from the room. "Moldy old fossil!" he was saying in warm admiration as they disappeared. "That was rich, Hilda. That was terrific."

Kate turned back to Raymond, who seemed noticeably calmer. Mamie stood close to him and spoke in low comforting tones, while the major rummaged busily through the adjoining room, examining the new dining room furniture.

"Okay," Raymond said abruptly.

Kate looked at him in surprise. "I beg your pardon, Raymond?"

"Okay, I'll install the boiler by next weekend for the price in the estimate. And I can't refund the money on the woodwork in the lobby because I spent it already, but I'll do some other work instead. I'll put the French door in your room for free. Is that all right with you?"

Kate gaped at the man, then at Mamie, who gave her daughter an urgent little nod.

"Why, Raymond... yes, of course. That will be wonderful."

She watched as the contractor turned, hitched up his overalls and stalked from the room with some of his old swagger. Kate turned to Mamie. "Mom," she said, "I just don't know what to say. I'm speechless."

"All it takes," Mamie said with a tranquil smile, "is a little firmness."

"It's so hard for me to be firm," Kate said glumly. "I think it's a talent I was born without."

"I know, honey," Mamie said, coming over to pat Kate's cheek. "You've always been that way. You're a lover, not a fighter. That's why you need people to fight your battles for you."

"But I don't want that," Kate said. "I want to make a success of this on my own. I don't want you and Tom dealing with the contractor on my behalf, or Nathan Cameron writing checks to help me, or you making arrangements with Adam about my life! Can't you understand that, Mom?"

But Mamie wasn't listening. She'd already joined Tom in the other room and was involved in a lively discussion about the unfinished tables. Defeated, Kate turned and wandered out into the lobby by herself.

CHAPTER NINE

Friday, December 16, 1904

What a marvelous day! Our first-ever Christmas concert proceeded without a single hitch. Well, that may be a mild exaggeration. There were one or two small hitches, but nobody seemed to mind in the least. For example, Mrs. Goldman, who is a very large woman, fell through our makeshift stage while delivering a stirring rendition of "Little Nell," but was rescued almost immediately by her husband and several other gentlemen.

And shortly after Mrs. Goldman's mishap, Herman Mueller caught the edge of his robe on an exposed nail and ripped it from his body, becoming, for an instant, an utterly naked pink cherub in front of everybody until I rushed to swathe him in one of the shepherd's robes. But Herman is so fat and sweet and the crowd was in such high spirits that his small accident merely added to the overflowing holiday good cheer.

I should start at the beginning—although I would dearly love to report what happened at the end of the evening! But I am a grown-up woman now, and I will restrain myself with proper decorum.

It has been such a long and momentous day. Because the concert was tonight, I did not even return to the hotel after work, but took my navy shirtwaist with me to school in the morning. Many of the children did the same, bringing their holiday costumes, and remaining after school to help prepare for the concert. By the time night fell and the first people began to arrive, the school was fairly bursting with excitement.

And they kept arriving! I simply could not believe that our little building was able to contain so many people. They came on foot and by horseback, in hay wagons and sleds and cutters, crowding into the schoolhouse with warm greetings to one another. By seven o'clock, there were several rows of horses outside, standing at ease, their breath steaming in the moonlight.

The women brought mountains of cakes and sandwiches and huge pots of coffee, which were later set to brew on top of the stove. The men supplied additional refreshments in a more surreptitious manner. Bottles were slipped from hand to hand while groups disappeared outside regularly to "tend the horses."

My students all gave inspired performances. I was tremendously proud of them, although it would not have mattered if they had faltered and stumbled. The audience was so warmly appreciative that every poem and song was greeted with roars of approval. At the end, I, too, was given a wild round of applause. In fact, standing before that adoring crowd, I was almost overcome by a wholly uncharacteristic shyness and could barely restrain myself from bursting into tears.

Joshua Cameron sat near the front and led the applause. He looked so handsome in his starched white collar and tie, and he kept smiling up at me with a warmth that added greatly to my confusion. Once again, I was deeply grateful for my navy shirtwaist, which has helped me so much on other occasions. Regardless of how stressful a situation may be, I always feel quite composed and confident when I am wearing that particular garment.

At the conclusion of the concert, Father Christmas arrived and distributed gifts. Each child was given an orange and a small sack of candy. Many of them have never seen an orange, and the smaller ones were so excited that they could scarcely contain themselves. Mrs. Goldman, fully recovered from her accident, sat on the jolly saint's knee and received a ruffled apron. Father Christmas looked quite pale as he supported her substantial bulk. I, too, had my turn to sit on his knee and was presented with a new ruler; some of the boys had destroyed my old one while playing swords and have been very contrite ever since.

But that was not my only gift! At the very bottom of his sack, Father Christmas discovered an object wrapped in gold paper which was "for the teacher." It is sitting next to me on my bed as I write, and I can hardly believe how lovely it is. My gift is an illustrated volume of *Pilgrim's Progress,* calfbound, with pages edged in gold and decorated with exquisite watercolors. Nobody would admit to purchasing this costly item, but I certainly have my suspicions, and I must restrain myself from hugging the book to my bosom in a most indecorous manner!

After the concert and the distribution of gifts, the evening shifted gears and became a rowdy celebration. Babies were put at the back of the room to sleep, wrapped in shawls and stacked like cordwood. The

chairs were cleared away, the stage was removed and
Mr. McLean took his place at the front of the room
with his fiddle and bow. I would never have suspected
dour Angus McLean of having artistic leanings, but
the man is truly an artist with the violin. His merest
touch is enough to set feet tapping and hands clap-
ping. He played some lively reels and then turned his
hand to a series of slow waltzes. I was busy oversee-
ing my younger students for most of the evening, but
I derived great pleasure from watching those hard-
working pioneer couples take a few hours to enjoy
themselves. The women spun and dipped in their husbands' arms, as carefree and graceful as society ladies, their weathered faces sparkling with delight.

Toward the end of the evening, some rogue managed to suspend a sprig of dried mistletoe from the
lamp hook in the middle of the ceiling. By this time,
the party was in full swing—greatly aided, I fear, by
the men's regular trips to tend the horses. There was
much hilarity among the unmarried couples as they
either sidestepped the hanging branch or maneuvered
their way beneath it. Everyone knows that kissing beneath the mistletoe is practically an announcement of
one's engagement. Judging from the activity at our
Christmas concert, there will be quite a number of
marriages in Wolf Hill in the coming spring!

While the dance was ending, I sat near the cloakroom with Herman asleep on my lap and Gunter and
Elsa both drowsing against my shoulders. Joshua
Cameron appeared with Karen Mueller beside him,
but I had no idea of their intention until Karen urged
me to get up, then took Herman from me and sat in
my place.

"So you can dance," she whispered, her face pink with happiness. Karen had spent the evening dancing with young Steven Oates who is visiting from Calgary. Her eyes were shining like stars.

"But I had no intention of dancing, Karen," I protested. "Besides, I have no partner."

"Ah! I beg to differ, Miss Livingston," Joshua said with a sweeping bow, acting so much the part of the courtly gentleman that I was moved to laughter, as he clearly had intended.

"I have never been a good dancer," I warned him as he led me onto the floor. "I tend to get the steps all mixed up."

"That's because you think too much," he told me with a smile. "Just relax, Ellen, and let me do the thinking."

He swept me into his arms and we began to circle the floor. I was astonished to find that he was right. When I relaxed in his grasp and allowed him to lead the way, my feet performed the steps so automatically that I felt quite graceful and elegant. Still, it was not entirely pleasant for me to yield myself so completely to another's will. I fear that I am probably far too strong-minded.

I soon forgot my reluctance, caught up in the sheer wonder of being in his arms. I have never been so close to him, although I must confess—but only to you, dear diary!—that I have often thought about it. He held me quite firmly, and I can hardly believe how strong and hard his body is. I could feel his arm and shoulder muscles rippling even through his jacket. I still shiver when I recall the sensation.

The music slowed for the final waltz, and Joshua spun me to the middle of the floor with calm deliberation. I had no idea what he intended until he paused beneath the sprig of mistletoe and bent to kiss me. When I think of it now, hours later, I am still overcome with emotion.

I have never really, seriously been kissed until tonight, and I had no idea what to expect. I will try to report the feeling with some accuracy. His mouth was so sweet, and although he looks hard as iron, his lips were soft. The sensation was almost unbearably pleasant. I confess to my shame that I wanted it to go on forever. I was so taken aback that I was only dimly conscious of the crowd's laughter and rowdy shouts of approval when Joshua finally drew away and we swept calmly through the final steps of the waltz. Nothing was said between us, but as he delivered me back to my seat, he looked at me with a sober, intense purpose that rendered me temporarily speechless.

"The two of you are practically engaged," Mrs. Oates said later when we were driving home in my little red sleigh. "I would look on that kiss under the mistletoe as a definite statement of intention."

"Well, I certainly do *not* agree," I said with some heat. "The intention cannot be only on his side, you know. I have some say in the matter, as well."

"Do you not want to get married, Ellen?" she asked.

Thinking about his sweet kiss and all that marriage entails, I blushed furiously and was grateful for the sheltering darkness. "I suppose I do," I said at last. "But not yet! Not while I am still so young, and I love teaching so much. I have no desire to end my career when it has barely begun."

"Well," she said calmly, "judging from the way Joshua Cameron looks at you, my dear, I rather doubt that he will be willing to wait very long."

Despite my turbulent emotions, I felt a growing stubbornness and resentment at the thought that a woman must automatically yield herself and her future to a man's wishes. But I said nothing to Mrs. Oates. I was too tired and too happy at the success of our concert to argue the point.

And, I must admit, too confused. Because whenever I think about that kiss, I begin to wonder if a career is really so important, after all.

RAYMOND APPEARED bright and early the next morning, ready to go to work on Kate's window. She followed him into the bedroom, amazed by his good cheer. His tantrum of the previous day had vanished as completely as one of those prairie storms that came howling out of the mountains, battered the land with punishing force and then swept away leaving sunshine in its wake.

"Hey, Kate, what happened to that old book you found in here?" he asked, lifting the loose piece of windowsill and peering inside.

Kate tensed. "Oh, I put it away," she said with forced casualness. "It's just some sort of old ledger. Parts of it are really faded and hard to read," she added truthfully.

Raymond nodded without interest and began to pry at the side moldings with a small crowbar.

"Good morning, all," Mamie said from the doorway. "Isn't it a gorgeous day?"

"Hello, Mom," Kate said with a smile. "You look chipper this morning."

"Hilda fed me some of her fresh coffee cake. It was divine. Hello, Raymond."

"Hi, Mamie," the contractor said with a wide grin. "Glad you're here. I could sure use an extra carpenter if you want to go to work."

Kate stared at him in astonishment. When had he and Mamie progressed to a first-name basis? If she hadn't known him better, Kate would actually have suspected Raymond of flirting.

"You're amazing, Mom." Kate shook her head in wonder as Mamie came in and sat on the edge of the bed. "You're truly amazing."

"The girl is thirty-one years old," Mamie said, rolling her eyes, "and she's just realized that now. Have you seen Tom, dear?"

Kate glanced cautiously at Raymond who was whistling as he pried the molding away from the wall. "Tom's already gone out for the morning," she said. "He's over at the hardware store, I believe."

"The hardware store?" Mamie asked in surprise. "Whatever for?"

Kate grinned. "He's got a little tape recorder with him. Apparently, he's going to tape some of the local speech patterns. He says he's fascinated by regional dialects."

Mamie shook her head, and her dangling turquoise earrings glittered and tinkled brightly. "The man's insane," she said with a fond smile. "Utterly insane.

Raymond, honey, will that opening really be big enough to hang a door?"

The contractor shook his head. "I'll have to enlarge the opening and reframe it," he said, squinting at the wall with professional speculation. "Nothing to it," he added, preening happily when Mamie gave him an admiring smile.

"So this is where everybody is," a deep voice said from the doorway. "Good morning, folks."

Kate turned to see Nathan in the doorway. She was embarrassed to find herself staring at his mouth, remembering the sweetness of his kisses.

Nathan's manner was as courteous as always. "You look nice this morning, Kate," he said. "Real fresh and rested."

"Isn't she?" Mamie agreed from her perch on Kate's bed. "This rugged frontier life seems to agree with her, Nathan. I've never seen my little girl looking so well. Of course, she's always been—"

"Never mind, Mom," Kate said, her cheeks flushing. "Nathan isn't interested in all my personal history."

"I sure am," he said quietly. "I'm interested in everything that's ever happened to you, Kate."

Kate hesitated, conscious of Mamie's eyes resting on them with bright speculation. "Well," she said at last, "I'm afraid nothing much has ever happened to me, Nathan. I'm really a very boring person."

Nathan looked at her thoughtfully for a moment, but Kate ignored both him and her mother. She took a shovel and began to scoop up pieces of the splintery old window molding, piling them along one wall.

"What are you doing over there, Ray?" Nathan asked after an awkward silence.

"Kate wants this window ripped out. She's got a French door she wants to hang, so her room opens onto the terrace, or whatever she calls it."

"More like a slab of cracked concrete full of weeds," Mamie said, looking out the ragged window opening. "But I'm sure it's going to be lovely, dear," she added hastily, "when you have time to repair the yard and do some landscaping."

Nathan frowned at the window, which Raymond was now approaching with a chain saw and a purposeful expression. "I forgot about that plan," he said. "Are you sure it's a good idea, Kate?"

"Why not?" she asked, gathering an armful of wood and preparing to carry it into the hallway.

"I don't know if I like the thought of a door opening into the backyard like that. Your fence isn't in very good shape."

"What does the fence have to do with anything?"

"Anybody could get into the yard, and if they wanted to force this door, they wouldn't be visible from the street while they were doing it. I'm just not sure it's safe."

"You know, that's a very good point," Mamie said. "The major and I never thought about the safety factor. Of course," she added with a meaningful look at Kate, "Nathan is very concerned about your welfare, dear. *That's* certainly obvious."

"Oh, for goodness' sake!" Kate said. "This town is hardly a hotbed of violent crime, you know. I don't see why any of you should be concerned."

"We have crime around here," Raymond observed, hefting the chain saw. "Just last spring we had a panty thief."

"A panty thief?" Mamie said in delight.

Raymond nodded. "Stole ladies' underwear off clotheslines at night. Never did catch the man."

"Who says it was a man?" Mamie asked, giggling. "Maybe it was just a lady who needed underwear."

Raymond made a strange sound. After a puzzled moment, Kate realized he was laughing. "Well, now, I don't know if anybody ever thought of that," he said, pulling the cord on his saw.

Nathan watched Kate, who was gathering another armful of wood. "I hear that Aggie came by to see you," he said over the roar of the saw.

Kate paused with her arms full of wood and nodded miserably. "It was so embarrassing. We were having sort of a...little problem at the time." She dropped her voice and glanced over at Raymond who ignored them, concentrating on his sawing.

"Yeah," Nathan said with a brief grin. "I heard that, too."

"And I'm sure she thought I was..." Kate grimaced, thinking about the woman's reaction.

"Nobody knows what Aggie thinks," Nathan said, reaching out to touch Kate's arm. "I've known her all my life and she's still a mystery to me."

Kate trembled at his touch. All her responses to this man seemed to happen on some complex physical level that was fully removed from rational thought processes. Even when she was feeling annoyed or distant from him, a part of her still yearned to feel his arms around her and his lips on hers....

"I guess Aggie wanted to discuss her damned petition," Nathan was saying. "What are you going to do about that, Kate?"

"I'm going to call and ask if I can talk with her," Kate said. "What else can I do? I need the liquor license, and she's the one who's got the power to block it. If I can't convince her to leave me alone, I don't have a chance."

"Well, you'll have to hurry," Raymond said, shutting off his saw in time to hear Kate's words. "She's sending it in by the end of June."

"I know," Kate said gloomily. "I guess I'd better call her this afternoon."

"I'll go with you, honey," Mamie offered. "We'll go see her together. I'm not afraid of the woman," she added darkly.

"I'm not afraid of her, either," Kate said. "I'm just..." She paused as Nathan reached out with a gentle hand to wipe a streak of plaster dust from her cheek. His fingers rested against her face, and he stared down at her with a sober intensity that made her feel breathless, almost dizzy. She drew away from him, still clutching her armful of wood.

"Do you want me to go with you?" Nathan asked. "I can usually manage to reason with Aggie, if I try real hard not to lose my patience."

Kate turned away from him. "I think," she said quietly, "that I'd just as soon do this on my own, if it's all right with everybody."

She carried her pile of wood out into the lobby, conscious of Nathan and Mamie watching her departure in silence.

NEXT MORNING, Kate trudged through the sleepy town
on her way to the Krantzs' home on Elm Street, wishing she felt as brave as she'd pretended to be yesterday.

The June morning was so beautiful that it seemed
almost otherworldly. In the fields nearby, meadow-
larks filled the air with their sweet warbling and the
breeze was fragrant with the scent of lilacs and wild
roses. Beyond the little town, the prairie glistened in
the sunlight like a vast bowl of liquid gold, while lawn
sprinklers, bright with rainbows, played gently on the
yards and flower gardens of Wolf Hill.

Most of the beauty, though, was lost on Kate, who
was brooding over all the problems that filled her life.
This unexpected difficulty with the liquor license, for
example, was an obstacle she couldn't come to grips
with. It seemed so bizarre, almost unthinkable, that a
group of strangers could mount an irrational opposition to her project and doom it to defeat in spite of all
her efforts to succeed.

Kate was also growing increasingly discouraged by
her inability to take control of her own life. Her
sweeping resolve at the time of her divorce seemed to
be deserting her. She was still far too dependent on
others for help. Everybody bullied her, some overtly,
like Raymond, some gently, even lovingly, like Hilda
and Mamie. They were all very fond of her, but nobody seemed to have much confidence in her ability to
make a success of this business.

She thought of Ellen's strength and fortitude at the
tender age of twenty, and marveled at the young
woman's courage. But thinking about Ellen was a
mistake because it led Kate inevitably to thoughts of

Joshua Cameron and his great-grandson, and that was the most distressing thing of all.

If only, Kate kept thinking in despair, remembering Nathan's dark eyes and handsome face, his laughter and warmth and the sweetness of being in his arms.

If only she'd met him when her life was better organized and she wasn't recovering from the pain of a failed marriage. If only he didn't have a family and life-style that threatened to swallow up the identity of any woman who got involved with him. If only...

Kate arrived at the picket fence that bordered Aggie's home. She sighed and put her hand on the latch, gazing up at the house that had probably been standing on this very street when Ellen Livingston lived at the hotel. It was a big broody old mansion covered with dark brown shingles and surrounded by tall trees that blocked the sunlight.

The place suited its owner, Kate thought. No wonder Aggie's soul was dark, living in this mausoleum.

Quelling an urgent, cowardly desire to flee to the warmth and safety of the hotel, Kate took a deep breath and opened the gate. The trees and windows seemed to watch her silently as she went up the walk, mounted the steps and rang the bell, shivering in the musty dimness of the old veranda.

Aggie came to the door and looked at her without expression. "Come in," she said, stepping back into the foyer.

Kate entered reluctantly and looked around at the interior of the big old house, which had probably not changed much since the time it was built. "This is beautiful, Mrs. Krantz," she said, genuinely impressed by the ornate woodwork and wallpaper, the antique chandeliers and furniture. "Are all the fittings original?"

"Yes, they are. Clarence inherited the house from his mother," Aggie said, leading the way into the living room and indicating a velvet wing chair. "She never wanted anything changed."

Kate looked at her hostess with interest as she seated herself in the chair. "What was her maiden name?"

"Clarence's mother? She was an Oates. They were one of the early families, but she married young and moved away. We came back here in the sixties when Clarence inherited the house, and he opened the hardware store downtown."

Kate nodded. This must have been the home of Mrs. Oates, whom Ellen described as her friend and mentor. Ellen had probably sat many times in this very room, drinking tea as she chatted about her life and her students.

In a roundabout fashion, Aggie Krantz was even related to the kindhearted Mrs. Oates. It made her seem a little less formidable.

"Would you like some coffee?" Aggie asked, pausing by the sofa. She wore a brown print dress instead of her customary polyester slacks, and had obviously taken some care with her makeup and hair. Kate was encouraged by this evidence of concern on Aggie's part.

"It's nice of you to offer," she said, "but I have to get back right away. Raymond's starting to install the new boiler today, and I promised to help him drain the radiators."

Aggie seated herself on the couch. "I thought Raymond refused to do the boiler."

Kate stared at her, momentarily taken aback. Was there anything in this town that didn't become common knowledge within ten minutes?

"He changed his mind," she said quietly. "We're all anxious to have the hotel finished and ready to open early in July, Mrs. Krantz."

"I see. And what do you want me to do about it?"

"I think you know what I want. I've come to ask if you'll reconsider and drop your petition to block the liquor license."

"There's no need for a beer parlor in this town," Aggie said coldly. "Drink just causes all kinds of misery and problems."

"I agree," Kate said. "Abuse of alcohol, like any other kind of abuse, can cause terrible social problems. Used judiciously, though, it's not necessarily an evil in itself."

Aggie smiled unpleasantly. "I see. And you're going to be able to control this place, are you? You're so wise and all-powerful that you can actually keep people from abusing alcohol on your premises?"

Kate struggled to maintain her composure. "Are you and your husband total abstainers, Mrs. Krantz? Do you occasionally serve alcoholic beverages to your guests?"

"Sometimes," Aggie admitted. "A little sherry, some whiskey sometimes, eggnog at Christmas. Things like that. We're not teetotalers, if that's what you mean."

Kate, who'd known this already, chose her words carefully. "Do your guests ever get...drunk, would you say? A little rowdy and out of control?"

"Of course not!" Aggie snapped, glaring at her.

"Then it is possible to serve alcohol but maintain a controlled atmosphere while doing so. You would agree that it's possible, because you do it here in your own home."

Aggie stiffened. "That's a different thing," she said coldly. "Completely different. When there's a bar in town, family life suffers."

"Why?" Kate asked.

"Because if there's a drinking place, the men spend all their time there. They neglect their wives and families."

Beneath the hostility, Kate heard something in the other woman's tone, a distant kind of sadness.

"But aren't the men entitled to a gathering place of some kind?" she asked gently. "Women visit for hours over at Julie's beauty shop, and down at the bingo parlor, and in one another's homes. Men don't tend to do that as frequently."

"I have nothing against the men getting together to talk," Aggie said stiffly, as if regretting her brief lapse. "But I certainly don't see why women should sit alone night after night in their houses because their men are down at the beer parlor."

Kate looked at her in thoughtful silence. "What if I was able to do something about that?" she asked.

"I beg your pardon?"

"What if I could think of a way to keep that from happening? If I could come up with some kind of plan to keep the bar from damaging family life, would you continue to oppose it?''

Aggie snorted in derision. "You certainly have a high opinion of yourself, my girl. You think you can change human nature? You can give liquor to a bunch of men and then control their behavior? Well, maybe you're not as smart as you think."

Kate smiled wanly. "I really don't have as much confidence in myself as you seem to think, Mrs. Krantz. But I do agree that there could be a problem here, and I think perhaps there's something I can do about it. Will you give me a chance to organize some ideas?''

"How can you change anything? If there's a bar, there are going to be problems.''

"Please give me some time," Kate said, leaning forward earnestly. "Don't send your petition before I've had a chance to come up with a way to convince you that the hotel bar won't be bad for the town. If I haven't managed to change your mind by then, you can send in the petition. All right?''

Aggie hesitated, looking skeptical.

"Please," Kate urged. "Please give me a chance. You're obviously a woman with a sense of history," she went on, indicating the old house and its antique furnishings. "If you weren't, you wouldn't have preserved all this. And the hotel bar is a part of Wolf Hill's history. It's been operating for almost a hundred years. Mrs. Krantz, give me a little time to prove to you that the bar can be restored without doing harm to anybody.''

Aggie was silent, fingering the edge of a velour arm cover on the sofa. Finally, she looked up. "All right.

Two weeks," she said. "I'll give you two more weeks, not a day longer, and then the petition goes in."

"Oh, thank you," Kate said fervently, getting to her feet. "Thank you so much. I'll call you sometime next week," she added, "as soon as I have time to get my ideas worked out."

"I'll be waiting," Aggie said, looking grim.

But Kate wasn't at all discouraged by the chilliness of her adversary. She felt lighthearted and confident as she left the house and went back out into the sunshine. After all, she'd tackled the problem on her own and solved it.

Almost solved it, she reminded herself. Aggie Krantz still needed to be convinced, and it wouldn't be an easy task. But at least Kate had managed to buy some precious time.

Now she just had to find a way to make use of her reprieve.

Thursday, January 12, 1905

What a winter! Coming from Ontario, I thought I had seen plenty of cold and snow but I have never experienced anything like the winter we are enduring here. Shortly after our Christmas concert, the temperature plunged to a bone-chilling minus forty degrees, and it has seldom risen above that mark since.

And the snow! It falls and falls. The drifts pile higher each day, covering some of the lower windows and rising above the eaves of the houses. On many days, howling winds create blizzards that engulf the countryside in snow and ice. People are afraid to leave their houses, and dark tales have begun to come in from the countryside, news of farmers who have been lost and frozen to death as they tried to get out to the barn to feed their livestock.

I have not seen Joshua Cameron since the evening of our school concert, and nobody has heard from him. I shudder to think of him all alone out there in his cabin with nobody to mount a search if he should become lost or stranded somewhere. But I must not allow myself to harbor these thoughts. Joshua is a capable man. He has survived terrible hardship, loneliness, even Indian wars. I am sure he can survive a winter storm.

Meanwhile, it is quite cozy and gay here at the hotel. A fire roars in the dining room at all hours, and our bedrooms are kept warm with mountains of coal and the hot bricks that Mrs. Goldman is constantly heating in the kitchen. A few travelers have been trapped by the storm, and many of the townspeople have taken to dropping by regularly, perhaps to relieve their sense of isolation and fear. They crowd into the lobby exhaling great gusts of frosty air and stamping snow from their boots.

There has been no school since the Christmas holiday. Consequently, I have had a great deal of free time to relax and prepare lessons. Too much free time, perhaps, because I sometimes find myself sitting here in my room and brooding for hours on end. On the rare occasions when the snow does not obscure my vision, I stare out the window at the hotel yard, which is an unending sea of white. All the shrubs have been obliterated, and even the smaller trees are now buried under mounds of snow.

For the first time since my arrival, I am suffering dreadful bouts of homesickness. Perhaps until now, I have been too busy to be really homesick. I miss the order and civility of my hometown, the tidy streets and houses standing neatly in rows, the conviviality of the Christmas season and the pleasant social round. I miss Mama and Papa and Auntie Grace, and all the dear little cousins. But most of all, I miss the cultural amenities, like the library and the concert hall where we used to enjoy so many entertaining programs.

Perhaps I am not the pioneer type, after all. I feel sad and disconsolate, almost giving way to irrational tears as I gaze at the swirling whiteness beyond my window and wonder what on earth I am doing in this bleak place.

Enough of these morbid thoughts! I will not sit here any longer and indulge in such weakness. Instead, I will go down to the kitchen and offer to help Mrs. Goldman, who has been laboring like a Trojan to feed and care for all the people stranded under her roof.

Sunday, January 22, 1905

The world has changed a great deal since my last diary entry. Several days ago, a chinook wind came sweeping down from the Rocky Mountains, and the result was astonishing. I had heard of the phenomenon of the chinook, but I had never actually witnessed it. Within an eighteen-hour period, the temperature rose almost eighty degrees!

By Friday afternoon, the glass stood well above freezing, and water flowed in rivers through the streets of the town. The warm wind howls with unbelievable force, licking the snow from the prairie like icing off a cake. Mountains of snow have vanished in a few days, and now the prairie is actually showing bare patches. I have never, never seen anything like it.

School will start tomorrow, but I fear that many of my students will still find the back roads impassable. Mr. Mueller was able to make it into town yesterday, though there was not enough snow for his sleigh, and his wagon wheels were heavy with mud. He reports that Joshua is well and sends his regards, but is so busy tending his herd through these abrupt changes of weather that he will not be visiting for some time. I am glad to hear that he is safe, and not greatly disappointed to learn that he will be away for a while. I am too confused these days to deal with *that* particular set of emotions in addition to everything else. Especially after what happened today!

This afternoon, we took advantage of the break in the weather to hold a meeting of the ladies' auxiliary in the church hall. We are already planning the celebration this coming summer that will mark our territory's incorporation as a province, and a lavish affair it is going to be. My students will be much involved, although the concert and community picnic will be held on Dominion Day, July first, long after school has been dismissed for the summer.

Everyone assumes that I will be here, and I have not said anything to the contrary, although I still have deep uncertainties about my future plans. My doubts were compounded today when I was in the church cloakroom taking my turn to make sandwiches for the ladies and had a most unpleasant confrontation.

Amy Lord came in, ostensibly to help me, but I could tell that she had something besides sandwiches on her mind. We stood side by side, mixing egg salad and slicing pickles, talking aimlessly about the weather while emotions simmered almost visibly beneath the surface of our conversation. At last, she took a deep breath and turned to me. "I think you should know," she said with a challenging look from her doll-like blue eyes, "that Joshua Cameron and I are engaged to be married."

I was shaken, but took care not to show it. "Are you, Amy?" I murmured. "I was really not aware of that. When was the formal announcement made?"

She flushed and glared at me. "It's not a formal thing," she said. "It's just been...understood. For years and years."

Understood by you, perhaps, I thought, but refrained from saying anything.

"And you're making a terrible fool of yourself," she went on harshly, "chasing after him the way you've been doing, and making him...making him look at you."

My anger began to rise, but I kept my voice deliberately light. "I have the impression that nobody makes Joshua Cameron do anything. I believe he does exactly as he pleases."

I buttered bread with firm strokes, trying to keep my hands from shaking. Amy gave up all pretense of slicing pickles. She pushed the jar aside and turned to me, her face white with anger.

"What do you hope to accomplish by this?" she asked. "You come here from someplace nobody's ever heard of and turn everything upside down. You've got no right to do this!"

"I have no idea what you mean," I said calmly. "May I have those pickles, please?"

She shoved the jar across the counter, still glaring at me. "You don't even want him," she accused. "Why do you keep trying to steal him away from me when you don't want him?"

"Steal him!" I echoed, trying to laugh. "You make him sound like a brooch for your dress. I am quite sure that a man cannot be stolen."

"You know well enough what I mean," she muttered sullenly. "Always smiling at him, and talking to him about... about poetry, and all those silly things. What good is poetry here on the prairie?"

"I think poetry is valuable anywhere," I said mildly, frowning as I arranged pickles on the plate.

"That's just what I mean," Amy said. "This isn't a play or parlor game, Ellen Livingston. It's a hard, lonely life. Out here, women need to be tough as old boots. You don't really want to marry Joshua and live on that godforsaken ranch of his. You want theaters and books and nice conversation. You're just playing some kind of game, and I think you're a perfectly dreadful person!"

I looked at her curiously. "If life with Joshua Cameron would be such an awful drudgery, why do you want it?"

"I was born to this," she said bluntly. "And you weren't. I've wanted Joshua Cameron since I was ten years old, and I aim to have him. I'm warning you!"

With that, she seized one of the plates of sandwiches and swept away into the church hall, leaving me alone with my pickles and my brooding thoughts.

CHAPTER TEN

NATHAN SPRAWLED on the couch by his empty fire-place, reading a newspaper and listening to classical guitar on the stereo.

He sighed and tossed the paper aside, looking out the window at the moonlight. Although the summer night was balmy and still, Nathan found himself thinking about the storms of winter, the howling winds and drifting snow, the dark nighttime feeling of being isolated from the rest of the world by miles of barren landscape.

Usually, he enjoyed the winter months, but this year he found himself dreading the prospect.

Getting to his feet, he wandered across the big room and peered out the window again. He felt restless and lonely, tense with sexual need and other emotions he was afraid to analyze.

He looked at the dark shifting leaves of the cotton-wood trees along the driveway, and saw Kate's face in the moonlight. These days, he saw her face every-where—in the gentle prairie skies as he worked and in the cool darkness of his room when he lay in bed alone, staring at the ceiling and yearning for her.

This driving, frustrated need for a particular woman was something new to Nathan Cameron, and not at all pleasant. Usually, women threw themselves at him with embarrassing directness. His only problem was deciding whether or not he wanted to respond.

But Kate Daniels was not only different from other women, she was maddeningly unpredictable. Sometimes when he held her, like that afternoon in the porch swing, she responded to him with an urgency that seemed to match his own, and a warm passion that took his breath away. Whenever he tried to pursue her, though, she drew away as if something about him troubled her, something that kept her from letting herself yield to him.

He couldn't for the life of him figure out what the problem was, and she wouldn't tell him....

Frowning with sudden impatience, he turned off the stereo and strode through the silent kitchen. He had to get out—go for a drive—do anything but stay here alone with his thoughts. At the doorway, he pulled his boots on, left the house and walked down the path to his truck, climbed inside and, without thinking, headed off toward Wolf Hill.

As he drove, he tapped his fingers on the steering wheel, gazing absently at the silvered landscape. The moon was round and full, creating an eerie impression of almost daylight. Though it was past midnight, he would have been able to drive without headlights, following the glittering ribbon of highway into the distance. In the countryside around him, herds of cattle drowsed silently and the white-tipped grasses swayed and rippled in the nighttime breeze.

Nathan pulled into town and drove slowly along Main Street, conscious of the hushed stillness and the darkened buildings. Wolf Hill still had no streetlamps, and the only illumination was the moonlight that spilled across the wide streets and reflected in the windows of the stores and houses.

He drifted slowly toward the hotel, looking up at its massive bulk, still thinking about Kate.

He was troubled, even frightened by the depth and urgency of his emotions. He suspected that this must be the way a man felt when he was ready to get married and settle down with one woman for the rest of his life, to be faithful and true, to raise a family and share everything in his life.

Until this spring, Nathan had always wondered what brought a man to those momentous decisions, causing him to give up all his freedom and privacy in exchange for the confines of domestic life. But now he was beginning to understand, and he no longer felt scornful of his friends who'd succumbed to the nesting urge.

Before he realized it, he'd parked by the hotel and got out, leaning against the door of his truck and looking up in silence at the weathered brick facade.

His mind was full of Kate, in all the ways he'd seen her over the past months.

He pictured her that very first day, trapped in the cluttered basement of her old hotel, looking at Raymond Butts in panic like a timid little bird watching a snake. He recalled her stubbornly pushing a wheelbarrow loaded with scrap iron, her face covered with grease and dust. That image gave way to one of her riding next to him through the spring wildflowers, her curly blond hair lifting softly on the breeze, her cheeks pink with happiness. Lying in his arms in the porch swing, returning his kisses . . .

Nathan's groin tightened with longing and he moaned softly under his breath. From the very beginning, this woman had attracted him so powerfully that he could hardly keep his hands off her. Leaning against his truck in the moonlight with his arms crossed, Nathan tried once again to analyze her appeal. It wasn't just her shy prettiness, though he'd always found her lovely. The attraction had something to do with the touching gallantry of the woman, the way she'd tackled this huge, unlikely task and was trying so hard to do it all on her own. And she was succeeding, too, although Nathan was pretty sure that she didn't even realize how much she'd accomplished since the day she'd first arrived in Wolf Hill with her armful of plants and her look of terrified resolve.

"You're so hard on yourself, Kate," he whispered, gazing up at the old hotel she was struggling to restore. "You don't even know when you're doing well, and you won't accept praise from anyone. It's one of the nicest things about you, and the most frustrating..."

He felt a quick stab of pain, wondering again if the mysterious barriers between them had anything to do with Kate's feelings for the famous husband she'd just divorced.

Or maybe the guy had been such a bastard that she just distrusted men in general. In that case, her experiences since she'd come to Wolf Hill, particularly with Raymond Butts, wouldn't have done much to reassure her.

Thinking of Raymond, he recalled the scene in Kate's bedroom, and the contractor hacking cheerfully at the wall with his chain saw.

Nathan took a couple of steps toward the building, wondering if her door was installed by now and if it was fully secure. Raymond was a good carpenter, but he probably wasn't as concerned about Kate's safety as he should be. It was entirely possible that Raymond might not even have finished the doorframe or put a lock on her door yet. A cloud drifted across the face of the moon, plunging the hotel into shadow. Somewhere in the trees down by the river an owl hooted a hushed, mournful call that quivered eerily on the warm night air. Nathan's hair prickled at the back of his neck.

He couldn't stop wondering about that newly hung door in the sheltered backyard, possibly not yet secure, and Kate lying alone and unprotected behind it. The idea of something happening to her, hurting or even frightening her, was more than he could bear.

Finally, he moved away from his truck, crossed the hotel veranda and went quietly down the steps at the far side, then began to walk around the ragged fence that bordered the hotel yard.

He edged his way between a couple of broken planks and stood in the shadows of the fence, looking at the backyard. The cloud had passed and the moonlight spilled over the broken cobbles and the tufted, weedy grass in a wash of pure silver.

Suddenly, Nathan drew in his breath sharply, flattening himself against the wall as he stared at Kate's terrace. A faint glow came from behind the closed drapes, but bright enough to illuminate her quiet figure as she sat outside on a cushioned lounge chair with a book in her lap. She had some kind of small reading lamp, a pinpoint of light in the shadows. As Nathan watched, she settled drowsily against the padded chair and her body relaxed. The book slid lower and her hand fell away, trailing over the edge of the chair.

Nathan moved closer, edging out onto the moonlit terrace so he could look down at her as she slept. The night was warm and she wore nothing but shorts and a blue cotton shirt. Her long legs were slim and silvery in the moonlight, her face and hair like pale burnished platinum. Her eyelashes cast dark shadows on her cheeks and her mouth looked childlike and tender.

Nathan felt a surge of love so intense that he swayed on his feet as he looked at her. He felt clumsy with longing, ashamed of himself for spying on her while she was asleep and vulnerable.

But he wanted her so much...

If she woke up, Nathan thought desperately, he'd have to make up some kind of story about being worried about the lock on her door. Otherwise, how would he ever explain this?

KATE WAS DREAMING.

In her dreams, as often happened these days, her soul and Ellen's had somehow become mysteriously intertwined, so that she was both women as she stumbled along the darkened road at midnight, hurrying toward the safety of Wolf Hill.

She was Kate, worrying about the hotel and brooding over the fact that Raymond, for some reason, kept insisting that he wanted to suspend the tables upside down from the ceiling in Hilda's dining room. The cook was furious. She threatened to abandon the coffee shop and take up a career in taxidermy if Raymond didn't change his plans and leave the tables on the floor.

But in her dream, Kate was also Ellen, wearing a long dress and trim black buttoned boots. As she lifted her skirts and hurried along in the darkness, she worried about Gunter who had developed a fever but wouldn't stay away from school. In fact, on this dark night, she was returning from the Mueller farm where she had taken Gunter forcibly and told his father to keep him at home until he was better.

The prairie night was dark and still, pressing around her, chilly with menace. She could hear an owl hooting near the road, a mournful cry that made her shiver. She quickened her steps and hurried into a shadowy grove that swallowed up the road. Rustling cottonwood trees lined both sides of the lane, arching overhead, their branches wrapped together in a leafy embrace.

She felt even more frightened as she entered the dark avenue, but inside the grove, all the danger seemed to vanish. It was an enchanted place, silvery and quiet in the moonlight. The road was gone, replaced by a sparkling pool of water bordered with grasses and flowers. She stepped toward the water and looked down, down, into its smooth platinum depths, wondering what mysteries lay in that bottomless pool.

Suddenly, she became aware of a man approaching through the trees.

He came quietly toward her, pausing at the edge of the pool just a few feet away from her. His face was in shadow, but she could see the breadth and strength of him, the powerful grace of his body. He wore tall buckskin moccasins, woolen breeches and a linen shirt tied with a thong of rawhide.

He turned and smiled, his high cheekbones and firm jaw etched with moonlight. In the strange, disjointed manner of dreams, the man was both Joshua and Nathan. She stared at him, wide-eyed and silent, lost in a kind of wondering desire.

His smile faded as he strode across the grass to reach for her. She shivered, knowing that his embrace was going to be the most wonderful pleasure she'd ever known. She drifted into his arms and their lips met, blending fire and ice in a sensation that left her breathless, limp with passion.

"I love you," he told her soberly. "I've always loved you."

The words were so sweet to her that she wanted to go on hearing them forever. She wanted to stay in this man's arms, here in this enchanted place, and never leave him again.

"I love you, too," she whispered. "I love you so much." He smiled and reached to caress her face with a gentle hand.

Kate's eyes fluttered open. She stared at the dim shape by her chair, still lost in her dream, struggling to orient herself.

"I'm sorry," he whispered. "I didn't mean to frighten you, sweetheart. I was just worried about your door, and I . . ."

Kate listened without comprehension. His words meant nothing at all to her. She was too stunned by the way her dream had materialized, taken on shape and substance. Moments ago, she had been in this man's arms with their lips crushed together, her heart singing with joy at his embrace. Suddenly, she felt chilled and bereft without him, as lonely as an abandoned child.

"Please," she whispered, reaching up toward him. "Please . . . hold me."

She heard his sharp intake of breath and saw his look of surprise, but she wasn't really conscious of anything except her need to be in his arms again. Almost impatiently, she grasped him and pulled him down toward her. He lay on the chair with her, gathering her into his arms. Kate sighed with pleasure at the warmth and power of his embrace.

"So good," she murmured. "Feels wonderful when you hold me."

"Oh, Kate . . ."

He held her and kissed her with rising passion.

Gradually, Kate began to wake up, to understand that this was really Nathan in her arms, not Joshua, and that they were lying together in the moonlit backyard of the hotel. I should tell him to go away, she thought. I shouldn't be doing this.

But he felt so good in her arms, so completely satisfying and right. . . .

At last, she managed to draw away and look at him. "This isn't very comfortable, is it?" she whispered. "Why do we always wind up in these cramped spaces, like teenage kids stealing kisses?"

He smiled and hugged her. "That's how you make me feel, Kate. Like a teenager again, all hot and bothered about a girl."

She laughed. "Nathan, why are you here? It must be past midnight."

"I was restless. I went for a drive and then started worrying about your door, and if Ray had put a lock on it yet."

"A likely story," Kate scoffed.

He began to kiss her again. She struggled to sit up, reaching for the diary. "Since you're here," she said, "do you want to come in for a minute? We'll have coffee and talk."

"Kate, sweetheart, I'm not all that interested in talking right now."

"Okay," she said, getting to her feet and looking at him with quiet intensity. "We won't talk."

"Oh, Kate..."

He followed her inside and glanced around at her bedroom, now almost completed, with its bright chintz-covered bed, its braided rug and hardwood floor and framed prints. Kate put the diary away in her dresser and turned to him.

"Kate," he said, hesitating by the door. "Kate, honey, please don't invite me in unless you mean it. I couldn't stand it."

Kate looked at his handsome face and lithe muscular body, and felt a hunger that almost overwhelmed her. All her months and years of loneliness seemed to crash over her in a dark wave of passion, robbing her of caution, making her ache for this man. With sudden recklessness, she turned off the overhead light and reached for him.

"Oh, yes, I mean it," she murmured. "God help me, Nathan, I really want to do this."

He drew her into his arms with an incredulous laugh, then held her and began to run his hands over her body, caressing her hips and thighs, pulling out her shirt so he could touch her naked skin.

"Kate," he whispered against her neck. "Kate, darling..."

Shameless with need, Kate reached to undo the buttons on his shirt and stroke his bare, hard-muscled chest. She kissed his skin, ran her tongue along the warm silky line of his shoulder and nuzzled against him hungrily.

Beneath her hands she could feel the powerful shudder that ran the length of his body.

"Lord," he whispered. "Darling, do you have any idea what you're doing to me?"

Heedless of his words, Kate unsnapped his belt buckle and tugged at the zipper in his jeans, then watched as he peeled off his clothes. He stood erect in the moonlight, his face and shoulders glistening, while she gazed at him in pleasure. "Beautiful," she whispered, reaching to trail her fingers along the bulging muscles of his upper thigh. "Such a beautiful man."

He lifted her and carried her to the bed, drew back the covers, lay her tenderly on the cool sheets and began to take off her clothes.

Kate moved to help him, arching her back so he could tug the shorts down, sitting up to pull off her shirt.

"No bra," he teased as he leaned forward to kiss her breasts. "I thought you'd be the type to wear a bra all the time."

"There are all sorts of things you don't know about me," Kate whispered, shivering as his tongue caressed her nipples.

Nathan drew her panties off and tossed them on the floor, then sat next to her. He began to stroke her, running his hand down the length of her body, tenderly cupping her breasts and releasing them, letting his fingers trail slowly over her waist and abdomen and down her thighs. When his hand slipped between her legs, she moaned softly at the pleasure of his touch and reached for him, trembling with urgency.

He lay beside her and drew her into his arms. She nestled in his embrace again, enchanted by the way their bodies seemed to blend so perfectly. His skin was cool and silky but where their bodies merged, they burned together like fire in the moonlight.

"So sweet," Kate murmured against his face, kissing him. "So sweet, darling."

"Kate, my love..." But their disjointed words were halted by another kiss, so deep and passionate that it left both of them shuddering. Kate reached down to cup and caress him, marveling at the thrusting strength of him.

"I want you so much," she whispered in his ear. "Wanted you since... the first time I ever saw you."

He groaned at her touch and moved above her, gentle but deliberate. "Are you sure, Kate?" he whispered. "I mean, is it all right if I...?"

She was so consumed with passion that she could no longer hear him at all. She gripped his shoulders and drew him forcefully toward her, into her, gasping with joy when she felt him begin to move inside her body.

"Oh!" she whispered. "Oh, Nathan..."

Nathan held her tenderly, full of concern for her, while his gentle thrusting power carried both of them to a place she'd never known before. Kate moved in his arms, gasping and drowning in rapture. The moonlight blossomed all around her and bathed her face in a warm radiance that was almost blinding.

"Oh, Lord," she murmured. "I never knew..."

"Kate," he whispered, his body shuddering with release. "Darling, I love you so much. I've never felt this way about anyone. I want you with me all the time, Kate. I want to keep holding you and looking after you for the rest of my life."

She smiled sleepily, limp and drowsy with fulfillment. "That sounds nice," she murmured.

He leaned up on his elbow and looked at her intently, tracing the line of her mouth with his fingertips. "Are you saying yes?" he whispered. "Will you marry me, Kate?"

Her drowsiness fled and she felt a sudden chill. "You're serious," she said, gazing up at his moonlit face. "You really mean it."

"More than I've ever meant anything in my life."

"Nathan," Kate whispered in despair, "I can't marry you."

"Why not?"

"Because of...so many things," she said, feeling a rush of sadness. She drew away from him and huddled under the blankets.

"Like what?" He pulled her into his arms again. "We love each other. And I don't want to live without you. So what's keeping us apart? What are you afraid of?"

"Nathan," she pleaded, "I've just managed to get free of a really smothering marriage. I'm trying to figure out who I am and where I belong in the world. I don't want to lose my life in yours right now, no matter how pleasant it would be. I just can't take on all the responsibilities of...of you and your ranch and your family's expectations. Not now.''

"So what do you want? What do you see for us in the future?''

"Do we have to talk about the future? Can't we just ... be friends for a while?''

"I've already got lots of friends, Kate,'' he said quietly. "The feelings I have for you can't be satisfied by friendship.''

Kate stirred in his arms, feeling helpless. "Let's not argue,'' she whispered against his throat. "Let's love each other again, and forget all about the arguments for a while. Please?''

She began to caress him and tease him until he was groaning with passion. Before long, all talk of the future was lost in the sweetness of the moment.

KATE WOKE in the early light of dawn and listened to the birds singing beyond her window. She gazed up at the ceiling, her body slowly flooding with warmth as she recalled the night before. Smiling, she turned to look at the early sunlight as it flickered through her new glass door.

Nathan must have dressed and slipped away sometime during the night while she was sound asleep. Her lover was gone, but her memories of him were still rich and vivid. Even her body felt different, languid and fulfilled, as if all the physical tensions of the past months had been magically released.

She couldn't believe how hungry she'd been for him and how shamelessly she'd pulled him into her room and flung herself upon him. Even worse, Kate thought, her euphoria dissipating abruptly, they'd used no protection of any kind. She might even be pregnant!

Not really all that likely, she assured herself, considering the timing. But still, after so many years of desperately wanting to conceive and having it never happen, it was a strange, breathless feeling to be worrying that she might be pregnant....

She got out of bed and stumbled into the bathroom to brush her hair and dab on some lipstick. She recalled his proposal of marriage and his obvious surprise at her refusal.

Probably, when a man grew up as son and heir to the Cameron family, he wasn't accustomed to being refused anything he wanted.

"Katie?" her mother called from the hallway. "The major and I are going for breakfast. Are you up?"

"I'll be right there," Kate called back, wondering how she was going to face her mother.

Mamie was a perceptive woman, and Kate was sure her nighttime adventure was branded on her face for everybody to see. She shivered, hugging her arms as she thought about Nathan's embrace, and the sweet fire that had burned between them. The man's lovemaking had been such a marvelous, shattering experience.

Kate pulled on her jeans and an old plaid shirt, slipped into a pair of moccasins and hurried through the lobby to the coffee shop, then paused in alarm. Mamie and Tom sat together at a table near the window. Nathan was opposite them, sipping coffee as he listened to something Mamie was saying.

Kate took a deep breath, staring at him. Her heart stopped, then began to thud painfully. She remembered everything...his gentle mouth and hands, the rich thrusting strength of him, his incredible tenderness...

Tom caught sight of her and waved a greeting. Slowly, Kate made her way through the crowded room and paused by their table.

"Hi, honey," Mamie said, smiling at her. "Did you sleep well?"

Involuntarily, Kate glanced at Nathan who gave her a warm grin and saluted her silently with his coffee mug.

"I...slept all right," she murmured.

"Did you have sweet dreams?" Nathan asked innocently, holding out a chair for her to sit next to him. Kate hesitated, then sank helplessly into the chair, conscious of his bare tanned arm next to hers and the pleasant scent of leather, sunshine and shaving cream that always seemed to be part of him.

"Kate?" he asked, leaning toward her.

"Yes," Kate muttered, staring down at the table, conscious of Mamie and Tom looking at her curiously. "I had...nice dreams."

"Glad to hear it," Nathan said, smiling.

He stroked her arm with a casual gesture and Kate shivered at his touch.

"Did Ray get a good heavy lock installed on that door yesterday?" Nathan asked, sipping his coffee again.

"Not yet," Kate whispered, then looked up in relief as Hilda arrived with the coffeepot. "He's doing it today."

"My word!" the major exclaimed. "You aren't telling us that you've been sleeping in that room with no lock on your door!"

"It's all right," Kate murmured. "Really, Tom. I pushed a carton of floor tiles against it."

"But, Katie...anybody could have come in!" Mamie said in horror.

"Anybody," Nathan agreed solemnly, his eyes sparkling.

Kate concentrated on adding sugar to her coffee, but she could feel Mamie's eyes resting on her and Nathan.

The major seemed unaware of any nuances, apparently far too outraged by this new evidence of Raymond's perfidy. "I'll trounce the little devil," he muttered darkly. "I'll turn him inside out and hang him from the ceiling."

"You'll do no such thing," Mamie said calmly, patting his hand. "For one thing, you've bullied that poor man enough already, and if you push him any further, you'll undo all the good you've done. And besides, we're leaving this morning, remember? You probably won't even see him before we go. I rather think," she added thoughtfully, "that Raymond will make sure of that."

Kate felt a powerful mixture of relief and panic. "Are you and Tom leaving, Mom? So soon? You just got here."

Mamie nibbled a slice of toast and stabbed at the sweet grapefruit that Hilda had grudgingly stocked since their arrival. "The major has to get back to

Vancouver. Apparently, there's some kind of problem with the veterans' association that he belongs to."

"Irregularities in the books," Tom agreed, scowling. "Most upsetting. Need to get to the bottom of it at once."

Kate looked at his pugnacious expression, briefly feeling sympathy for the hapless person responsible for those "irregularities."

"Anyhow," Mamie went on, waving her toast with an expansive gesture. "I have no concern about leaving you alone, honey. Not with all the help you have here, and a nice man like Nathan to take care of you."

"You've got it all wrong, Mom," Kate said calmly. "Nathan doesn't take care of me. I'm taking care of myself, and I intend to keep on doing it," she added, pushing her chair back. "I need to make out a big order for sheets and blankets this morning. Be sure that you both stop by the office before you leave. Goodbye, Nathan. I can recommend Hilda's blueberry waffles if you're staying for breakfast."

Before he could reply, she walked out of the coffee shop, conscious of his dark eyes resting on her.

NATHAN TRIED for more than a week to get Kate alone again, but all his attempts failed. She was too busy to take his calls, and whenever he managed to get her on the phone, she sounded distant and preoccupied. On the occasions when he stopped by the hotel hoping to catch her off guard, she was either away in the city buying supplies, or surrounded by workmen and immersed in some job that she couldn't leave.

As the time passed his frustration increased until he felt that unless he could make her talk to him, he would simply explode. She was so maddening, such an enigma to a man who was accustomed to success in his dealings with women.

More than anything, Nathan was haunted by the memory of their lovemaking. In bed, Kate had been everything he'd hoped and dreamed, so utterly fulfilling and exciting that he felt breathless with yearning whenever he thought about her slim body in his arms.

He pushed the disturbing memories from his mind and strode across the hotel lobby. A noisy clatter erupted from the dining room, where Hilda was supervising a group of workmen installing wooden louvers at the new windows. All the taxidermy supplies had been removed, and the restoration, with Raymond's grudging cooperation, was almost finished.

Nathan paused in the doorway and forced a smile. "Hi, Hilda," he said. "Where's the boss?"

Hilda turned and beamed at him. "Hi there, honey. Look at this place!" She waved her plump arms to take in the polished hardwood floor, the new tables and chairs, the oak paneling and ruffled paisley curtains. "Isn't this the most beautiful sight you ever saw?" she asked with a blissful sigh.

Nathan tried to look interested. "It's real nice, Hilda. Will there be some romantic touches, like candles on the tables? People like romance when they're dining out."

"Even better," Hilda told him smugly. "We're installing replicas of the old gas lamps they used to have in here. Kate ordered them last week."

"That's great. What's she busy with this morning?" Nathan asked with forced casualness.

Hilda turned back to the workmen, who were arguing over shutter heights. "Kate? I think she's out in the backyard," she said absently. "Working on that god-awful mess she calls her terrace."

Nathan nodded, then went out through the lobby and around the hotel to the backyard. He paused in the shadows by the corner of the building, trying not to think about the last time he'd walked through this yard in the moonlight and found her lying outside, warm and passionately welcoming, almost as if she'd been waiting for him....

Nathan swallowed hard and crossed the weed-covered space to reach Kate, relieved to find that she appeared to be alone. She hadn't seen him yet, absorbed in her task of pulling up weeds and hauling broken pieces of concrete into a pile near the wall.

"Need help?" he asked quietly, coming up behind her. "That looks like a pretty tough job."

Kate stiffened and glanced up in alarm, then went on tugging doggedly at a heavy chunk of concrete. "No, thanks," she said. "Actually, I'm enjoying the fresh air."

Nathan leaned against the wall and watched her. "What's wrong, Kate?" he asked.

"I'm not sure what you mean."

He bent and lifted the piece of concrete she'd been struggling with, tossing it effortlessly onto the pile. "Yes, you are. The other night I was sure you loved me. Now you're treating me like a stranger."

"I'm busy, Nathan. I have so many things to do, and hardly any time left before our grand opening." She tugged furiously at a weed stalk almost as thick as her wrist. "I can't spend all my time thinking about my relationships."

"You know, I hate those words," he said with sudden coldness.

"What words?"

"All the trendy buzzwords. Commitment, relationships, personal space, all that garbage. Don't people ever talk about real things anymore?"

Kate stood erect and wiped a gloved hand across her forehead, giving him a level glance. "Like what? What's your definition of real, Nathan?"

"Love," he said curtly. "Marriage. Kids. Sharing a life. That's what reality means to me. And you won't even talk to me about it."

"We're talking," she said, stooping to attack the weed again. "Aren't we?"

"Kate, stop it." Nathan stepped forward and took her arm, drawing her upright and holding her as he looked down at her. "Tell me what's going on here."

Kate shook his hand away and met his eyes with a calm blue gaze that he could never begin to fathom.

"Nothing's going on here, Nathan," she said. "That's just it, don't you see? You keep insisting there has to be something important between us, but it's not true. I'm a businesswoman trying to make a success of this project. You're a single man living your own life. We had fun together the other night, but it doesn't mean anything earthshaking is going on."

"Like hell!" he said, fighting to control his anger. "I can't believe I'm hearing this. You know damned well there's something going on. Come on, Kate. Talk to me."

She bit her lip and looked away. "Nathan, please don't..."

"I love you," he said. "I want to marry you. I don't know what it means to you, but my whole life is tied up in this."

"Nathan, stop to think about it for a minute. What about my life? What about my home—the Wolf Hill Hotel. You'd expect me to live out at the ranch, wouldn't you?"

"Of course," he said, looking at her in astonishment. "That's my home, Kate. Where else would you live?"

"Has any woman ever lived on that ranch and worked somewhere else? In fact, has any Cameron woman ever had an existence beyond the ranch?"

He hesitated. "The ranch is a full-time job, Kate," he said after a moment. "It's my life. I'd expect my wife to share it."

"But what if I wanted a life of my own? What if I didn't want to live out there and spend all my time being your helpmate and hostess?"

"Kate, it's a good life I'm offering you. It's happy and secure and full of comfort. Is that such a bad prospect?"

She turned away, looking troubled and sad. "Of course not," she said. "For the right woman, it would be a marvelous prospect. I'm just not sure if I'm the right woman for you."

"Well, I'm damn sure of it," Nathan told her stubbornly.

"What would your mother think if you married someone who wanted to have a career of her own?"

Nathan considered the question while she watched him in silence. "Why does it matter?" he asked finally. "We're both over thirty, Kate. Is my mother's opinion so important to us?"

"Only if you happen to share it," Kate said quietly.

With that, she crossed the yard and vanished inside her room, closing the door firmly, leaving a baffled Nathan staring after her.

CHAPTER ELEVEN

KATE SAT in the Camerons' living room, sorting through piles of yellowed newspaper clippings that flooded the coffee table. Josh and Marian, both in reading glasses, studied the papers with her while Nathan worked alone at a desk nearby, itemizing piles of tax receipts.

Kate stole a glance at him but he kept his head lowered, working steadily. He'd dropped by the day after their argument to offer her a ride into Calgary, saying casually that his mother had some more papers for her to look at it, and been visibly surprised when Kate accepted.

Their trip to the city had been a little strained and quiet, but peaceful enough. Kate didn't want to fight with him anymore. She scarcely had enough energy for all the things she needed to do, and she was in no mood for conflict. Mercifully, Nathan no longer seemed bent on pressing her for a commitment....

"I love all these 'Society Corner' things," Kate said wistfully. "I wish I had time to read every one of them. Listen to this. It's from June 1912."

Marian and Josh settled back to listen while Kate read aloud from the old paper. " 'Mrs. Sarah Oates recently entertained her sister from Calgary during a pleasant interlude on the Oates veranda. The ladies fared sumptuously on iced lemonade and a tempting array of fancy cakes and sandwiches.'"

Josh chuckled. "It's a different world now, isn't it? If Wolf Hill had a society column nowadays, that article would probably say, 'The ladies scoffed down burgers and beer, then played a mean round of golf. Mrs. Oates beat the pants off her sister, winning a dollar a point.'"

"I love nostalgia," Marian observed, "but I think I'd still rather have the golf and burgers than the pleasant interlude. How about you, Kate?"

"Hmm?" Kate was studying an item from December 1904, describing the stunning success of the first Christmas concert at the Wolf Hill school and praising the efforts of "our talented and gracious schoolmistress, Miss Ellen Livingston."

"Kate doesn't believe in romance." Nathan looked up from the tax receipts he was working on at a desk in a corner of the room. "She lives entirely in the present. A very practical woman, Kate is."

"Women have to be practical," Marian said calmly. "They're the ones who keep everything running smoothly. Women have most of the responsibility in our society, and not many of the rewards."

"I think Kate must have a lot of romance in her soul," Josh protested. "If she didn't, she'd never have taken on that old hotel in the first place."

Kate smiled at him. "Will the two of you be coming to our grand opening?"

"We wouldn't miss such an important event in Wolf Hill," Marian said. "Here's what you're looking for, Kate. A menu from Sunday dinner at the Wolf Hill Hotel, dated July 23, 1905."

"Oh, perfect!" Kate took the clipping and read it eagerly, then looked up in dismay. "Hilda was right! I thought she was just teasing me."

"Hilda's usually right," Josh said placidly. "Always has been."

"What do you mean, Kate?" Marian asked. "Hilda was right about what?"

"In the summer of 1905, they served buffalo prime rib in the dining room for Sunday dinner. Where am I ever going to find buffalo meat?"

"There's a place downtown that sells it in commercial quantities," Nathan contributed from his desk. "We can stop by there later and order your prime rib for July, if you like."

Kate looked at him in disbelief, then turned to his parents. "Really? They sell buffalo here in Calgary?"

Marian nodded. "Josh and I have bought it a few times. It's quite good, really. Leaner than beef and very tasty, isn't it, Josh?"

"That's amazing. I had no idea." Kate thought it over, her mind kindling with excitement. "This is going to be ideal!" she said. "We can advertise in the city papers, and we'll have a huge crowd there. The word-of-mouth promotion will be tremendous. We'll have the very same menu as they had in 1905. Mashed potatoes, prime rib of buffalo, fresh spinach salad, rhubarb pie with homemade ice cream and dandelion punch!"

"My mouth is watering already," Josh told the women solemnly. "How about you, Nathan?"

"I'll volunteer Bessie for the occasion if Hilda promises not to hurt her," Nathan offered. "Bessie's rhubarb pie is a thing of wonder."

Kate smiled, thinking about their grand opening, the restored dining room, the newly wallpapered bedrooms with their crisp sheets and blankets, a vase of fresh-picked flowers in every room...

Marian looked over at her. "Kate, I've been meaning to ask you something."

"Hmm?" Kate looked up cautiously, hoping that Marian wasn't going to ask about Ellen's diary. The book hadn't been mentioned since their first conversation, but Kate was certain the woman hadn't forgotten about it.

"I've been wondering... What's happening with Aggie Krantz and your liquor license?" Marian asked.

"I have to go and see her tomorrow. I've been putting together some proposals about the bar, and I hope she finds them acceptable. If not," Kate said gloomily, "all this planning is more or less academic. I won't be able to keep the hotel running if I can't open the bar."

"What's your plan?" Josh asked. "Is there any way we can help?"

"I'm hoping to convince her the bar can be a couples place, a kind of social center for the town. A lot of neighborhood pubs are doing that nowadays. I hope she's willing to listen to me."

"Aggie's never been much of a listener," Marian said thoughtfully. "We went to school together, you know. By the time Aggie was six years old, she was already running everything and she's never stopped."

"I think she's a lonely woman," Kate said, surprising herself a little. "After you've talked to her for a while, it's really hard not to feel sorry for her."

"Aggie takes far too much on herself," Marian said with sudden coldness. "She'd be happier if she looked after her own home instead of insisting on being center stage, managing everything."

Kate wondered if those words carried a subtle message for her, as well. She always had the uncomfortable feeling that Marian disapproved of the ambitious project Kate had taken on. And if she suspected that her son had much more than a passing interest in the new hotel owner...

Nathan's mother got to her feet with her usual briskness and started toward the kitchen. "I'll make some coffee," she called over her shoulder to Josh and Kate. "You two keep reading."

"Can I help?" Kate asked.

"No, thank you. If I need anything, I'll get Nathan to help me. Bessie has him very well trained."

Nathan smiled at his mother and went on recording figures in his ledger.

"Listen to this, Josh," Kate said, holding up a clipping. "Here's something about your namesake, Joshua Cameron."

"What does it say?"

Kate frowned as she tried to decipher the faded print. "It's from the fall of 1904. 'Mr. Joshua Cameron has generously donated a piano to the Wolf Hill school. The piano is a finely wrought upright grand in a solid mahogany case, and was built in the Verdeuil Brothers' factory in Montreal, taking all of seven weeks to travel from there to Calgary by rail. The instrument was picked up in Calgary on Tuesday by Mr. Angus McLean, who required six strong men from the Wolf Hill district to assist him in transporting our new instrument to its place of honor in the schoolhouse.

'Miss Ellen Livingston, our schoolmistress, has described the gift as being exceedingly generous. Miss Livingston is an accomplished pianist and says that she plans to use the piano as a featured part of the upcoming Christmas concert, a social event which the entire district awaits with keen anticipation.'"

Josh chuckled. "Keen anticipation," he said. "For a school Christmas concert. It really was a different world, wasn't it?"

"A piano would have been awfully expensive in those days, wouldn't it?"

"I suppose so," Josh said, leafing through clippings. "It sounds like quite a production, getting it delivered all the way to the school."

"Your grandfather must have been a very generous man," Kate said, trying to sound casual.

Josh looked at the window, his handsome face clouding briefly. "If he was, I never saw any evidence of it."

"But he—"

"Kate!" Marian called from the kitchen. "Would you prefer tea? I can make a pot if you like."

By the time they settled the issue of what to have for lunch, the opportunity had passed. Kate couldn't think of a way to return to the mysterious topic of Joshua Cameron.

A FEW HOURS later, Kate and Nathan were driving back to Wolf Hill after stopping to order two hundred servings of buffalo prime rib, a proceeding that made Kate feel quite giddy with terror.

"What if nobody comes?" she brooded aloud, staring out the window at the late-afternoon shadows.

"Then you and Hilda and Luther will be eating a whole lot of buffalo stew this winter," Nathan said comfortably.

Kate groaned and pressed her face against the glass.

"Don't worry." Nathan reached over to pat her shoulder. "People will come. You're right about this. It's a terrific advertising gimmick."

"But what if I can't get the liquor license? Nathan, my money's practically gone. After I pay the advance on that meat we ordered, I'm going to be broke."

He looked straight ahead, his profile etched with gold in the fading light. "Look, Kate," he began awkwardly, "why don't you let me—"

"No!" she said, "Please, Nathan, don't even say it, or else we'll have another fight."

"But it's so—"

"I'm warning you," she said firmly, and he fell silent.

Kate watched as a coyote loped up to the crest of a nearby hill, then turned to look down at them, his tail waving like a soft plume on the afternoon wind.

"Nathan..."

"Yeah?"

"What does your mother really think about this whole project? I mean, my plans to restore and operate the hotel. Does she disapprove?"

"What makes you think so?"

"I don't know. I always get the impression that she thinks it's...unseemly, somehow. Your mother's pretty much of a traditionalist, you know."

"I think you're altogether wrong about that. I believe she envies you."

Kate looked at him in astonishment. "She envies me? Why?"

He frowned and steered expertly around a pothole in the road. "I think my mother would have loved to do something like this when she was younger. She's a capable woman, and she would have enjoyed the challenge."

"Then why didn't she?"

"Because she married my father," Nathan said quietly, "and moved to the ranch, and it occupied her life from then on. She had no time or opportunity to do anything else."

Kate shivered and gripped her hands in her lap. She watched in silence as they approached the outskirts of Wolf Hill, drowsing sleepily in the summer twilight. But when Nathan pulled his truck onto Main Street, the town suddenly began to appear anything but sleepy.

The dusty avenue swarmed with people, most of them teenagers, who massed in front of the hotel, staring up at its brick facade and yelling lustily. They milled about in tattered plaid shirts and baggy pants, caps askew, some on skateboards and Rollerblade skates, bumping into one another and creating a general air of wild confusion.

"What the hell?" Nathan muttered, peering at the melee in astonishment.

But Kate had witnessed similar commotions many times. She'd also caught sight of the low-slung red sports car parked in front of the hotel.

"I think," she said, looking bleakly at the milling crowd, "that my ex-husband has probably dropped in for a visit."

Grim faced and silent, Nathan pulled into the lane and parked his truck out of sight behind the hotel. He and Kate sneaked into the backyard, sprinted across the dusty ground and paused by the door of the bulkhead while Kate fumbled for her keys.

"God, I hope I have the basement key with me," she muttered. "If we have to go around the front, they'll probably—"

"Here," Nathan said curtly. "Give me your key ring."

He took the keys, squinted at them and selected the most likely one, fitting it into the lock. Kate sighed in relief as the door swung open and they hurried into the dim silence of the basement, edging their way down the stairs. The newly installed boiler dominated the lower floor, sleek and quiet, its metal sides gleaming faintly in the muted light.

Kate looked at the boiler, then cast a timid glance at the man beside her. "It looks a lot different down here now, doesn't it?" she ventured, trying to smile. "Do you remember that very first day, Nathan, when Raymond was telling me that all the beams needed to be replaced, and you came and rescued me?"

"Yeah," he said without expression. "I remember, Kate."

She paused next to the inner stairway and looked up at him, frightened by the coldness of his face.

"Nathan," she said hesitantly.

"Why is he here, Kate?"

"I don't know," she said. "Adam does whatever he wants. He always has."

"Did you call him and ask him to come?"

"No, of course not! Last time I talked with him, before my mother came to visit, I got the impression he was staying in Europe for the summer."

Nathan studied her, his face shadowy and unreadable in the darkness. Kate heard a clatter coming from upstairs in the lobby, accompanied by Hilda's outraged shouting. She looked at Nathan miserably, searching for something that would make his face relax and soften, make him smile at her again. But he was already heading up the stairs toward the commotion in the lobby.

Kate followed silently, emerging behind Nathan into the light and confusion of the floor level.

"Get away, you little varmints!" Hilda was shouting, glaring through the lobby window at the mass of screaming teenagers on the veranda. "Get out of here, all of you, or I'll call the police!"

Nathan brushed past her, opened the door and strode onto the veranda, tall and commanding in the midst of the rowdy group. He spoke to them briefly, looking so fierce that they subsided, muttering, and retreated to the sidewalk where they continued to stare up at the hotel.

Nathan came back inside, his glance moving past Kate to someone behind her. His face tensed, and his eyes were so piercing that Kate shivered. At this moment, Nathan looked exactly as she visualized Joshua Cameron.

"Hi, folks," a familiar voice said, making Kate's heart sink. "Katie, this is a great old place you've got here."

Kate turned to look at a slight man in ragged jeans and a black T-shirt who stood near the door of her office. "Hello, Adam," she said quietly. "What brings you here?"

Adam Daniels was of medium height, with unruly blond hair curling onto his shoulders, bright blue eyes and a square-jawed, boyish look that drove teenage girls wild with desire. This was the face—almost as well-known as the president's—that adorned posters and album covers all over the world.

Kate confronted her ex-husband, feeling strangely detached. Next to Nathan he looked like an overgrown child, willful and self-centered, almost as immature as his adoring fans who thronged the hotel entrance.

"I called Mamie last week," Adam said with a warm smile at Kate. "She said you were having a lot of problems out here. I thought maybe I could help."

Nathan watched her, his face cold and still, while Kate tried to think of something to say that would ease the tension.

She was rescued by Hilda who came bustling toward them with her hands on her hips. "I don't care how famous he is," she said to Kate, pointedly ignoring Adam. "If he can't get them little monsters off the veranda, I'm leaving and I'm not coming back."

"Adam," Kate said, turning to him, "can't you go out and sign some autographs? They'll leave peacefully if you just give them a few minutes of your time."

He shook his head, looking stubborn. "I'm on my holidays, Katie. You know how much I hate signing autographs when I'm not working. I don't want to talk to anybody but you, sweetheart."

In desperation, Kate glanced at Nathan, who turned away abruptly and began heading toward the door. "Nathan," she said.

"I have to get home," Nathan told her quietly. "Bessie's expecting me. See you later, Hilda. Goodbye, Mr. Daniels."

He nodded at Kate as if they were strangers, then let himself out, crossed the veranda and was swallowed up in the milling throng.

Adam watched his departure with an amused smile. "When did you start hanging out with cowboys?" he asked Kate.

"He's a friend of mine, Adam. I'm living a different life now."

"So Mamie tells me."

Hilda appeared in the entrance to the dining room, looking grim. "Kate, I want them kids out of here. If they don't settle down, they're going to break my new windows."

Kate gave her a pleading glance. "I'm sorry about all this, Hilda. I really am. Why don't you close up for the day and take the rest of the evening off? Nobody's going to come to the coffee shop while that mob's out there, anyhow."

"That's for damn sure," Hilda said, glaring at Adam who gave her a bland version of his famous smile.

"And on your way," Kate said, "you can tell them that Adam will be coming outside in a few minutes to sign autographs for them, if they stay off the veranda and wait quietly."

Adam's eyes widened in shock. "Look, Kate," he protested, "I told you I—"

"Tell them, Hilda," Kate said firmly. "In fact, you can tell them he's going to keep signing autographs until every one of them is satisfied, no matter how long it takes."

Kate watched as Hilda waded out into the crowd of teenagers. They listened to her and then backed reluctantly out into the street, where they stared up at the hotel windows in obvious anticipation.

Adam's fit of petulance faded as abruptly as it had come. "Well, well," he said with an admiring grin, coming forward and putting an arm around Kate. "When did you get so tough? You were never like this before."

"Well, I am now," she told him briefly, and realized in astonishment that it was true. Seeing Adam again made her realize just how far she'd progressed since her arrival in Wolf Hill. "And I don't appreciate your coming here without any warning, Adam. You spent years dropping in and out of my life on your own timetable, but those days are over now."

He gave her a hurt look. "You sound so cold, honey. I thought you'd be happy to see me. Mamie says you're almost broke, and you know I can write you a check and make your life a whole lot easier."

Kate sighed, wondering a little desperately if anybody had ever suffered like this from constant offers of help. Most people longed for some assistance and never got it. Kate, on the other hand, seemed to spend her life fighting off people armed with checkbooks who wanted to solve all her problems. "I don't need your money, Adam. Our business affairs were settled long ago. I don't want anything at all from you."

"Not even friendship? A little warmth in the chilly world?" he asked softly, tightening his grip on her shoulder. "Or something more..."

Kate thought of Nathan's arms around her, his laughter and gentleness, the sweet feeling of his body close to hers in the summer night.

"I'm afraid not," she said. "Friendship is fine, Adam, but nothing else. Those days are gone."

"Katie..."

Hilda came back into the lobby. "The animals are waiting," she announced with satisfaction. "I told them if he wasn't out there in five minutes, I'd let a couple of them in to carry him out."

Adam glowered at the plump woman, who gave him a smile as bland as his own and swept past him into the coffee shop.

Friday, February 17, 1905

Today has probably been the most momentous day of my life, though it certainly did not begin auspiciously. For one thing, I overslept and was required to rush through my morning routine, almost burning several locks of hair on my curling tongs. To make matters worse, poor Mrs. Goldman was preoccupied with some crisis involving her bread dough and was unable to heat water for the guests, so I had to wash and dress with only the ewer of water left in my room overnight. It was so cold that a skiff of ice had formed on top of the jug.

The temperature has dipped once again and snow has begun to fall, although the fierce cold and blizzards of early January have mercifully not returned. But our chinook is now only a distant memory. The roads are once again choked with snow, and people go about bundled up in fur and leather.

But the return of wintry weather was no deterrent to Amy Lord, who has long been determined to host the social event of the season in Wolf Hill. Amy's twenty-first birthday fell on Saint Valentine's Day, and she decided to hold a fashionable snow-and-ice party in honor of the event. These parties have become quite the rage out West, where people only now seem to be catching up with the fact that Napoleon and Josephine went ice-skating together at Auxerre more than a hundred years ago!

Despite the growing popularity of the sport, there are few residents of Wolf Hill who actually own a pair of ice skates. But this, too, did not discourage Amy, who announced that her party would also feature toboggans and sleds so everyone could participate. Of course, she only invited the singles and young-marrieds, as romance was intended to be the order of the day. Particularly her own romance! I fear that Amy expected this occasion to be the perfect opportunity for Joshua Cameron to tender his long-awaited proposal of marriage. But more about that later...

Because only younger people were invited, I fell into lucky possession of real ice skates. Mrs. Goldman, of all people, has a pair of skates and loves the sport! I should probably not have been so surprised. Despite her bulk, Mrs. Goldman is very light on her feet and dances beautifully. She urged me to take her skates, which are the clever sort that strap to the bottom of one's boots, so size is not a problem. Merely fitting the skates in place brought back wonderful, poignant memories of skimming across the pond behind our house with dozens of my school friends. For a moment, I felt utterly overcome by homesickness.

But when the school day finally ended and it was time to get ready for the party, I was quite giddy with anticipation. The event was held at the Lords' big house outside town, where Mr. Lord has dammed a natural waterway to provide summer watering for his cattle.

This is not at all like the river dams that are common back home. It is actually situated on a narrow, winding coulee that is dry for most of the year but catches enough water during chinooks and spring runoff to fill his dugout to the brim.

Amy intended her guests to toboggan down the sides of the coulee and skate on the surface of the dugout. The conditions were ideal because the heavy snowfalls and rapid melt not only filled the dammed area, it flooded the coulee for miles behind the dam and then froze, quite wide and smooth as glass. Consequently, we were treated to a superb toboggan run and an ice-skating rink that was miles in length!

I particularly enjoy parties that involve some kind of activity, finding them vastly more entertaining than a group of people sitting about and indulging in aimless chatter. When I arrived at the Lords' mansion with a crowd of young people from the church hall, I was feeling quite amiably disposed toward my hostess in spite of our recent conflict.

Amy and her mother had taken great pains with the decoration of the house. It was hung about with red-and-white streamers in honor of Saint Valentine's Day, and a proliferation of heart-shaped cakes, flowery messages of love, cupids with arrows and other coy adornments. I shuddered to think what sort of flirtatious entertainments might be planned for later in the evening.

In fact, I blush to confess that I had already resolved to leave the party early, after enjoying the skating and the lunch. Much of this resolve, I must further confess, was due to the fact that if Joshua Cameron and Amy Lord intended to announce their engagement at some time during the evening, I had not the slightest desire to witness the event.

Amy looked quite ravishing when we arrived. With predictable flair, she had traveled to the city and supplied herself with an actual skating costume, also in keeping with the red-and-white motif of her party. She wore a sweeping cape and skirt of cherry red velvet, trimmed with bands of white fur at the collar and cuffs. She looked exactly like a slender, golden-haired, female version of Father Christmas. I was sure that any man with eyes in his head would have been enchanted by her, and was not surprised when Joshua Cameron smiled warmly at her upon his arrival.

Standing near her, I felt like Oliver Twist in my oldest gray woolen skirt and a heavy brown knitted cardigan borrowed from Mr. Goldman, who is a somewhat smaller person than his wife. But Joshua's gaze shifted to me almost immediately as Amy turned to greet other guests.

"Hello, Ellen," he said, taking my arm and escorting me across the room. "Do you have ice skates, or will you be sliding?"

I showed him the skates in my leather pouch. "Mrs. Goldman loaned them to me."

He arched his eyebrows and grinned, looking so boyish and full of fun that my heart began to flutter in a most alarming fashion. "Well, that's fine news. I was hoping you might have skates," he murmured, leaning toward me. "Are you any good, or will I need to hold you up?"

"I am an excellent skater," I told him calmly. "I could probably beat you in a race. I always used to beat my cousins, even the boys."

He smiled at me with such warmth that I was forced to turn away in confusion. "I don't doubt it," he murmured. "I don't doubt it a bit."

At that moment, Amy called him from across the room. He departed from me to join his hostess and greet some of the newcomers.

Soon all the guests had arrived, the horses were cared for and the party moved outside with much laughter and shouting. It was a clear moonlit night with the temperature about ten degrees below freezing, ideal for outdoor entertainment. Mr. Lord, assisted by a crew of young men, had lit a huge bonfire at one side of the dam and drawn up kegs and logs for people to sit on. A number of couples scampered immediately up the coulee hill and began sledding down onto the frozen waterway, amid shouts of laughter and squeals of feminine excitement. Those of us who were lucky enough to possess ice skates moved onto the dam's surface, which had been cleared of snow and was as smooth as a professional skating rink.

I did a few turns of the pond, skimming along with my hands behind my back and enjoying the starry night, the soft glow of moonlight, the happy company and the cheerfulness of the bonfire. People massed around the flames, their faces bright with a coppery glow, singing lively songs and teasing one another.

As I neared the pool of shadows at the end of the dam, beyond the glow of the fire, a figure came racing up behind me. It was Joshua Cameron, very handsome and dashing in beaver hat, fur topcoat and leather breeches. He skated beyond me into the darkness and then came gliding back, stopping next to me with a flourish and a spray of ice chips.

"You are showing off, Mr. Cameron," I teased him, barely able to see his face in the shadows. "It is quite unseemly behavior. My little cousins used to do exactly the same thing."

"You're right, I am. Tell me, Ellen, are you impressed with me?" he asked, coming nearer, his eyes bright with laughter.

Of course, I had not the slightest intention of telling him how impressed I truly was, and how handsome he looked with his hawklike face all swathed in fur. Instead, I turned away and started back toward the fire. But Joshua grasped my hand and drew me toward him.

"Come with me," he said quietly. "I want to show you something."

Startled by the feeling of his hand holding mine, warm and disturbing even through my woolen mitts,

I yielded and allowed him to lead me farther into the shadows. We began to skate together along the coulee floor where the water had frozen in a ribbon of glass. Soon we drifted far away from the party, so distant that the partygoers' happy shouts carried only faintly on the still night air. As we glided deeper into the silence, the moonlight became eerily bright, wrapping us in a warm cloak of platinum.

I forgot all about propriety and decorous behavior, or even my concern over the fact that our absence might be noted and commented upon. All I wanted was to go on skating forever with my hand in Joshua's, into whatever fairyland this enchanted ribbon of silver would carry us. After a while, Joshua paused and looked down at me, his face etched with silver and very serious. He gathered me into his arms and kissed me with such passion that I was quite overcome. But I did not want him to stop. In fact, I am ashamed to confess that I kissed him back, so enthusiastically that I feared he would be shocked!

But Joshua seemed to be not at all dismayed by my wanton behavior. Instead, he laughed softly with delight and stroked my face.

"Ellen," he whispered in a husky voice. "Ellen, darling, I love you."

I trembled in his arms though I was not at all cold. Far from it!

"Will you marry me, Ellen?" he asked.

His words so astounded me that I could think of nothing to say. I merely stared at him, openmouthed.

I know Joshua Cameron has said things to me in the past that might have led me to expect this. But I always thought his proclamations were a show of male bravado or muscle flexing, merely an arrogant type of flirtation. I honestly had no inkling that he might seriously be intending to propose marriage, even though Mrs. Oates sometimes teases me about that very thing.

"What's the matter?" he asked with a gentle smile. "Do you want me to go down on my knees, Ellen? I will if you insist, but this ice is pretty cold."

I held him to prevent the man from suiting actions to his words. "But, Joshua," I said in confusion, "are you not supposed to be proposing to Amy tonight?"

He threw back his head and laughed. Then he sobered and looked at me intently. "A man can't propose to a woman just because she wants him to, Ellen. I haven't married until now because I've been waiting for the woman I could love with all my heart. I knew the first time I saw you, last summer in the hotel lobby. Ever since, I've wanted you and nobody else."

Still I gaped at him, searching for words. I was so full of confusion and fear. Part of me clamored to say, "Yes! Yes!"

In fact, I had an urgent desire to throw myself into his arms and feel more of those sweet kisses that left me so breathless.

But another part of me kept waving flags of caution. I saw my teaching career cut short by babies and all the responsibilities of a home. Worse, I recalled Amy's words and saw the dismal lot of a pioneer farmer's wife, the drudgery, the lack of intellectual stimulation...

As if he were reading my thoughts, Joshua gave me a sober look. "I promise it'll be different for you, Ellen," he said. "I swear I won't treat you the way these other men treat their wives. You'll have everything you need to make you happy. Books, concerts, trips back East to see your family, whatever you want."

I stared up at him, mesmerized by this vision of a life in which I would be able to have not only Joshua, but all the other things I valued.

"And trees?" I whispered at last, no doubt sounding like an idiot. But it was terribly important to me. "Will there be some trees, Joshua? I need them in order to be happy. I can't bear a life without trees. The sound of their leaves rustling in the wind, the patter of rain amongst the branches, the bird song at dawn... I need trees, Joshua."

He waved his arm at the endless vista of silvered prairie that surrounded us. "It's February," he told me solemnly, like a man taking a vow. "When April comes and the snow has melted, I'll start setting out your trees. I'll plant you a forest, Ellen, and I'll keep it alive. I swear I will."

I hesitated, then gave him a pleading glance. "May I have a little time to decide?" I asked. "A few weeks? May we not speak of this again until I have been able to think it over?"

Joshua seemed not at all troubled by my indecision. In fact, he relaxed and began to smile, almost as if by not refusing him, I had given him all the encouragement he needed.

"Take as much time as you want, my dearest," he said, tucking my arm in his. After kissing me again, very gently, he escorted me back to the lighted area with gentlemanly aplomb.

It seemed to me that a lifetime had elapsed since we'd left the party, but apparently nobody had missed us or remarked on our absence, not even Amy who was busy organizing a game of crack-the-whip.

I remained so stunned and preoccupied for the rest of the evening that I scarcely recall what happened, or how I found my way home. Now I stare out my window at the hotel yard and wonder what the remainder of my life will hold.

I am as confused and torn by indecision as I was when Joshua first uttered his proposal. But my body, alas, feels no such indecision. What my body truly wishes...shameless, brazen hussy that I am...is for Joshua Cameron to be waiting in my bed at this moment, ready to hold me and teach me all the sweet mysteries of life and womanhood!

CHAPTER TWELVE

KATE SAT at her usual table in the coffee shop, looking out the window with a brooding expression. The sun was already climbing, flooding the street with a wash of pale golden light.

The day promised to be beautiful, but Kate felt too tired and out of sorts to appreciate it. She'd lain awake most of the night, then fallen into an uneasy sleep near dawn, worn out by the tumult of the previous day which had seemed endless.

In fact, she could hardly remember the morning when she'd been working out on her terrace, pulling weeds, and Nathan had come along....

"Look at them black circles under your eyes," Hilda said with cold disapproval. "You mustn't have slept a wink."

"Not much," Kate agreed. "This is all getting to be too much for me, Hilda."

"Well, honey, you can't weaken now." Hilda lowered herself into the opposite chair. "We've got the grand opening coming up right away, and a few guests already booked for next month. Things are just starting."

Kate sighed and nibbled her toast, looking out the window again.

"Are they still out there?" Hilda asked.

Kate squinted at a group of teenagers hanging around near the hotel entrance. "Yes, they are. They're really persistent, aren't they?"

Hilda shook her head in wonder. "Now that school's finished, I never thought anything could make them kids get out of bed so early. I surely don't know what they see in that man, but he must have something."

"Charisma," Kate said with a bleak smile. "Star quality. That's what they call it. I've never been sure what it is, either, but Adam's certainly got it. He always has."

"It's a good thing Luther's sitting out there keeping them away from the door."

"I know. But we can't ask Luther to protect us forever," Kate said.

"How long is the man planning to stay, for God's sake?"

"Not long. He never stays anywhere for very long, Hilda."

"Speak of the devil," Hilda said with a sour glance at the door, where Adam had appeared and was looking around. He was tanned and casual in shorts, sandals and a cotton shirt, and his long golden hair shone in the morning light. He looked, Kate thought, almost unbearably handsome.

Adam's eyes brightened as he caught sight of Kate by the window. He flashed his famous smile, then strolled across the room toward her, clearly aware that all eyes were upon him.

"Hi, girls," he said. "Lovely morning, isn't it?"

Hilda heaved herself to her feet and moved impassively toward the kitchen. Adam took her chair and smiled at Kate. "Do you eat all your meals in here, honey?"

She nodded. "I was planning to have a kitchenette installed in my suite so I could make a few salads and omelets for myself, but I probably won't bother now."

"Why not?"

"Because I won't likely be staying here," Kate said. "I told you about the liquor license, Adam. If I can't open the bar, the hotel will never be commercially viable no matter how many people come to stay. I'll have to sell and try to start all over again somewhere else, I guess."

Adam toyed with the napkin holder, trying to see his reflection in its polished surface. "Look, Katie," he began, "I've been thinking. I can see how much this whole thing matters to you. It's not just a whim, is it?"

"No, it's not. I've had a hard time getting people to take me seriously, but I really want to make a success of this."

"I could hardly believe it when Mamie told me what you were doing here. It seemed so... out of character."

"Isn't that strange? And I feel like I'm finally doing the right thing, after years of trying to figure out who I was and what I wanted out of life."

Adam shifted in the chair and looked out the window, drawing back quickly when he saw the growing crowd of young people. "Until I talked to Mamie, I never knew how much it mattered to you, Kate, the whole idea of having kids."

Kate felt a wave of sadness. "We never talked enough, Adam. It was my fault as much as yours. I should have told you how I felt."

"And I should have listened. I was always too busy to give you enough of my time, and now I've lost you."

"Adam..."

"I still love you, Katie." Adam took her hand in both of his and looked at her earnestly. "I need to keep traveling because it's my job, but I thought maybe we could try again and make a go of it now that you've got this place to keep you busy. I'll give you all the money you need to keep it running, and you can adopt a baby. *We* can adopt a baby," he said hastily when she opened her mouth to speak.

Kate's eyes stung with tears. "There was a time," she murmured, "when it would have meant the world to me, hearing you say that."

"But not anymore?"

"Adam, what kind of family could we give a baby? How much would you be home?"

"You're the one who wants the family. I just want you. I'm being honest about it."

"It's not enough, Adam. I can't be content with half a marriage and an occasional husband I have to share with other women."

"But I won't ever cheat on you again, Kate. I'll be a real faithful guy, all the time. And I'll try to get back home a lot more often. At least once a month or so. I swear I will."

Kate looked at her former husband, remembering a long-ago coulee in the moonlight, a man's face swathed in fur, a sober vow to love, cherish and honor the needs of a woman's gentle heart. . . .

"I'm afraid I couldn't possibly live with you again, Adam," she said quietly, getting to her feet. "But if it's any comfort, I like you better now than I have for a long time. I have to go," she added before he could say anything. "I'll talk to you later, all right?"

He sat watching in astonishment as she turned and left the coffee shop without looking back.

"I THOUGHT you were divorced."

Startled, Kate looked at Aggie Krantz who eyed her with cold appraisal.

They were in Aggie's living room, once again surrounded by the antique furniture and lavish decor of a bygone era. Aggie, though, had a somewhat more modern look. She was wearing a summer-weight suit that Kate hadn't seen before, of soft yellow linen with a silk blouse. Her gray hair was carefully styled.

"I am divorced," Kate said after a moment. "My divorce was finalized before I came here to buy the hotel."

"So why is your ex-husband back? The town doesn't need all this upset and confusion, you know. Will he be coming around often?"

"No, I don't expect he will. I think this visit is an isolated occurrence, just a whim of his."

"You mean you're not living with him again?"

Kate looked up in astonishment. "Of course I'm not. What makes you think that?"

Aggie sipped her tea calmly. "Everybody thinks so. After all, the whole town knows that you spent the night with him."

"Spent the *night* with him!" Kate echoed in horror. "Is that what people are saying?"

She remembered Nathan's cold face as he left, and her heart twisted with pain. Did Nathan, too, think that she and Adam had spent the night together? And why did it matter so terribly if he did?

Aggie watched in silence as Kate struggled with her thoughts.

"It's a hotel, Aggie," she said at last. "Anybody can spend the night if they choose. There's nothing... nothing immoral going on."

"Your morals are your own business," Aggie said coldly. "I'm just concerned about peace and quiet in this town."

"Well, I can assure you that Adam Daniels is not going to become a regular part of my life, or upset the life of the town. I have no desire to see very much of him. He made me really unhappy," Kate said impulsively.

Aggie's eyes widened in surprise behind her steel-framed spectacles. "Folks seem to think it would be real exciting," she ventured, "being married to somebody so famous."

"Well, it isn't. It's a lonely, miserable life. He was always gone, and I never knew what he was doing, and women throw themselves at him...."

Kate bit her lip as she recalled the pain of Adam's many infidelities, a pain that she'd never really allowed herself to suffer. For years, she'd even managed to blame herself for his unfaithfulness, as if she'd failed him in some way.

Aggie set her cup down and watched Kate in silence.

"We weren't able to have a child," Kate went on quietly, staring into the depths of her cup, amazed that she was confiding these things to Aggie Krantz, of all people. But she didn't seem able to stop herself. "I wanted desperately to adopt a baby, but he wouldn't even consider it. He just wanted me to be available when he needed me, able to pack up and go away on holidays with him at a moment's notice. I was . . . so lonely."

She glanced up at Aggie, who nodded. "It's real hard," the older woman murmured, "being lonely."

"Nobody can understand if they haven't gone through it. You can be surrounded by tons of money and all the comforts anybody could ever want, and still be dying for somebody to take an interest in you."

"So why didn't you get a job, or something?" Aggie asked, but her face no longer looked quite as severe and disapproving.

"I don't know," Kate told her honestly. "Partly I guess I was hoping all the time that he'd change his mind about adoption because I wanted a baby so much. But mostly I was just so shy and insecure, and it got worse as the years went by. I had a couple of part-time jobs and I did some volunteer work at the hospital, but I was afraid to build a career of my own or take on anything really challenging."

Aggie looked at her thoughtfully. "You seemed so confident when you came to Wolf Hill, like you weren't afraid of anything."

"Me?" Kate asked in disbelief. *"Confident?"*

"Sailing in and taking over that big old hotel, sleeping there all alone every night . . . Folks thought you were a real tough city woman. Hard as nails."

Kate smiled wryly at this description of herself. "I guess I looked on this as my last chance. And if I wasn't scared, it was just because I was too naive to recognize all the problems. I'd certainly be scared to tackle it *now,* I can tell you that."

Aggie actually smiled back, a rearrangement of her features so brief and fleeting that Kate could hardly believe she'd seen it. Immediately, as if regretting this lapse, the older woman sat up and busied herself with the coffee tray.

"So," she said briskly, "what's this big plan of yours? You were going to tell me something about the hotel bar."

Kate nodded and reached into the briefcase by her chair. "I have some activity sheets and timetables I wanted to show you, and profiles of some places in the bigger cities and how they're organized. What I'm hoping is to set up a kind of neighborhood pub at the hotel, with a family atmosphere."

Aggie looked skeptical and amused. "A family atmosphere? In a bar?"

"A bar doesn't have to be a smoky den of sin and corruption," Kate said. "It really doesn't. I visualize a nice, airy place with a big nonsmoking area, lots of plants and framed prints on the walls and a games room attached where we can hold tournaments, with husbands and wives competing against other couples—"

"What kind of games?" Aggie interrupted.

"All kinds. Shuffleboard, darts, cards, electronic games on a big-screen television . . . You should see some of these other places, and how they're run. It seems like so much fun."

Aggie looked at the sheets Kate spread on the coffee table, studying the pictures and descriptions with a noncommittal expression.

"I've been thinking a lot about your objections to this bar, and you're right. What I'm hoping for," Kate went on with rising enthusiasm, "is exactly the opposite of what you've been afraid of, Aggie. I'd like to see a place that will encourage couples to spend more time together, not less. This town doesn't have much of anything that men and women can do together. The men congregate in some places and the women go to others. I'd like to operate a place where couples can go out for the evening together, meet their friends and enjoy themselves."

"I never heard of such a thing." Aggie glared at the papers. "It sure doesn't sound like any bar I've ever been to."

"Times are changing," Kate said. "Women aren't content to be left at home anymore, waiting for men to come back from their entertainment. At least," she added, remembering the lonely years of her marriage, "they certainly shouldn't be."

"I don't think the men would even want a place like this," Aggie said, gesturing at the pictures of laughing couples playing shuffleboard and sitting at tables together. "I think men want a bar where they can get away from their women. They'd still all go to bars in other towns and you'd end up losing money."

"I thought about that, too," Kate said. "And you're partly right. According to the market studies I've read, at first, men are really nervous about these places. But as soon as they get adjusted, they seem to enjoy the atmosphere as much as the women do. I guess men actually feel better when their wives are contented and not upset with them."

"I don't know," Aggie said again, continuing to leaf doubtfully through the papers.

"And the studies show that there's less incidence of intoxication and related problems," Kate went on, pressing her advantage.

"So how do you make your profit?" Aggie asked shrewdly. "If the men aren't drinking as much, you're going to lose money, right?"

Kate smiled. "Not if they stay longer. And they bring their wives, too, so there'll be twice as many customers."

"But people don't have to drink if they don't want to? They can still play the games and so forth, even if they aren't drinking?"

"Of course. Hilda will be serving a full lunch menu from the kitchen, and there'll be a wide variety of nonalcoholic drinks available."

Aggie studied a sample timetable Kate had drawn up, outlining a week's activities in the bar. "It'd be a real big job, running all these tournaments and things. What if it gets to be too much for you after a while and you just let it go? Then we'll be stuck with a regular bar like we've always had, and the women sitting at home again."

Kate hesitated. So much was riding on what happened at this meeting. "Actually, I was ... hoping for some help from you," she confessed. "You're such a good organizer, Aggie."

"Me?" Aggie's eyes widened in disbelief. "Helping you to run your bar?"

"I wanted to set up a social committee," Kate told her. "I thought you could be our first president and help with the planning and scheduling of activities, telephoning people about the tournaments, that kind of thing. I wanted to start with a darts tournament for the grand opening. I know it's really putting you on the spot and you have every right to refuse, considering all that's happened between us, but I—"

"Clarence and I won a darts tournament once when we lived in Calgary," Aggie said with a faraway look. "It was so much fun. We kept beating people and moving higher in the competition, and when we won the championship, he said…" Suddenly aware of Kate watching her, Aggie flushed and gathered herself together. "It was a long time ago," she said coldly. "We were younger then. Times have changed."

"But would you consider my plan?" Kate asked. "Please? I mean, you don't have to be involved in any way if you don't want to, but would you please drop your petition and give me a chance to try this?"

"We've gone to a lot of work organizing that petition," Aggie said. "All the paperwork and everything. If I drop it now, I'll probably just have to do it all again later on."

"All I'm asking is a chance," Kate said earnestly. "If I open this bar and it turns out to cause the kind of problems you expect, I won't even argue with you. I'll revoke the license voluntarily."

Aggie's eyes were cold and unrevealing behind her glasses. "We'll have to hold a meeting," she said. "The committee needs to vote on it."

Kate looked at her, knowing that the committee was firmly under Aggie's thumb and would vote exactly as their chairwoman dictated. But she couldn't think of anything else to say. She got to her feet and picked up her briefcase. "May I at least leave the papers for you to look at?"

Aggie inclined her head. "I won't need them for very long. I'll drop them off at the hotel tomorrow."

"All right." Kate paused by the door, searching for some argument that would sway this implacable woman. At last, she gave up, murmured her thanks for the coffee and emerged into the sunlight, hurrying down the walkway toward the picket fence.

Her heart sank when she saw a familiar truck parked by the curb, obviously waiting for her. Nathan Cameron leaned against the fender, arms folded, whistling quietly between his teeth as he studied the row of houses drowsing in the sunlight.

"Hello, Nathan," Kate said as he came around and opened the passenger door for her.

"Hilda told me you'd gone to pay Aggie a visit. I thought I'd stop by and give you a ride back to the hotel."

"Thank you." Kate climbed into the truck, then looked out the window in alarm as he drove off along the street and turned at the corner. "Nathan, where are you going?"

"I thought we could go for a little drive in the country before we go back. Is that okay? Or would you rather we talked at the hotel, and included your ex-husband in the conversation?"

She shook her head and settled back reluctantly against the padded seat.

"Did you get anywhere with Aggie?" Nathan asked, pulling off the highway and parking in an approach road beside a small grove of poplars. A hay meadow spread beyond them, full of sweet clover and alfalfa. At the edge of the field, a row of beehives hummed with activity in the morning sunlight.

Nathan opened his window, filling the truck cab with the scent of clover. Kate rested her head against the back of the seat, eyes closed, desperately wishing that a little of the peace all around her could somehow find its way into her troubled spirit.

"Kate?" Nathan prompted. "Did you talk Aggie into cutting you some slack?"

"I don't think so. I doubt that anybody could change the woman's mind. I think she's planning to roll over me and squash me."

Nathan was silent, but Kate could feel his eyes resting on her.

"Aggie tells me that the town suspects me of sleeping with Adam, since he spent last night at the hotel," she said. "Everybody seems to know every detail of my private life."

"They seem to," Nathan agreed calmly. "At least, they think your marriage is back on track and we're going to have a celebrity in our midst."

"And what do you think?"

"Does it matter what I think?"

She hesitated, reluctant to let him know just how much it mattered. "You and I are friends, Nathan, if nothing else. I certainly value your good opinion."

"Well, then, you've still got it. After all, I can hardly blame you for loving somebody."

"I don't love Adam!" she said. "And I didn't sleep with him, either. I could hardly believe it when Aggie said that."

He nodded, his face unreadable.

"Adam proposed to me this morning," Kate went on, gazing out at the sun-washed field. "He said he'd even be willing to adopt a baby and let me have all the things I wanted from life. But it's too late."

"Was that one of the main problems in your marriage? Not having kids?"

Kate nodded. "Adam can't have children, and he simply refused to adopt. I think he didn't want children because he's still a child himself, in spite of all his fame and money. He probably always will be."

"You told me that once before, the day we were out at my ranch. I asked if you wouldn't prefer to have a man instead of a boy, and you never gave me an answer."

Kate stared at the row of beehives while Nathan leaned toward her. "Look, Kate, I'm not the kind of man who begs a woman for love. It's not easy for me to do this, but I'm begging you right now to listen to me. I want you, Kate, and I want a family, too. I'm promising you that I won't let you down or disappoint you. If you tie your life to mine, you'll be safe and you'll have all the things you want."

"But that's the problem!" Kate said in despair. "You can tell me that, Nathan, and I believe you really mean it. But how can you make a promise like that? If I marry you, I'll be giving up all the independence I've tried to achieve. I'll be putting my life into a man's hands, just like I did with Adam, and hoping he'll be kind to me. That's what my mother wants me to do, but I'm not willing to risk it another time."

Nathan drummed his fingers on the steering wheel. "Look, Kate," he said abruptly, "I've been thinking about things."

"What things?"

"About my mother, and the way she looks at life, and what you're trying to accomplish with your hotel. I'm starting to realize that I'll have to change some of my attitudes if I want a woman like you."

"What do you mean?"

"For one thing, I have to quit looking at my ranch as if it represents some kind of powerful dynasty that matters more than anything else. I can't expect you to be as wrapped up in the business of being a Cameron wife as my mother and grandmother were. If a man loves a modern woman," he added with a fleeting grin, "I guess he has to be willing to give her some freedom."

Kate glanced at him in surprise, then looked out the window again. "You know what? I feel the same as I did with Adam this morning," she said at last. "You're saying all the things I wanted to hear, but I'm afraid it's too little, too late."

"Why?"

"I guess," Kate said simply, "I've finally outgrown the belief that I need to have a man's permission to be happy. You say that you're willing to give me some freedom. I don't believe my freedom or my happiness is up to you. I have to make myself happy. Every woman does."

"And you honestly believe you'll be happiest on your own? You're content to go through your life without ever having a husband and children, just so you're not answering to anyone else? You won't mind sleeping alone in that bed every night?''

In spite of herself, Kate remembered the night this man had come to her bed, the tender sweetness of his kisses and the utter fulfillment of his lovemaking. She thought, too, about all the good times they'd had, the way they always laughed easily together and shared such similar tastes and outlooks. But these memories were too dangerous to consider. She banished them with firm resolve.

"Let's leave all that out of it, shall we?"

"Leave what out of it?"

"Sex," Kate said. "Physical attraction. God knows, people make terrible mistakes over the issue of sex, and who they'd like to sleep with. I enjoyed sleeping with you, Nathan," she added, forcing herself to look straight at him. "You know I did. There's no doubt that we're terrific in bed. But that doesn't mean we could have a happy marriage."

"Why not?"

"Because I don't really *know* you," Kate said in despair. "I don't know what I can expect from you."

"Kate, you know me better than any woman ever has. We've spent hours talking to each other about the things that matter to us."

"Maybe so. But can a woman ever know a man well enough to trust that he won't change his ways once she's put her life in his hands?"

Nathan took her arm and drew her closer to him, his eyes blazing. "Look, Kate," he said tightly. "You may have dealt with men like that in the past, but I wasn't raised that way. I'm not the kind of man who betrays a woman's trust. That's not how the men in my family behave. If I promise you freedom and independence, then you can be damned sure you'll have them."

"Can I?" she asked, knowing she was being completely irrational, but unable to stop herself. "Can I, Nathan? And what about your great-grandfather, old Joshua Cameron? Why were those cottonwood trees at your ranch not planted until he was over seventy years old, if all the men in your family are so great at keeping their promises?"

He stared at her, his eyes widening in bewilderment. "Trees?" he asked blankly. "When did we start talking about *trees?*"

"Never mind," Kate said, drawing away from him and huddling against the passenger door. "Take me home, please. I have a hundred things to do. I can't sit here all day arguing with you."

"Kate..."

"Please," she repeated firmly. "I want to go home now."

Nathan swore under his breath, turned on the engine and headed toward town. Kate sat next to him, silent with a growing sense of loss that made her eyes burn with unshed tears.

"Look, Kate," Nathan said at last, his voice quiet and tightly controlled, "I'm not as patient as Luther Barnes. I can't hang around forever, waiting for you to change your mind and decide to give me a chance."

Kate stared out the window, not trusting herself to speak.

"So if this is your final word, you likely won't be seeing me again," Nathan went on. "I won't keep calling you and bothering you. If you need my help with anything, let me know. Otherwise, I'll just wish you well and hope things work out for you."

"Oh, Nathan..." Kate gave him a pleading glance, but his face was hard and unyielding. "All right," she said formally when he stopped in front of the hotel. "Thank you for the ride."

He inclined his head with distant courtesy, waited as she got out and shut the door, then drove off. Kate stood watching while his truck was swallowed up in a blurry lake of heat waves that shimmered on the road.

At last, feeling lonely and unutterably weary, she turned and trudged up the steps to the hotel entrance.

CHAPTER THIRTEEN

Friday, March 10, 1905

In the course of writing this diary, I note that I have referred to quite a number of occasions as the most momentous day of my life. The problem with superlatives is that when something truly momentous happens, one is left with nothing to say. I suppose I really must learn to be more disciplined in my use of language.

Still, I cannot resist saying that today was truly astonishing, and the next few days will surely be the most important I have yet lived through! For one thing, this weekend I am sternly required to reach my final decision and let Joshua know what I have decided about his proposal.

"March twelfth," he told me last Sunday when we went for a drive together. "I'll give you until March twelfth, and not a day longer."

"Why is that such a significant date?" I asked, smiling.

"Because it's my birthday," he said. "And I want you, sweet Ellen, to give me the nicest birthday gift I've ever had."

He will be thirty-four years old.

I like to think of Joshua thirty-odd years ago, a little dark-eyed boy in short pants. What a beautiful child he must have been, with such fire and intelligence. If I choose to marry him, my children will be like that. The thought warms my heart. But I am not going to waste this entire diary entry with still more descriptions of Joshua Cameron! Another event has intervened, something so incredible that my decision is no longer the forgone conclusion that I had come to believe it was going to be.

Let me start at the beginning of my day or I will never get to the meat of the story.

When I arrived at school, I found the attendance even more sadly diminished than it has been in recent weeks. Apparently, we are having an unseasonably mild spring for this region, and many of my older students are already helping to clean seed and prepare machinery for the spring planting. In addition, a number of the smaller children are sick with the colds and sore throats that are common with the advent of milder weather.

"Spring fever," Joshua says. "That's what they've got, poor little duffers, and I don't blame them. I feel like a sick calf myself this spring."

How funny he is! He makes me laugh so much that ladies turn and frown at me on the street, thinking my behavior most unseemly for a lady schoolteacher.

I am afraid that Amy Lord and her mother do not merely frown. They glare at me with an intensity of hatred that is quite unsettling. I am sorry to anger them, but as Joshua says, he can hardly be compelled to court Amy simply because she wants him so fiercely.

He assures me that he has already ordered a thousand cottonwood seedlings, and plans to set them out as soon as his crop is planted and the cows have finished calving. Oddly enough, the seedlings are to be shipped by rail from a nursery quite near my home back in Ontario. In years to come, if I should decide to accept Joshua's proposal, those trees would be such a comfort to me! Every time I looked at their rustling green branches, it would seem like a little bit of home in the midst of this strange landscape....

But enough of such fruitless daydreaming, and back to school.

There were only thirteen students in school when the bell was rung and I called the roll. Every class was lacking at least one or two of the regular attendees, and so I was reluctant to embark on any new work. Besides, the day was so lovely. We left the door open, and the scent of damp earth and the call of birds drifted inside, enticing all of us.

Soon I abandoned the arithmetic exercise we had been doing and announced a day of field trips and nature study. A chorus of lusty cheers greeted my suggestion. Without delay we all put on our coats and galoshes, gathered up our lunch pails and set off to roam the fields around the schoolhouse.

What fun we had! We collected bugs, picked various kinds of plants to dry and press, studied bird and insect life and wrote down as many signs of spring as we could find, everything from the arrival of two crows to the sluggish stirring of big red ants on an anthill.

We found a dry spot at the top of a knoll to have our lunch. The day was warm enough that most of the children shed their coats and sat on them, basking in the bright sunlight. We sang songs and chattered so freely that I found it hard to believe these same children were once so coldly suspicious of me. I truly love being a teacher. I enjoy nothing more than the challenge of planting seeds of knowledge in the minds of children and watching as they take root and grow.

Knowledge is so liberating! Some of these children will grow up to do things I cannot imagine. Perhaps they will travel the world, become heads of state, writers or scholars, and all because at an early stage they were inspired with a love of books and learning. I feel quite awed and humble when I contemplate the scope of my influence. I also feel dreadfully troubled about the decision I am now forced to make. But more of that later.

By midafternoon, I realized that I had miscalculated the time. Distances are terribly deceptive here because one can see so far, all the way to a horizon that can be more than forty miles away. The sun was dropping and the air grew cool, and we were still a couple of miles from the school. We began to hurry along the road, hoping to arrive in time so the parents would not be kept waiting.

Karen and I took turns carrying little Herman, who seems to be coming down with the spring cold that has afflicted so many of the children. He was feverish and fretful, too tired to walk any farther on his fat little legs.

But sick or not, he is a very solid lump to carry, and I was quite relieved when Joshua came along in his wagon, heading back home from town. He gave all of us a ride to the school, where I was pleased to find that Mr. Mueller waited to take his brood home. On many days when their father is busy, they are required to

walk the four miles to their farm. I delivered Herman
into his care, advising that Karen put the poor little
fellow to bed with some hot tea and a mustard plaster.

Joshua looked on, smiling, as they drove away.
"Karen's a motherly soul," he commented when he
saw my concern. "She'll take good care of Herman."

"I wonder if she knows how to make a mustard
plaster," I fretted. "If the mixture is too strong, or if
she leaves the paper on too long, it will burn his skin.
But it still needs to be—"

"Ellen, Ellen," he murmured, taking me into his
arms and kissing me in masterful fashion—fortunately, all the children had left the schoolyard by then,
and we were quite alone. "My dearest, you can't look
after everyone. Herman will be all right. Come on,
let's go. I'll give you a ride to town."

"But I have my pony cart here, and Mouse is in the
barn waiting for me."

He grinned. Joshua is always tickled by the fondness I have for Mouse, who is a wonderful horse, sweet
tempered and reliable. Over the winter, Mouse and I
have become fast friends.

"All right," he said at last, laughing. "Leave me if
you insist. Go your independent way, my darling Miss
Livingston. But I'll be calling for you on Sunday afternoon and I expect you to have an answer for me."

"I will have an answer," I assured him, walking
with him to the barn to fit the harness on Mouse. And
at that time, I felt quite confident that I would. I was
certain that I would be saying, "Yes, Joshua, I will
marry you and share your life." I still want to say it,
most desperately. But I am in such a quandary!

When I arrived at the hotel, Mrs. Goldman had left a bundle of guest mail on the desk in the lobby. Mr. McLean collects the mail on Friday when he travels to the city, and we await it here with such eagerness. I found several letters for myself, one from Auntie Grace, one from Mama and Papa and a nice fat letter from my friend, Emily. It is so hard to believe that Emily is now expecting her second baby. She is just one year older than I am!

I clutched my bundle of letters with happy anticipation. Suddenly, my eye was caught by an official-looking envelope addressed to me, lying near the bottom of the pile.

The letter is open on my desk as I write, and I can still hardly believe what it says. My letter is from the director of the Calgary School Board. He congratulates me on the work I have done in Wolf Hill during the current term, and offers me—I tremble even to think of it!—the position of vice principal in one of the larger city schools, effective this coming September.

This is an unheard-of honor. I believe that I might well be the first female in all of western Canada to hold such a lofty administrative position, and I have not yet reached my twenty-first birthday.

But perhaps they are not aware of that. I am sure this job was offered to me because of a presentation I made at a school board meeting in January in the city, when I spoke about the problems of educating children in rural areas and urged the development of a more unified curriculum. I wore my navy shirtwaist, of course, and dressed my hair in a rather severe fashion, so perhaps they thought I was more grown-up and formidable than I really am.

At any rate, I am sorely tempted. I would have the opportunity to test many of my beliefs and principles related to education. And I would be able to teach in a setting where I would have access to all the most modern equipment, and the opportunity to make a real difference. The thought makes me quite giddy with excitement.

But what would I tell Joshua? And even if he should be willing to wait for me, can I bear to live without him? I know it would not be easy. I have grown so accustomed to spending time with him, and so attached to the prospect of sharing our lives that I feel desolate at the thought of postponing all those dreams.

Whatever am I to do? My head aches with the effort of this decision.

I suppose I can only follow Papa's suggestion for the best course of action when one has a difficult choice to make. Papa always advised me to sleep on the problem and look for inspiration in the morning. That is probably the best advice, because at this hour of the night when the moon is shining and the owl hoots down by the river in such mournful fashion, all I can think of is Joshua and how terribly I want him!

KATE LAY IN BED with her reading lamp on, struggling to decipher Ellen's faded handwriting. She turned eagerly to the next page, then stopped in dismay.

The rest of the diary was blank. There were four pages remaining at the end of the book, but nothing was written on them at all, not even a hint about what Ellen had finally decided.

Kate stared at the empty pages, startled and disappointed. What if she never learned what had finally happened to Ellen? Maybe she could ask Nathan if...

She sagged miserably against the pillows, remembering that she and Nathan weren't even speaking to each other these days. Probably his mother could help, but Kate was reluctant to approach Marian Cameron, considering the way things stood between herself and Nathan. She'd just have to think of some other way to solve the mystery.

A FEW DAYS LATER, Kate sat on the floor in the hotel dining room, surrounded by a small mountain of packing crates and invoice slips.

"Hilda," she called, "it looks as if they've made a mistake. We have ten boxes of dessert forks, and only six cartons of soupspoons. It that what you ordered?"

Hilda bustled in from the kitchen, looking harried. "Lord, no!" she muttered. "We'll be serving far more soup than dessert. Folks these days are just plain stupid when it comes to desserts."

"Why?" Kate asked, diverted as always by her cook's vigorous opinions.

Hilda snorted in contempt. "They got some idea that rich food ain't good for them. Damn fools."

"But isn't that true?" Kate asked innocently.

"Maybe so." Hilda frowned at the soupspoons. "But it don't make a whole lot of difference if they eat bits of lettuce in my dining room, then go home and stuff themselves with cake and potato chips when they figure nobody's looking.''

Kate chuckled. ''You're certainly right about that.'' She looked up as Adam approached, carrying a shoulder bag and a large suitcase.

Kate hadn't seen much of her ex-husband since the morning when he'd tried so earnestly to talk her back into his life. Never one to brood over a lost cause, Adam had spent the remainder of his holiday traveling around the countryside, setting the quiet little towns on their ears. He especially liked to go into a local bar, sit down with his guitar in a corner and start singing, then watch as the word spread and the place filled up with screaming fans, most of them too young to be on licensed premises.

''It's really good for my image,'' he'd told Kate earnestly.

''To say nothing of your ego,'' she'd answered dryly.

''You quit picking on me, Katie. I'm not such a bad guy. And I've learned some good stuff, too,'' he'd retorted. ''A lot of the weird minor chords they use in these old cowboy ballads are fantastic, you know.''

Remembering, she smiled and got to her feet. ''Are you off for good, Adam?''

''I'm flying out of Calgary this afternoon, headed for the Big Apple. We're planning a major tour of New York, Pennsylvania and the Eastern Seaboard this summer.''

''It sounds great.''

Adam gave her one of his winning smiles. ''You could still come with me, Katie. I'd love to have you.

We'll go first class all the way, stay at the Plaza, do all the tourist stuff..."

Kate patted his arm. "A lovely offer, Adam, but I have this hotel to run. See, I'm counting spoons today. How could I possibly go to New York?"

He chuckled, but there was a wistful look in his eye as he lifted his big suitcase and headed for the door.

"Adam, you're welcome any time you'd like to drop in. You know that."

He turned and nodded. "Thanks, I might take you up on that in the fall. Luther and Carl promised to take me hunting. I like this place, Katie."

"It's a nice place," she agreed quietly. "Oh, one more thing..."

He stopped in the doorway and gave her an inquiring glance.

"Adam, don't believe everything my mother tells you. She means well, but she's not always as right about things as she believes."

"You know, I'm not so sure about that."

Kate looked at him with sudden suspicion. "Why not?"

"Well," Adam said, grinning, "Mamie told me that you and the cowboy were made for each other, and if I didn't get here pretty soon, I'd be losing you forever. And you know what? I think she was right."

Stunned into silence, Kate watched while he crossed the lobby and left the hotel, swallowed up immediately by a throng of his loyal fans on Rollerblade skates and skateboards.

She stood erect with her hands full of spoons, thinking about Nathan.

This was a luxury she seldom allowed herself these days because it brought her so much suffering. Only after she'd sent him away did Kate begin to realize how much she valued the man, how dependable and passionate and funny he was. When she pictured his keen dark face, his tall body and the lithe ease of his step, she felt an actual physical pain that stabbed all the way to the core of her, leaving her feeling weak and shaky with desire.

But that was all it was, Kate told herself firmly. It was just desire. That last day, she'd told Nathan that people made terrible mistakes in the name of sexual attraction. There were far more important things to be considered, things like...

"This big celebration we're planning," Hilda announced from the kitchen as if continuing the conversation in Kate's head. "I been thinking."

Kate dragged herself back to reality with an effort. "Yes, Hilda? What have you been thinking?"

Hilda appeared in the doorway with her hands wrapped in an apron. She actually looked, if Kate's eyes weren't deceiving her, a little shy and tentative.

Kate gazed at her in astonishment. "Hilda?" she asked.

"Well, this whole celebration thing, it's about union, right? About the province of Alberta joining Canada and us becoming one country, and the hotel joining the town again and all that, so I thought it might be a pretty good time for a..."

"For what?"

"A wedding," Hilda said, her fat cheeks turning as pink as her apron. "Me and Luther."

"Oh, *Hilda!*" Kate hugged her warmly. "What a wonderful idea. We can serve wedding cake after the meal and have toasts to Canada, to Wolf Hill and to the bride and groom. Three happy occasions, and lots of chance to sell champagne. If I get my liquor license by then," she added, suddenly gloomy.

"Still no word from Aggie?"

"Not a whisper. I'm getting really worried." Kate brooded over the scattered boxes of utensils, all monogrammed WHH. "I've done my very best, Hilda. If she's still opposed, I'm a dead duck."

"Poor Katie." Hilda hugged her with such surprising tenderness that Kate had to fight back a sudden rush of emotion.

"We shouldn't be talking about *me,*" she murmured, smiling at the plump little woman in her candy-striped apron. "You're the blushing bride, after all. What does Luther think? Is he overjoyed?"

"Luther doesn't exactly know about it yet," Hilda said. "But," she added serenely, "there's no doubt that he'll be tickled."

"Hilda, Luther will have to be told in advance, you know. He can hardly turn up in a plaid shirt and bib overalls for his own wedding."

"Luther," Hilda said with dignity, "will look very spiffy. You just wait and see."

She started toward the kitchen, then paused and turned to Kate with a shrewd glance. "Why don't we make it a double wedding?"

"I beg your pardon?" Kate frowned at a carton of salad plates. "Look, Hilda, these plates are smaller than the ones we ordered, aren't they? I thought we wanted the nine-inch size, but these are..."

"No problem," Hilda said grandly, waving her arm. "We can use the smaller ones for pie and toast. I *said*, why don't we have a double wedding? You can get married at the same time."

"I'd love to, but you've already gone and nabbed Luther and he's the most eligible bachelor in town."

"Don't tease me, girl. Nathan Cameron is the sweetest man in the world, and he's crazy about you. Furthermore," Hilda went on relentlessly, coming a few steps back into the room, "you feel exactly the same way. I can see it whenever you look at him. You're just dying to get your hands on him. Every time he walks into a room, your eyes light up and your face goes all pink and full of smiles, and you start to bounce. If that ain't love, I sure don't know what is."

Kate hesitated, staring at the other woman's face without really seeing her. "Hilda," she said abruptly, "tell me something."

"Sure. What do you what to know?"

"Is there any way I can find out about something that happened in this town a long time ago?"

"How long ago?"

Kate looked down at the salad plate in her hands. "Say, about ninety years ago. Right around the time we happen to be honoring in our celebration. If I wanted to know what happened to a specific person in the town back then, where would I look?"

Hilda frowned, thinking. "There was a time you could go to the newspaper office. They kept copies of all the old papers."

"But the first newspaper office burned down in the sixties, didn't it?"

"It got struck by lightning, and they lost everything in the fire. Now, the only record of town history is the stuff in people's scrapbooks. But most folks just save the clippings that have something to do with their own family."

Kate frowned. "I'm not really sure if this person... if she married into a local family or not."

"Then your best bet would be checking with somebody who saved a whole lot of stuff, general-interest things and old newspapers."

"Somebody like Marian Cameron," Kate said, her heart sinking.

Hilda nodded calmly. "Marian's got the best collection of local history in the province."

"But, Hilda, I..." Kate gripped the plate and looked nervously out the window.

"Marian Cameron's a good woman," Hilda said gently. "She may seem a little high-and-mighty sometimes, but that's mostly for show. Deep down, she's always been a real generous neighbor and a good friend to folks around here."

"I know. But I feel so—"

"If there's something you want to know about town history, you go see Marian Cameron," Hilda said firmly. "Meantime, finish getting that china unpacked if you want to help me. I got two hundred people to feed, and a couple of weeks to get ready, and I'm getting married besides."

THE NEXT MORNING, Kate was still brooding over the mystery of Ellen Livingston. She stood in the hotel lobby, leafing though a bundle of mail on the desk.

Ellen must have stood here exactly the same way, looking for her name on the—

Kate stiffened, clutching an official-looking envelope with a government seal. She glanced nervously around the empty lobby, then carried the envelope into her office, closed the door and sat at her desk. The letter read:

Dear Mrs. Daniels,

Regarding the petition filed against your liquor license by the townspeople of Wolf Hill: we are pleased to inform you that this action has now been suspended. Because all necessary paperwork has been filed as of this date, we will proceed summarily with...

Kate's eyes blurred with tears. She dropped her face onto her folded arms and sat for a long time listening to the hum of bees in the flowering spirea beyond the window.

At last she drew herself together and got slowly to her feet.

There was so much to do, so many plans to make. Kate knew that she should settle at her desk and get to work right away. She needed to start calling people, place some orders, hire staff and organize a schedule of activities in the bar. She also had to ask Raymond to polish the floors and do an initial touch-up of the place. The bundles of wallpaper needed to be looked at and...

But she did none of those things. Instead, she left the room and moved slowly across the lobby, climbing the stairs to the second floor, then the third. All alone, Kate walked through her hotel, gazing into the quiet bedrooms with their pretty brass headboards and flowered wallpaper, their antique dressers and bright hooked rugs.

She made her way downstairs again, running her fingers along the polished banister. Everything she looked at, everything she touched bore the stamp of her hard work and effort. Much of the restoration she'd done with her own callused hands, stripping paint, polishing woodwork, applying endless rolls of wallpaper.

At last she passed through the main floor to her bedroom, the room where she and Ellen Livingston had shared so much, even though ninety years stood between them.

"I did it, Ellen," Kate murmured aloud, crossing the room to stand by the French door where Ellen had once hidden her diary. "I really did it."

She looked at the charming bedroom, wondering again what Ellen had finally decided about her own life and the momentous decision she had to make. Kate felt fairly certain that the young schoolteacher hadn't married Joshua Cameron. Had she ever seen him again? Did she take the job in Calgary and make a success of it? Most intriguing of all, what woman did Joshua finally marry, if not Ellen?

But Ellen's diary lay silently in the top drawer of Kate's dresser, yielding up no answers to these questions.

"KATE, you got to get this woman under control," Hilda said darkly, a few days after the liquor license was formally granted. "I'm warning you, I can't stand much more of it."

Across the table, Kate labored over a pile of bar menus, a calligraphy pen in her hand. "How do you spell 'amaretto'? Is it all double consonants, or what?"

"G-o-n-e," Hilda said.

Kate glanced up, startled.

"That's me, if you don't get Aggie out of my hair pretty soon."

Kate chuckled. "There, there," she murmured soothingly. "You just have a touch of bridal jitters, dear. It'll be all right. We'll have a little talk about what to expect on your wedding night, and you'll be fine."

"Oh, sure," Hilda said with a wicked grin. "I could likely tell you a thing or two, my girl. But that Aggie," she went on, her smile fading, "is just too much for me."

Kate sighed and set her pen down. "What's the problem now?"

"She's got this big darts and shuffleboard tournament organized in the bar for opening night, right?"

Kate nodded. "I asked her to do that. She's a wonderful organizer, Hilda, and she's got that committee right under her thumb. You should see the charts they've drawn up. And she's got all the local merchants bullied into donating huge prizes, too. It's going to be so much fun. I wish I had a partner," Kate added, feeling a little melancholy.

"Sure, the woman's a good organizer," Hilda said heatedly, "but that don't give her any right to organize my kitchen."

"Is she trying to?"

"She's got it scheduled right here on her fancy little program. Lunch, it says. And she's got the nerve to come around and tell me what I'm supposed to prepare and how to serve it, like I'm one of them dumb little maids in a black dress and frilly apron."

Kate tried without success to picture Hilda in a maid's outfit. "I'll talk to Aggie," she promised.

Hilda snorted. "A fat lot of good that'll do."

"Oh, you're wrong. I can handle Aggie," Kate said calmly. "We've reached an understanding."

Hilda gave her a shrewd glance. "You've come a long way, haven't you, honey?"

"Not all that far," Kate said dryly. "I'm still terrified of Raymond. I'm putty in his hands. But I think I've finally learned to accept it as an understandable weakness."

Hilda smiled at her, then sobered. "So why ain't you happy?"

"I beg your pardon?"

"Talk to the man, Katie," Hilda urged her gently. "Anybody can see you're dying for him, and Bessie says poor Nathan feels the same way."

"He does?" Kate bit her lip and stared at her friend.

"Bessie says she's never seen him so cut up over anything. He just mopes around his ranch, spends hours out riding, won't talk to anybody, face as dark as a thundercloud..."

"Hilda, aren't you afraid?" Kate asked abruptly.

"Of what?"

"Of marriage. Of giving up your independence after all these years. Don't you worry that it might not work out? It seems like such a terrible risk, marrying someone and agreeing to share his life.''

Hilda took Kate's hand across the table and squeezed it gently. ''Everything's a risk, honey,'' she said. ''Getting up in the morning, that's risky. Driving your car on the highway is a terrible danger. Every time you ride in an elevator, it means putting your life in the hands of fate. I s'pose,'' she added thoughtfully, ''it's harder for you, when you're getting over a bad experience. But me, I look on this marriage to Luther as a calculated risk.''

''Because you—''

''Because I know,'' Hilda said with a placid smile, ''that life don't come with guarantees, not ever. But if a woman's real careful about picking her man, she can't go far wrong. She just needs to get the right man, that's all.''

Kate sat for a moment, staring at the pile of menus she was lettering. Finally, she capped her pen, pushed the work aside and got to her feet. ''Look after things here for a while, would you, Hilda?'' she asked. ''I'm going into the city this afternoon.''

CHAPTER FOURTEEN

THE SUN SHONE warmly on Kate's shoulders as she walked up the tree-lined path to the condominium, feeling a little nervous about her reception.

But when Marian answered the door, her manner was as gracious as ever. "Hello, Kate," she said. "It's always so nice to see you. Come in and tell me all your news. I hear that wonderful things are happening in that old hotel."

"Isn't Josh home?" Kate asked, crossing the room and seating herself in one of the comfortable leather armchairs.

"No, he's gone to the stock show with a couple of neighbors from Wolf Hill. For some reason, men just love to walk around those smelly pens and look at all the prize cows."

Kate smiled, enjoying the thought of Josh Cameron and his friends wandering through the pens of fat, glossy livestock.

"So, what's all this I hear about Aggie?" Marian asked, seating herself opposite Kate. "You've really got her on board? She's dropped her petition altogether?"

"Not only that, but her committee's taken over the scheduling of social activities in the bar. Which reminds me, I'm supposed to ask if you and Josh want to enter the darts tournament on opening day. They've got a couple of spots open.''

"Certainly," Marian said without hesitation. "What time does it get under way?"

"That's still tentative, but you're going to be there all day, aren't you? We're cutting the ribbon in the lobby at noon, and then everybody's going down to the park for the wedding picnic, and speeches from the mayor and the town council..."

"There hasn't been a day like that in Wolf Hill for years. You've done a lot of good things for the community, Kate."

"It hasn't been easy," Kate said with a sigh.

"Worthwhile things usually aren't. Has Hilda's buffalo meat been delivered yet?"

"Yesterday. Walter Hamill sold us his two big freezers.... You know, the ones that used to be in the dining room, full of animal carcasses?"

"Oh, yes. I remember Walter's taxidermy business."

"Well," Kate said, "Raymond moved them downstairs and Hilda's got them stuffed full with rhubarb pies and buffalo cuts. Sometimes I wake up and can't believe the things that are happening in my life."

"I'm not surprised. How's the hotel end of things going?"

"We're fully booked for opening weekend with all the people who are coming for the celebrations. This whole thing has turned into a kind of town reunion as well as our grand opening. And we're also booked through hunting season, even though it's months ahead. And with the bar opening, too..."

"You're going to make a go of it," Marian concluded when Kate fell silent.

"Yes." Kate leaned forward to rap the coffee table superstitiously with her knuckles. "I believe I am."

"Good for you. And Hilda's really marrying Luther after all these years. I can hardly believe it. Talk about miracles."

"The ceremony will be in the park under the rose arbor. Bessie's going to be her maid of honor, and I'm a bridesmaid."

"And Nathan will be Luther's best man."

Kate tensed. "I know. I haven't...talked to him lately."

Marian raised her eyebrows, but said nothing.

Kate stared at the rustling green trees beyond the window. "Marian," she said at last.

"Yes?"

"Did you ever hear of a woman called Ellen Livingston?"

Marian frowned in concentration, then shook her head. "The name rings a bell," she said at last, "but I can't put my finger on it. Should I know her?"

"She was the first schoolteacher in Wolf Hill, back in 1904. You have a picture of her in one of your old photograph albums. I thought she might have... married Nathan's great-grandfather."

"I'm afraid she didn't, but she probably would have been around when he got married. Why do you ask?"

Kate hesitated, struggling with her emotions. Part of her was bitterly disappointed to learn for certain that Ellen had decided against marriage to Joshua. But in a way, she was also relieved because Joshua, despite his charm, had apparently turned out not to be a man of his word.

No doubt he would have made Ellen miserable....

"Kate?"

She shook her head. "I'll tell you the whole story later. First, I'd really like to find out what happened to her. I was hoping you'd let me look at some of those old newspapers from the end of the first school term, the spring of 1905, and see if they mention Ellen Livingston."

Marian brightened, always happy at the thought of historical research. "Of course. I'll get the papers and you can make us some tea. You know where everything is, don't you?"

A few minutes later, Kate brought the teapot and a pair of cups into the living room where Marian was already sorting through the stacks of yellowed papers, her reading glasses perched on her nose. "The spring of 1904, you said?"

"No, it was 1905. I think she probably finished the school term and then went to Calgary, but I'd really like to know for sure. They would have held some kind of going-away ceremony for her, and I'm certain it'll be mentioned in the paper."

Marian returned to her task. There was silence in the room as both women leafed through the piles of pages.

"Here's something from June 1905," Marian said, then frowned. "It talks about the close of the school term, and says Mrs. Oates was the teacher."

"Mrs. *Oates?*" Kate looked at the paper in confusion. "But...I don't understand. Surely Ellen wouldn't have left before the term ended. She just wasn't that kind of person."

Marian gave her a thoughtful glance, then returned to the papers. "Well, let's see if there's something earlier. You know, I really should go through all these papers and put them in some kind of chronological order, shouldn't I? They're such a hodgepodge. Oh," she murmured softly, looking up at Kate.

"What?"

Silently, Marian handed over a sheet of paper and indicated an article at the top of the page. Kate read it, her eyes widening in horror.

Saturday, March 25, 1905

The townspeople of Wolf Hill were saddened today to learn that the recent diphtheria epidemic has claimed another victim. Miss Ellen Livingston, our beloved schoolmistress, passed away yesterday evening in her hotel room in Wolf Hill. Dr. Wilson, called in from Calgary to attend the victims of the epidemic, said that Miss Livingston's death was due to heart failure brought on by the disease, after a courageous two-week battle with her illness. Her dearest friends, Mrs. Sarah Oates and Mr. Joshua Cameron, were at her bedside at the time of her passing. Miss Livingston will be sorely missed by all who knew and loved her. Funeral services will be held on...

The faded print blurred in front of Kate's eyes. She was dimly conscious of Marian hovering nearby, looking at her in concern. "Kate? My dear, what is it? What's the matter?"

Kate buried her face in her hands. After a while, she looked up, sniffling, and rummaged in her pocket for a tissue. "Isn't this silly? The woman died ninety years ago. If she'd lived, she'd be a hundred and ten by now. And yet I feel as if...as if I'd just lost my best friend."

"Who was she, Kate? How did you happen to know about her?"

Kate shook her head, unable to speak.

She wondered why it had never before occurred to her that there was something really odd about finding that diary in her hotel room. She should have realized right from the beginning that a woman like Ellen would never have gone away and left her diary in its hiding place. Of course she would have retrieved it and taken it with her if she'd been able.

But she hadn't gone away. Ellen had died in the very room that Kate slept in. Her final diary entry had probably been the last thing she wrote in her lifetime. She'd recorded the details of her momentous day and the decision she had to make, then hidden away her diary under the window ledge. Within days, perhaps even hours, the disease had struck, ravaging her body and weakening her gallant heart.

Kate thought of the young schoolteacher plodding wearily down a prairie road, carrying little Herman and worrying over his sickness, grateful because Joshua came along in his wagon to give them a ride....

Suddenly, Kate was struck by another thought.

"Marian," she said slowly. "Who did Joshua Cameron marry? Who was Nathan's great-grandmother?"

"I barely remember her, though she outlived old Joshua by quite a few years. I'm not sure of her maiden name, but her first name was Amy."

"Amy Lord," Kate said. "That's who she was. Her name was Amy Lord."

Marian looked at her in surprise. "Josh says she wasn't a nice person at all. She used to scream at his grandfather until the windows rattled. But I guess old Joshua gave back as good as he got. He was a real tartar, Kate."

"That's not true," Kate said. "He was a generous, loving man with a wonderful sense of humor. No wonder he got so bitter and miserable, being married to Amy. He only married her because she chased him, and after Ellen died, he had no will to resist. His heart was broken."

Suddenly, Kate remembered the cottonwood trees.

As clearly as if he were there in front of her, she saw the lonely old man, disappointed in his marriage and crippled by arthritis, paying homage to a dear love he'd lost forty years earlier and never forgotten.

"The trees," she whispered. "He planted Ellen's trees before he died. It was the last thing he did."

"It sure was. Josh says the old fellow was like a man possessed. Once he got it in his head that he wanted those cottonwood trees planted, there was no stopping him. He practically worked until he dropped."

"And now they make a lovely green avenue, all the way up to the house," Kate said softly. "They're like a forest on the prairie."

Marian nodded. "I've always been grateful to old Joshua for those trees, although nobody really knew why he planted them. He seemed driven to it by something inside him."

"He loved her," Kate said. "He never stopped loving her. Oh, Marian..."

She began to cry helplessly while Marian patted her shoulder and murmured soothing words. Kate struggled to get herself under control, but so many feelings raged inside her.

At last she managed to pull herself together and give Marian a rueful, teary smile. "I'm sorry about this. I feel like such an idiot."

"You've been through a difficult time," Marian said gently. "No wonder your emotions are a little frayed."

Kate rummaged in her shoulder bag and took out the old diary, putting it into Marian's hands. "This should be yours," she said, her voice shaking. "Once you've read it, I think you'll understand Josh's grandfather better. I'm sorry I kept it so long, but I was..." She fell silent for a moment, then looked up at the other woman. "Marian, do you know anything about...about what's happened between me and Nathan?"

"A little. Nathan talked to me last week. And I feel so ashamed of myself," Marian confessed. "I'm afraid I've given you a terrible impression of the Cameron family."

"Oh, no," Kate protested. "It's just that I was—"

"I've been snobbish and overbearing," Marian went on firmly, fingering the covers of the old diary. "Acting as if that ranch and its history mattered more than anything. Nathan heard it so often while he was growing up, I think he just automatically accepted it as the truth until you came along and forced all of us to look at things differently. I realize that what you've accomplished with your hotel is every bit as important as Nathan's job running the ranch."

Kate looked at her in astonishment. "You really believe that?"

"Kate, I think perhaps I exaggerated the importance of being mistress of the ranch in order to justify my own existence. After all, it was the focus of my life."

"But, Marian, you did so much. You raised a family and helped Josh build the ranch to what it is, entertained all kinds of important people, decorated the house so beautifully..."

"Oh, I'm not dissatisfied with my life. But I need to be more tolerant of other people's goals. I'm sorry if I caused problems for the two of you, Kate. I truly am."

"It wasn't that," Kate said, staring out the window. "Not really. Mostly it was my own cowardice. I've been so afraid of finding myself trapped in a smothering marriage again, after just escaping from one."

"Nathan's a good man," Marian said gently. "And he loves you more than anything."

Kate looked at the woman's beautiful, finely drawn face, thinking about Hilda's homely practicality and her opinion that all a woman needed to do was pick the right man.

Suddenly, she felt a fierce longing for Nathan, a deep aching need that stabbed all the way to the core of her.

"Is he...do you know if he's at home today?"

"I'm sure he is," Marian said quietly. "Nathan hasn't been going out much lately."

"I need to see him," Kate said. She got to her feet, compelled by an urgency she could barely contain. "I'm sorry to rush off like this, but I really need to see him right away."

Marian gave her a brief hug, then moved with her to the door. She stood watching, holding Ellen's diary in her arms, while Kate ran down the path toward the parking lot.

But Kate was no longer aware of Marian or anything at all except the man she was hurrying to see. Her eyes were still blinded by tears, and her heart sang wildly with fear and excitement.

She drove along the highway toward Wolf Hill, oblivious for once to the sweep and grandeur of the landscape. All she could think of was Ellen, not yet twenty-one years old, dying in a hotel room before she'd ever known what it was to lie in her lover's arms, share his life and bear his children.

That was what really mattered. Kate understood the truth so clearly now, she couldn't believe how confused and troubled she'd been all these months.

It didn't matter that Ellen had never become the first female school administrator in all the western provinces. Kate grieved because Ellen had died without knowing Joshua's love, and left him alone to endure a life of desolation and bitterness. She thought again of the old man setting out his row of trees, and brushed at the tears that still trickled down her cheeks.

A woman could certainly have lofty goals. She could strive for success just as validly and energetically as any man. But if she sacrificed love for worldly accomplishment, what had she gained?

In the same way, the Wolf Hill Hotel could become a model of efficiency and generate a tidy profit, year after year. It could win prizes and acclaim in the tourism industry. But if Kate lost the one man she could laugh with, the man who would love and understand and cherish her through the years, she knew her success would be a hollow thing.

She thought of Nathan, her mind dwelling lovingly on a thousand scattered images of his face and hands, his broad shoulders and lithe springing walk, the way his dark hair fell onto his forehead and his mouth lifted in a crooked smile. She remembered the tenderness of his lovemaking, the gentle way he seemed to understand all her thoughts and feelings.

"Nathan," she whispered through her tears. "Nathan, my darling, I'm so sorry. Please forgive me. I hope it's not too late. Oh, I hope it's not too late...."

SHE REACHED Wolf Hill and drove through town without stopping.

The hotel hummed with activity as she passed. Hilda was outside sweeping the veranda while two of Raymond's helpers cleaned the upstairs windows and a delivery van unloaded supplies at the sidewalk. Raymond lounged next to the van, giving orders to the window cleaners who glowered from their scaffold. He looked up in surprise as Kate swept by, then said something to Hilda who waved and stood on the veranda, one hand shading her eyes against the afternoon sun.

Kate hardly saw them. Her eyes were fixed on the horizon and her heart pounded as she waited for her first sight of that line of cottonwood trees leading to the Cameron ranch house.

Soon the trees came into view, and then the sprawl of corrals and outbuildings. Kate's courage almost

failed her when she saw the roof of the big house that
Joshua Cameron had built all those years ago. He'd
planned his house with such care, but the woman he
loved had never lived there with him. . . .

When she drew closer to the avenue of trees, she
could see a small tractor moving among them, pulling
a cultivator. Nathan drove the tractor, and seemed to
be unaware of her approach. Kate parked at the side
of the road and got out, gazing at him hungrily
through the screen of leaves.

He wore jeans, work boots and an old plaid work
shirt. His shoulders strained at the faded blue fabric
as he drove carefully in and out among the rows of
trees, working the rich soil above their roots. She
edged closer, watching while he stopped the tractor
and climbed down to haul a broken branch out of the
way.

"Nathan," she said, moving through the trees to
stand near the tractor. He straightened and whirled to
stare at her, his eyes widening in surprise beneath the
peak of his cap.

She came closer, looking at him nervously.
"I . . . wanted to talk with you."

He bent and tugged at the branch. "Must have
blown down in that big wind we had last night," he
muttered. "It was sure howling across the prairie."

"Nathan, I love you."

It felt so good to say the words aloud. She realized
that she'd never allowed herself to express her love for
him, except in dreams.

He lifted the branch and hauled it over to the edge
of the grove. "I'll have to come out later with a chain
saw and cut that up for firewood."

Kate watched him, confused by his behavior. "I just told you that I love you," she said.

He straightened and looked at her directly. "I heard you."

"I'm sorry for the way I acted," Kate said. "And I don't blame you if you hate me. I just wanted you to know that . . . that I love you. I think I fell in love with you the first time I saw you, but it's taken me such a long time to come to my senses."

He looked at her so steadily that she began to feel awkward and shy. "What made you change your mind?" he asked finally.

"I just . . . I'll tell you all about it later. Something happened to make me realize that there's not much sense to life if you can't be with the person you love. I want to marry you, Nathan. I don't want to waste any more of my life."

His eyes flashed with emotion but his face was still rigid and noncommittal.

Kate looked at him in sudden dread, wondering if she'd squandered her chance at happiness. Had she rejected him too harshly, hurt him so much that he could never forgive her? Had she driven away the only man she could ever love?

"What about your hotel?" he asked, moving back to lean against the tractor with his arms crossed.

"I don't want to give up my hotel," Kate said. "I've worked so hard, and a lot of people are depending on me to make a success of it. I think . . ." She faltered, feeling increasingly nervous under his quiet gaze. "I think we could work things out if we tried."

"Do you?"

"Yes, I do." She lifted her chin and forced herself to look directly at him. "I think we could find a way to balance our lives and share responsibilities if we really wanted to.''

"I wanted to, Kate," he said. "I told you I was willing to try.''

"I know. I wasn't listening, Nathan. I was so afraid, and I didn't really understand what I wanted until today. But now I know.''

"And what do you want?''

Kate looked down at his feet, the scuffed toes of his boots, the faded denim jeans. "I just told you. I want us to be together. I want to...''

"What, Kate?" he asked softly. "What do you want to do?''

She looked up quickly and saw the teasing light in his eyes. Relief flooded her, so intense that she could hardly breathe. "Nathan," she whispered, moving closer to him, touching him.

But he continued to look at her with his arms folded, dark eyes dancing. "Tell me what you want, Kate.''

She stood on tiptoe and leaned against him, whispering in his ear.

"Yeah?" He put his hands on her shoulders, smiling. "And what else?''

Again she whispered. He laughed with delight and seized her in his arms, lifting her off her feet as he kissed her.

Kate sighed in bliss and nestled close to him, loving the feel of him, the scent of his sun-warmed body, the strength of his arms. She sighed as his lips moved on hers and his hands caressed her.

The years fell away, a century of love and longing. She looked up and saw Ellen's face, her hair blowing in the prairie wind, her contented smile.

This is for you, Ellen, Kate thought, pressing close to the man she loved. This is for you and Joshua.

Kate realized that part of their lives, as long as they were together, would be dedicated to the two who'd gone before.

The babies that would be born, the rich time of growing and sharing, the golden years when they sat on the veranda with their grandchildren tumbling at their feet . . . all of it would be shared with Ellen and Joshua, who'd never known those pleasures.

"Kate," Nathan murmured in alarm, touching her face. "Sweetheart, you're crying. What's the matter?"

"I'm just so happy," she whispered. "I'm so happy, I can hardly bear it. Nathan, a hundred years is a long time to wait for this kind of happiness."

He looked at her in surprise, but she smiled through her tears and reached up to kiss him.

"It's all right," she said. "I'll tell you all about it, dear. Everything's all right now."

Satisfied, he nodded and put his arm around her, then walked with her through the trees and onto the road. Arm in arm, lost in each other, they wandered under the rustling, sun-dappled canopy of leaves, moving up the shaded avenue toward the house.

HARLEQUIN SUPERROMANCE®

WOMEN WHO DARE
They take chances, make changes
and follow their hearts!

Too Many Bosses
by Jan Freed

According to Alec McDonald, Laura Hayes is "impertinent,
impulsive, insubordinate and totally lacking in self-discipline"—
all negatives in an employee. Mind you, he also has to admit that
she has the legs of a Las Vegas showgirl.

According to Laura Hayes, Alec McDonald is "a pompous
bigot who considers Kleenex standard issue for his female
employees." But while these are negatives in a boss, Laura
doesn't intend to remain his employee for long, because it's
obvious that Alec needs Laura—in his business and in his life.

Within twenty-four hours of their first meeting, Laura and Alec
are partners in a new business. *Equal* partners. Yet two bosses
is one too many for any business—especially when the boss is
falling in love with the boss!

Watch for *Too Many Bosses* by Jan Freed.
Available in May 1995, wherever Harlequin books are sold.

HARLEQUIN®

PRESENTS
RELUCTANT BRIDEGROOMS

Two beautiful brides, two unforgettable romances...
two men running for their lives....

My Lady Love, by Paula Marshall, introduces
Charles, Viscount Halstead, who lost his memory
and found himself employed as a stableboy by the
untouchable Nell Tallboys, Countess Malplaquet.
But Nell didn't consider Charles untouchable—
not at all!

Darling Amazon, by Sylvia Andrew, is the story of
a spurious engagement between Julia Marchant
and Hugo, marquess of Rostherne—an engagement
that gets out of hand and just may lead Hugo to
the altar after all!

Enjoy two madcap Regency weddings this May,
wherever Harlequin books are sold.

REG5

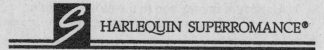

HARLEQUIN SUPERROMANCE®

presents

EVERY MOVE YOU MAKE
By Bobby Hutchinson

This May, meet the first of our FOUR STRONG MEN:

Mountie Joe Marcello. He was hot on the trail of his
man, but what he got was...a woman. Schoolteacher
Carrie Zablonski found herself in the wrong place at the
wrong time, and when Joe learned there was more to the
lady than met the eye—and she was quite an eyeful—he
assigned himself as her personal guardian angel. Trouble
was, Carrie didn't *want* his protection....

Look for *Every Move You Make* in May 1995,
wherever Harlequin books are sold.

4SM-1

Harlequin invites you to the most romantic
wedding of the season...with

MARRY ME, COWBOY!

And you could WIN A DREAM VACATION of a lifetime!

from HARLEQUIN BOOKS and SANDALS—
THE CARIBBEAN'S #1 **ULTRA INCLUSIVE**℠ LUXURY RESORTS
FOR COUPLES ONLY.

Harlequin Books and Sandals Resorts are offering you a
vacation of a lifetime—a vacation of your choice at any of
the Sandals Caribbean resorts—FREE!

LOOK FOR FURTHER DETAILS in the Harlequin Books
title MARRY ME, COWBOY!, an exciting collection
of four brand-new short stories by popular romance
authors, including *New York Times* bestselling author
JANET DAILEY!

**AVAILABLE IN APRIL WHEREVER
HARLEQUIN BOOKS ARE SOLD.**

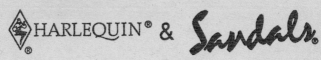

HARLEQUIN® & *Sandals*.